THE WRETCHED OF
MUIRWOOD

Legends of Muirwood Trilogy

The Wretched of Muirwood
The Blight of Muirwood
The Scourge of Muirwood

THE WRETCHED OF
MUIRWOOD

THE LEGENDS OF MUIRWOOD

Book One

JEFF
WHEELER

Published by 47North
P.O. Box 400818
Las Vegas, NV 89140

Cover illustration by Eamon O'Donoghue

ISBN-13: 9781612187006
ISBN-10: 1612187005
Library of Congress Control Number: 2012943279

To Jenna

There is a difference between a wretched and an orphan. An orphan is literally a child whose parents are dead. It is a pitiable state, to be sure, but the child still knows, by means of relations or guardians, who their parents were and what Gifts they have inherited. The necessary rites can or already have been performed for them, binding them through the Medium to their ancestral forebears and the consequences appertaining to them.

A wretched is like an orphan. They have no family, no relations, no one willing to own them or care for them. Their parents may be alive or dead. They are often born in secret, with no one aware of their coming into this second life, except for the unlucky souls who find them abandoned on Abbey steps in the dark of night. After laboring and searching the most ancient references, I have thus concluded that the original meaning of the word is this—a wretched is someone deserving pity. And by this definition, I say that those children found in this state are appropriately named.

—Cuthbert Renowden of Billerbeck Abbey

CHAPTER ONE

Cemetery Rings

Lia lived in the Aldermaston's kitchen at Muirwood Abbey. More than anything else in the world, she craved learning how to read. But she had no family to afford such a privilege, no one willing to teach her the secrets, and no hope of it ever happening because she was a wretched.

Nine years before, someone had abandoned her at the Abbey gate and that should have put an end to her ambitions. Only it did not. One cannot live in a sweet-scented kitchen without hungering after pumpkin loaves, spicy apple soup, and tarts with glaze. And one could not live at Muirwood Abbey without longing to learn the wisest of crafts—reading and engraving.

Thunder boomed above Muirwood Abbey, and water drenched the already muddy grounds. Lia's companion, Sowe, slept next to her in the loft, but the thunder and the sharp stabs of lightning did not wake her, nor did the voices murmuring from the kitchen below as the Aldermaston spoke to Pasqua. It was difficult waking Sowe under any circumstances, for she dearly loved her sleep.

Running drips dampened their blankets and plopped in pots on the kitchen tiles below. Rain had its own way of bringing out smells—in wet clothes, wet cheeses, and wet sackcloth. Even the wooden planks and the eaves had a damp, musty smell.

The Aldermaston's gray cassock and over-robe were soaked and dripping, his thick, dark eyebrows knotted with worry and impatience. Lia watched him secretly from the shadows of the loft.

"Let me pour you some cider," Pasqua said to him as she fidgeted among the pots, sieves, and ladles. "A fresh batch was pressed and boiled less than a fortnight ago. It will refresh you. Now where did that chatteling put the mugs? Here we are. Well now, it seems someone has drunk from it again. I mark these things, you know. It was probably Lia. She is always snitching."

"Your gift of observation is keen," said the Aldermaston, who seemed hurried to speak. "I am not at all thirsty. If you…"

"It is no trouble at all. In truth, it is good for your humors. Now why did they stack those eggs that way? I ought to crack one over the both of their heads, I should. But that would be wasteful."

"Please, Pasqua, some bread. If you could rouse the girls and start the bread now. Stoke the fires. You may be baking all night."

"Are we expecting guests, Aldermaston? In this storm? I doubt if a skilled horseman could ford the moors now, even with the bridges. I have seen many storms blow in like this. Hang and cure me if any guests should brave the storm tonight."

"Not guests, Pasqua. The rivers may flood. I will rouse the other help, maybe even the learners. If it floods…"

"You think it might flood?"

"I believe that is what I just said."

"It rained four days and four nights nigh on twelve years ago. The Abbey did not flood then."

"I believe it may tonight, Pasqua. We are on higher ground. They will look to us for help."

Lia poked Sowe to rouse her, but she mumbled something and turned the other way, swatting at her own ear. She was still completely asleep.

The Aldermaston's voice was rough, as if he was always trying to keep himself from coughing, and it throbbed with impatience. "If it floods, there will be danger for the village. Not only our crops chance being ruined. Bread. Make five hundred loaves. We should be prepared…"

"Five hundred loaves?"

"That is what I instructed. I am grateful you heard me correctly."

"From our stores? But…what a dreadful waste if it does not flood."

"In this matter, I am not seeking advice. I am impressed that we should prepare for flooding this evening. It is heavy on me now. As heavy as the cauldron in the nook. I keep waiting for it. For the footsteps. For the alarm. Something will happen this night. I dread news of it."

"Have some cider then," Pasqua said, her voice trembling with worry. "It will calm your nerves. Do you really think it will flood tonight?"

Straightening his crooked back, the Aldermaston roared, "Do you not understand me? Loaves! Five hundred at least. Must I rouse your help myself? Must I knead the dough with my own hands? Bake, Pasqua! I did not come here to trifle with you or convince you."

Lia thought his voice more frightening than the thunder— the feeling of it, the heat of his anger. It made her sink deep inside herself. Her heart pained for Pasqua. She knew how it felt to be yelled at like that.

Sowe sat up immediately, clutching her blanket to her mouth. Her eyes were wild with fear.

Another blast of thunder sounded, its force shaking the walls.

In the calm of silence that followed, Pasqua replied, "There is no use yelling, Aldermaston, I can hear you very well. You may think me deaf, by the tone of your voice. Loaves you shall have then. Grouchy old niffler, coming into *my* kitchen to yell at me. A fine way to treat your cook."

At that moment, the kitchen opened with a gusty wind and a man slogged in, spraying mud from his boots with every step. His hair was dripping, his beard dripping, his nose dripping. Grime covered him from head to foot. He clenched something in his hand against his chest.

"And who do you think you are to come in like that, Jon Hunter!" Pasqua said, rounding on him. "Kicking mud like that! Tell me that a wretched is found half drowned at the Abbey gate, or I will beat you with my broom for barging into my kitchen. Filthy as a cur, look at you."

Jon Hunter looked like a wild thing, a mess of soaked, sodden cloak, tangled hair with twigs and bits of leaves, and a gladius blade belted to his waist. "Aldermaston," he said in a breathless voice. He mopped his beard and pitched his voice lower. "The graveyard. It flooded. Landslide."

There was quiet, then more blinding lightning followed by billows of thunder. The Aldermaston said nothing. He only waited.

Jon Hunter seemed to be struggling to find his voice again. Lia peeked farther from the ladder steps, her long curly hair tickling the sides of her face. Sowe tried to pull her back, to get her out of the light, but Lia pushed her away.

Jon Hunter pressed his forehead against his arm, staring down at the floor. "The lower slope gave way, spilling part of the

cemetery downhill. Grave markers are strewn about and many..."
He stopped, choking on the words, "Many ossuaries were burst.
They were...my lord...they were...they were all empty, save for
muddy linens...and...and...wedding bands made of gold."

Jon put his hand on the cutting table. His other still clenched
something. "As I searched the ruins and collected the bands, the
part of the hill I was on collapsed. I thought...I thought I was
going to die. I fell. I cannot say how far, not in all the dark, but I
fell on stone. A shelf of rock, I thought. It knocked the wind out of
me. But when the lightning flashed again, I realized it was...in the
air. Do you understand me? Hanging in the air. A giant block of
chiseled stone. But there was nothing below it. Nothing holding
it up. I was trapped and shouted for help. But then the lightning
flashed anew, and I saw the hillside above and the roots of a with-
ered oak exposed. There is nothing but a tangle of oaks in that
part of the grounds. So I leapt and climbed and came."

The Aldermaston said nothing, chewing on the moment as if
it were some bitter-tasting thing. His eyes closed. His shoulders
drooped. "Who else is about tonight? Who may have seen it?"

"Only I," Jon Hunter said, holding out his hand, his mud-
caked hand. There were several smeared rings in his filthy palm.
"Aldermaston, why were there no bones in the ossuaries? Why
leave the rings? I do not understand what I beheld tonight."

The Aldermaston took the rings, looking at them in the flick-
ering lamplight. Then his fingers tightened around the gold bands
and fury kindled his cheeks.

"There is much labor to fulfill before dawn. The cemetery
grounds are forbidden now. Be certain that no one trespasses.
Take two mules and a cart and gather the grave markers and ossuaries and move them to where I shall tell you. I will help. I do
not want learners to discover what you did. The entire Abbey is

forbidden from that ground. Have I spoken clearly? Can there be any doubt as to my orders?"

"None, Aldermaston. The storm is raging still. I will work alone. Do not risk your health to the elements. Tell me what must be done and I will do it."

"The rains have plagued us quite enough. They will cease. *Now*." He held up his hand, as if to calm a thrashing stallion in front of him.

Either by the words or the gesture or both, the rain ceased, and only the water sluicing through the gutters and the plop and drip from a thousand shingles and countless shuddering oak branches could be heard. A tingle in the air sizzled, and Lia's heart went hot with a blushing giddiness. All her life she had heard whispers of the power of the Medium. That it was strong enough to master storms, to tame fire or sea, or restore that which was lost. Even to bring the dead back alive again.

Now she knew it was real. Empty ossuaries could mean only one thing. The dead bones had been restored to the flesh of their masters, the bodies reborn and new. When the revived ones had left Muirwood was a mystery. Lia was eager to explore the forbidden grounds—to see the floating stone, to search for rings in the mud herself.

And at precisely that moment, the moment when she realized the Medium was real, with her heart full of thoughts too dazzling to bottle up, she saw the Aldermaston turn, gaze up the ladder, and meet her eyes.

For the brief blink of a moment, she knew what he was thinking. How a young girl just past her ninth nameday could understand a world-wise and world-weary Aldermaston did not matter. This was the moment he had been dreading that evening. Not the washed out grave markers, the empty stone ossuaries, or the rings and linens left behind. It was knowing that she, a wretched of Muirwood, knew what had happened. That it was a moment that would change her forever.

His recognition of her intrusion was shared then by Pasqua and Jon Hunter.

"I ought to blister your backside, you rude little child!" Pasqua said, striding over to the loft ladder as Lia scrambled down it. "Listening in like that. Like you were nothing but a teeny mouse, all anxious for bits of cheese. A rat is more like it. Snooping and sneaking." Pasqua grabbed her scrawny arm.

"I won't tell anyone," Lia said, gazing at the Aldermaston fiercely, ignoring Pasqua and Jon Hunter. She tried to tug her arm away, but the grip was iron. "Not if you let me be taught to read. I want to be a learner."

Pasqua slapped her for that, a stinging blow. "You evil little thing! Are you threatening the Aldermaston? He could turn you out to the village. Hunger, my little crow, real hunger. You have never known that feeling. Ungrateful, selfish…"

"Let her go, Pasqua, you are not helping," the Aldermaston said, his eyes shining with inner fury. His gaze burned into Lia's eyes. "While I am Aldermaston over Muirwood, you will not be taught to read. You greatly misunderstand your position here." His eyes narrowed. "Five hundred loaves. Tonight. The food will help offer distraction." He turned to leave, but stopped and gave her one last look. It was a sharp, threatening look. "They would not believe such a story even if you told them." He left the kitchen, the vanished storm no longer blowing his stock of pale white hair.

Jon Hunter plucked a twig out of his hair and gave Lia another look—one that promised a thrashing if she ever said a word to anyone—then followed the Aldermaston out. Lia did not care about a thrashing. She knew what those felt like too.

Pasqua kept her and Sowe up all night, and by dawn their shoulders and fingers throbbed from the endless kneading, patting, and shaping of loaves. But Lia was not too exhausted, the next morning, to resist stealing one of the gold cemetery rings from a box in the Aldermaston's chambers. After tying it to a stout length of string, she wore it around her neck and hid it beneath her clothes.

She never took it off.

CHAPTER TWO

Knight-Maston

Four years passed. The Aldermaston was true to his word, and Lia was true to hers. She never told anyone about the floating stone, or the alcove she and Sowe had discovered in the hillside, or the cemetery rings. The storm raging outside reminded her of the previous one from years ago. Instead of sleeping in the loft with Sowe, she tried to get comfortable on the floor near the oven where it was warmer.

Thunder rocked the Abbey grounds, and even the thick stone wall thrummed with it. The rain dripped from several loose shingles on the roof, and the plunk-plunking on the mats kept her awake. She was not certain what would be worse, grabbing a few pots to catch the water and listening to the deep blooping sound or cramming her blanket harder against her ears to muffle it.

In the darkness, something heavy lurched against the double doors, and for a moment Lia remembered Jon Hunter bursting in, bearing the news of the landslide. She sat up fast enough to graze her head against the planks of the trestle table nearby. The sound was loud, like when Getmin or Ribbs shoved a barrel full of beans into place. She heard a few low whispers and curses just outside

9

the door, which meant it was likely a pair of learners. Sometimes they snuck out of their rooms at night to wander the grounds, but few were courageous enough to brave the Aldermaston's personal kitchen. On quiet, bare feet, she padded over and grabbed a skillet from the hook pegs, a wide, flat one made of iron. A heavy wallop on the head was usually all it took to stop a learner.

"Here we are," a man's voice whispered. "Easy there, lad. Let me look at you. Bleeding still. Let me see if the kitchen is open."

The handle rattled and shook.

"Locked. Won't be able to cross the river again if I stay here much longer...let me see if I can open it." A dagger came through the crack and struggled against the crossbar, making Lia skip back with shock. Learners did not carry daggers!

"There we go...oh piddle, the crossbar is too heavy. Sorry, lad. Looks like you will be bleeding to death here. How the Abbey help will love a corpse on the porch instead of a wretched. But what is there to do? Well, I suppose I could knock."

Lia clenched her hands around the skillet handle, wondering if she should open the doors. A firm pounding startled her. "For the love of life, is anyone there? I have a wounded man with me. Is anyone there?"

She bit her lip, wondering if she should sneak out the rear doors and waken Pasqua. The old woman snored so loudly, it would take more than distant pounding to wake her from her dreams, though sometimes she snored herself awake. Something thumped outside, and she thought she heard the chinking sound of spurs. What kind of man wore spurs? Few soldiers could afford horses. But knight-mastons could. At least she thought they could, knight-mastons and the nobles.

Thoughts of the Aldermaston did not make the choice any easier. She knew she could just as easily be scolded for deciding either way. *What were you thinking, Lia, letting two rough men into the kitchen in the dead of night? What were you thinking, Lia, letting a man bleed to death on the porch of Muirwood?*

Looking at it that way, she supposed there was really only one choice to make. How could she let a man die, especially if he was a maston? Would not the king be greatly angered if one of his knights died? Especially considering the king was renowned for his cruelty. Yet why would two of the king's men be wandering about Muirwood anyway? The gates were always locked during the night, so they must have approached the grounds from the rear instead of the village. Why? Would they treat someone kindly who helped? Perhaps a few coins? Or even greater generosity?

That decided her.

Lia set the pan on a table, lifted the crossbar, and pulled open the door—and fell over when a man stumbled inside.

"Sweet mother of Idumea!" the man gasped, flailing and sidestepping to keep from squashing her. He was dripping wet, smelled like the hog pens, and his face looked more scratchy than a porcupine. A body collapsed with a thump just outside, and she saw glistening red streaking down his face.

"You scared me, lass! Fans or fires, that is horrible to do to someone." He regained his balance, all quickness and grace, and grabbed her hand and arm to help her stand. After wiping his mouth, which caused a rasping sound, he turned and hoisted the other fellow under the arms and dragged him the rest of the way inside. As he pulled, she saw the sword belted at his waist. It was a fine sword, the pommel glinting in the dim light of the oven fires. It bore the insignia on the pommel—an eight-pointed star, formed of two offset squares.

"You are a knight-maston!" Lia whispered.

His head jerked and he looked her in the face. "How did you know?"

"The sword, it is…well you see, I have heard that they…"

"A clever lass. Quick as a wisp. Help me drag him over to that mat. Grab his legs."

She did, and helped move the wounded man in out of the rain. They set him down on the rush-matting. The wounded man was younger than she first thought, pale and clean-shaven, with dripping, dark hair.

She crouched down and studied him. "I can help," she said. "Bring me that lamp. The one over there." She was anxious to flaunt her apothecary skills, earned when a rush of fevers struck the Abbey two winters ago. He obeyed and produced it.

The injured one was no older than seventeen or eighteen—a man for certain, but one young enough to still have the blemishes of youth on his face. His hair was cropped short around his neck. His build somewhat resembled that of Getmin, the blacksmith's help who loved to torment her.

"Is this your squire?" she asked. "We should have carried him closer to the fire. He is bone cold. I can start the fire quickly."

"Squire? Well, he is…he is a good lad. Not my squire though. His father was a good man. How old are you lass? Sixteen?"

"I am thirteen. At least I think so. I am a wretched."

"I would not have believed you thirteen. You look tall enough to have danced beneath a maypole already."

"I am hoping to this year, if the Aldermaston lets me. I am near enough to fourteen and think he should." The blood flowed from a cut on the young man's eyebrow. She stanched it firmly with a cloth. It might take a while to make it stop as the cut was deep. She glanced up at the loft, half expecting to see Sowe cow-

12

ering there, but there was no one. Part of her was glad that Sowe was asleep.

"I always try to make it to Muirwood for Whitsunday. A most profitable day it is."

"You mean the tourneys or the trading?"

"Yes, yes, the tourneys. Nothing like bumping a man onto his hindquarters. And I most gravely apologize for knocking you onto yours just now. My, look at that wound. That is a nasty cut." He looked into Lia's eyes, and she felt a sudden jolt of warmth. "Rode his piddling mare right into an oak branch. Too many trees here, lass. Too dark and the storm made it worse! Praise the Medium, we are both still alive. Let me grab another cloth, and we can wring out that one. Wait here."

Lia knelt by the limp body, her stomach buzzing, and pressed the wound harder. She looked over her shoulder and watched the knight slice a shank from the spitted hog and stuff it into a leather bag at his waist. It was followed by three buttered rolls and a whole cherry tart.

"Those are for the Aldermaston's dinner tomorrow!" she whispered in a panic, knowing exactly who Pasqua would blame. "The hog is not even done cooking yet!"

"There we are, a cloth!" He snatched one of the fine linen napkins and hurried over, licking his fingers. He held out the napkin to exchange with hers.

"That is one of the Aldermaston's napkins!"

"Is a lad's life held so cheaply here? We must stop the bleeding. Here, put your hand on this and hold it tight. The linen will sop the blood better." He grabbed her wrist and pressed her hand against the bleeding.

"That is *not* the way to do it," she said. "Here, let me fetch some things. I can cure him." Lia ran to the benches and grabbed some clean dishrags, a kettle of warm water from the fire-peg, and a sprig of blue woad. She watched as the knight grabbed two more tarts, veins of grapes, and a small tub of treacle and stuffed them into his leather knapsack.

"What are you doing?"

"Hmmm? Victuals, lass. I will leave a little pouch with coins on the mantle." He pointed to the fire.

"Pasqua will be furious," Lia muttered under her breath, arranging the healing provisions near the young man's head. She steeped the cloth with some hot water and wiped blood from his face. He did not flinch or start, but his eyes darted beneath his eyelids. His body started to tremble. She grabbed his hand.

"He is too cold. Where is his cloak?" She poured more hot water and wrung out the cloth, bathing his face a second time before wadding it up and pressing it against the cut on his eyebrow. If Sowe were awake, she could have helped pestle the woad. But Lia was left to do it all herself.

The knight's shadow smothered her from behind. She turned her head and looked up at him.

He nodded. "Woad? Ah, you studied under a healer as well as a cook? It is a useful plant. You are a good lass. Make him well. I will be back for him in three days. Keep him hidden, if you can."

Panic. Pure and sudden panic.

"What? You are not going to... not leaving him..."

"I must throw the sheriff of Mendenhall's men off our trail, lass. It is dangerous for mastons in this part of the country. Especially this Hundred." He walked quickly to the door and the rain puddling on the entryway. "Keep him safe. If Almaguer comes, do your best to hide him. His life is in your hands. I am trusting you in this."

"No! He cannot stay here. I am only a helper. I cannot..."

"You do what you can, lass. You do your best. I am trusting you." And he ducked his head into the rain, clenched the hilt of his maston sword, and disappeared into the storm.

***

It is the tradition at abbeys throughout the lands to bestow on a wretched a surname until they are adopted into a proper Family. Thus if a wretched girl named Binne were trained in the laundry, she would be called Binne Lavender. Or a boy given to serve in the forge could be called Gilbert Smith. Thus it is not uncommon to find any number of individuals with the same surname of Tailor, Cook, or Shepherd. In time, and through the mercy of the Medium, they may be adopted into a proper Family, and by the Medium's power, it is as if they were born in that Family originally. Their blood changes and the stigma of their birth is washed clean.

—*Cuthbert Renowden of Billerbeck Abbey*

CHAPTER THREE

Blue Woad

Sowe could sleep through thunder, snoring, bumping, shaking, rattling, and on occasion, screaming. Even worse, she fell asleep moments after lying down. This made her a horrible companion, especially if Lia had something important to tell her, like the time that Getmin had shoved Lia's pitcher into the well because it was in his way and how she had managed to dye a noticeable swath of his hair and cheek blue in revenge. Woad was a useful plant, after all, and not just for curing wounds.

"Sowe, wake up! Wake up!" Lia shook her—hard.

Sowe moaned, mumbled something that sounded like "alderwort," and rolled over.

"Sowe! Wake up. Wake up. I need your help." This was accompanied with a lot more shaking, then harder shaking, and then a pinch.

"Lia—I hate you."

Even though the words hurt Lia's feelings, it sounded more like she was saying, "I was having a very good dream and you just woke me up from it." Lia forgave her instantly.

"Someone is hurt and we must hide him. Sowe—look. There is a knight on the floor. Well, not exactly a knight, but the other one was a knight-maston. He is hurt. Look."

"I am so tired, Lia. Just tell me in the morning."

"No! There is no waiting for the morning. We must hide him. The sheriff of Mendenhall is looking for him. The rain is mad right now, so there is no place outside to hide him. Help me lift him up here. Pasqua cannot make it up the ladder, so it would be perfect hiding him up here."

Sowe strained her neck a little, shifting her dark hair. Sowe's hair was straight and dark while Lia's was curly and gold. They were opposites in many other ways as well. Her eyes were still closed, and her expression was pouty. "There is not a knight sleeping on the floor."

"There is. Look if you do not believe me."

"This is just another one of your silly games. Lia—I am so tired. Why do you have to do this? Tomorrow is going to be awful enough already. There is so much work."

"You do not believe me. Look, Sowe. Just look."

Sowe sighed and shunted her way to the ladder edge on her elbows. "I like you sleeping on the floor these last few nights. Even though it is colder without you…oh my goodness! Who is that?"

"I already told you. Help me get him up the ladder."

"Up the ladder? Him? Up in the loft with us? No, I do not think that is a good idea at all. Where did he come from? Who is he?" Her eyes were wide open now.

"I do not think I even know. But he is a squire. The knight-maston that brought him here said he struck his head against a tree branch. He had a cut in his eyebrow, but I closed it up with some woad. See? My fingers are blue. I tried lifting him, but I cannot bear his weight alone."

"Then we should tell Pasqua."

Lia shook her head. "She will only summon the Aldermaston straightaway. The knight said his life was in danger if he was caught. He promised to return for him in three days with a reward. By morning, he will probably waken. We can learn more of him then. Do you want his life on your conscience?" She was more worried about losing a possible reward than she was about the squire's danger.

Sowe wrung her hands, looking down at the body and then at Lia. "But we sleep up here, Lia. We cannot...you know...we cannot let him sleep up here too."

There was stirring below, and a cough.

"He is awake!" Sowe said with a squeak.

Lia rushed to the ladder and hurried down as the squire struggled to his feet. He swayed, back-stepped, and collided with a trestle table. Gingerly, he touched his wound and the bandage covering it.

"You have been hurt," Lia said, coming into the lamplight. "By a tree branch."

His reaction to her voice made her stop. He stiffened with panic, then glared at her with undisguised loathing as if he could not believe his misfortune. He slammed his hand on the table to steady himself.

Lia bit her lip. "You are safe, sir."

The squire trembled as if his knees would fail him. As he surveyed the kitchen, the lamplight played over the grooves and angles of his face. The dried blood had been bathed away, but his hair was matted and unkempt.

"Where am I? Is this the Abbey?"

"Muirwood, sir."

The squire nodded, then another look clouded his face, and he doubled over fiercely. Lia went to help him, but he was merely being sick. All over himself and all over her. His knees collapsed then, and he fell to the floor, vomiting violently again. It was a noisy affair, and the smell of it made Lia turn her face away, nearly gagging herself.

Sowe descended the ladder, her expression a mixture of fear and wincing.

"Get him something to drink," Lia said, crouching down next to him. Sweat ran down his face and his body convulsed and trembled. She dabbed some spittle and flecks from his chin with a rag. "You have chills."

"Muirwood," he whispered, clenching his eyes shut and rocking back and forth. His face was white. He wiped his mouth on his sleeve and glared at her for the second time, a look that seared with distrust. "Who have you told?"

"What?"

"Who have you told I am here? You both are wretcheds, are you not? Who have you told?"

Lia felt a flush of anger rise to her cheeks. Your friend was warmer, she thought. "I am a wretched. It is not as if I can help that. I saved your life tonight, sir. Why would I risk it again by telling the Aldermaston you are here? Your friend said he would come for you in three days. So we will hide you until then."

"What friend?"

"The man who brought you here. The knight-maston."

The young squire blinked, regarding her coolly. "What was his name?"

"He did not give me one."

"Of course," he said. "And neither shall I. You may have surmised—guessed—but if not, let me tell you that I am a man of no small wealth. My presence at Muirwood…it must not be noticed. Can you…can you hide me then? Even from the Aldermaston? If I evade capture, I will amply reward you."

Sowe approached, quavering and trembling, with a flagon. She handed it to him tentatively, and he took it from her hand, gulping fast and hard. His breath was horrible.

After finishing the drink, he wiped his mouth, still bent double. His body shook with spasms of pain or cold. "I will say it again," he whispered. "No one can know I am here."

"It will be difficult keeping this secret," Lia said, looking into his eyes. "Pasqua notices everything. So do the other helpers. If you want me to…"

"I understand your meaning perfectly," he said, his mouth twisting with a cruel look. "And I promise you, again, that your reward will be sufficiently bold."

"You misunderstood me, sir…I…"

"I understand you very well. You are a wretched and risk a good deal sheltering me. Eviction from the Abbey, from your trade, from those who have raised you…despite how they have pitied you. You desire more than what you have been born to, and you can only get it with sufficient coin. I can appreciate that, and my promise is not hollow. You help me to seek a reward. I will gladly pay it. Do we understand one another? Do not pretend compassion for me. Do not claim you are doing this for anything other than very selfish reasons. As I said, I can understand that. Let us be honest in this at least."

The look he gave her challenged her to defy his conclusion. But he was right. She did want—no, she expected a reward. They both knew it.

"We do, sir." She rose and reached for his elbow to help him rise as well.

"Do not touch me," he said, grunting, and stood by his own power. He trembled like a newborn colt and wiped his mouth again. "Where...where can I hide?" He looked around the kitchen.

"Can you climb to the loft on your own?" Lia asked, cocking her head, feeling a bit impertinent. "Or would you rather retch on me again?"

CHAPTER FOUR

Pasqua's Kitchen

The Abbey kitchen was near the manor house where the Aldermaston slept. Like all of the buildings on the grounds, it was worked of large blocks of heavy, sculpted stone. It was a spacious square building dimpled with half-columns protruding from the walls and a steepled roof. The interior was not square because of four ovens, one in each corner, with the flues inset into the stone so the smoke could escape. Two of the ovens were tall enough that Lia or Sowe could stand within and sweep away the ashes. The other two were smaller, for baking.

Two sets of wide double doors serviced the kitchen, one set facing the Abbey itself, the other directly opposite in the rear, but it was seldom used. The wood and iron doors had windows in their upper portions, but only someone very tall like the Aldermaston would have been able to look in, not someone short like Pasqua or many of the learners. Enormous windows were also inset high into the stone walls to allow sunlight to brighten the space. The roof was held up by eight giant stays that rose high above the loft and sloped steeply to the cupola. There was no way down from that point except a direct drop to the stone-paved kitchen floor below.

The shape of the kitchen made it possible for the ovens to heat the room, which made it a comfortable place for the two girls to live. Lia and Sowe slept in a loft constructed of wooden beams and rails, with a sturdy floor, and a ladder connecting it to the ground below. Stores of spices—nutmeg, cinnamon, poaceae, cardamom—along with sacks of milled grain, sheaves of oats, pumpkins, and small vats of treacle crowded most of the space. The heavier barrels and sacks were stored beneath them on the floor.

The beautiful Abbey rose up beyond the Aldermaston's residence, and Lia could see it from the upper windows if she was sitting in the loft. The Abbey was enormous. To the east of the kitchen, past a row of scraggy oak trees, was the famous Cider Orchard where the apples came from that were renowned for making a favorite drink in the kingdom. Past the orchard was the fish pond. Directly to the north of the Abbey kitchen, across a small park, lay the learner kitchen and those who cooked and provided for the learners and the rest of the Abbey help, but not for the Aldermaston and his guests.

Pasqua slept on a bed—a luxury—in a small room in the rear of the Aldermaston's manor house, but it was scarcely two dozen steps away from the kitchen where she arrived, before dawn, ready to stoke the small fires, punch the dough, and command the girls around for the rest of the day until weak embers were all that were left in the eyes of the grand ovens.

As Pasqua butted the kitchen door open, her gray hair-ends dripping from the rain, she scowled when she found Lia working alone at a grain mill, looking very sleepy.

"Sowe! Get down here, lazy child. There is work to be done and I don't fancy having to…" She stopped, for she noticed at once that things were wrong. Lia could see the perplexed look on her face as she tried to interpret the changes, just as Jon Hunter would a new set of animal tracks in the woods.

The rush-matting on the floor by the door was fresh, not stamped and askew. She tapped the rushes with her shoe. A sour smell clung to the air—a smell of sickness. She smelled the air, used to its normal scents. Something in the air felt…wrong. Pasqua looked around quickly, gazing from the cauldrons, to the spitted meat, to Lia.

"Sowe is ill," Lia said and then yawned. She turned back to the grain mill, filling her apron with seeds. "She climbed down last night to tell me her stomach was ailing, only she retched over us both. I changed the rushes already."

"Has she a fever?"

"No," Lia said, carrying the seeds to a small pot of boiling water and emptying them in, then brushing her hands. She pinched some salt and added it. "Can we get help today from the other kitchen? I did not sleep well. My dress smells terrible, and I should like to clean it so it can dry today."

Lia observed Pasqua discreetly. Pasqua still felt something lingering in the air. It was obvious in her confused stance, her wary attitude. She shut the kitchen door, listening to the sounds Lia made as she worked. The only light came from the fires, hissing and spitting across the small logs, and from the lamp next to Lia. Shadows wreathed the loft where Sowe slept.

Then she noticed the table. Lia knew that she would sooner or later.

"Did she eat the cherry tarts, is that why she is ill?" Anger boomed and shook through her voice. "Sick are we now, Sowe? So sick we cannot help with our chores? A tempting feast was laid before your eyes. And you thought yourself worthy to eat the Aldermaston's food?"

Lia turned around, her eyes crinkling with worry. "I did not see her eat them," she whispered.

"I have half a mind to take a switch to you both," Pasqua said, hiking up her meaty sleeves. She grumbled to herself, although in reality she was complaining loudly. "Ungrateful wretcheds, both of you. As if you do not eat well enough. Pasqua sees the snitches. Pasqua sees the pinches of dough. Ought to pinch your skinny bottoms, I ought to."

Lia tried to interrupt her tirade. "Ailsa Cook came begging for a shank off the hog to season a soup for the learners' second meal."

"Did you give it to her? Or must I? Looking answers my own question. And there you let her cut it herself, did you now? She took a good portion of the meat too."

Lia shrugged.

"No doubt you were hopeful she would let a helper come and aid your chores. That is the truth of the matter. Well, Lia, you can both suffer for the misdeeds."

"*I* did not eat any of the tarts."

"But you knew they were gone. Cheeky girl. You could have told me when I came, but you were hiding it for her. Shame on you both. You wipe that sleep from your eyes, lass. You will be working a double share today. Sowe will get her own when she feels better, I promise you that."

There was a heavy creak from the loft. For a moment, Pasqua clutched her heart and looked with panicked eyes. Lia could see her mind going through spasms of fear, a fear that she could not exactly fathom. Even Lia recognized that little Sowe was not heavy enough to make a creak like that.

Looking crossly at the loft, Lia grabbed a bowl and marched over to the ladder. "Not again."

Pasqua stared up into the shadows, her face a mask of alarm. Soon daylight would come and dispel the darkness. "Boil some nettle," she directed. "That can cure an upset stomach. Or mint. Some mint in a tea. That would help settle her. If she has trouble sleeping, we will give her some valerianum."

Lia climbed up the ladder and disappeared into the loft, where she got ready to scold her friend for making too much noise. So far, her plan was unfolding surprisingly well.

***

"I hate this," Sowe whimpered. "Now it is my fault? I did not eat those tarts. Why did you blame me?"

"What else was I to say? Pasqua suspects everything."

"She suspects you because you always try to trick her."

"You could at least compliment me that my plan is working."

"Yes, Lia, you have done a perfect job making me seem a glutton. I cannot thank you enough."

"If you can do better, by all means try. I have to do your work and mine today. You get to sleep up here all day."

"I cannot sleep."

"What?"

"I cannot sleep," she said, even more softly, cringing.

"Why not?"

Sowe pitched her voice even lower. "Because he is up here."

Lia rubbed her eyes. "That is ridiculous. You cannot even see him behind the sacks."

"I hear him breathing."

"You do not."

"I can!"

"You are such a child. And since when has my breathing ever kept you awake? He is not going to do anything to you. He will hold still until Pasqua leaves for the night. He cannot make a sound."

"He is noisy when he breathes!"

Lia rolled her eyes. "If you get a chance, tell him I will clean his shirt at the same time I clean my dress. I will need your dress too."

"I am not changing dresses up here!" Sowe whispered indignantly.

"Then I will clean your clean one," Lia said, exasperated. "I need to clean two dresses. I think it best while the morning meal is delivered to the learners. There will not be as many people washing then. Besides, it is still raining. If I wait longer, I will not be able to do it until later, and it may not dry by tonight. Tell him to be ready when Pasqua leaves to use the garderobe."

"I do not want to talk to him."

Lia gave her a hard look.

"I am afraid!"

Pasqua's voice thundered from across the kitchen. "Lia! The pottage is boiling! Stop pinching her and climb down. Leave the bowl up there with her, silly girl! There is enough to do to fill the entire season before Whitsunday. Come down, girl. Let her alone."

Sowe grabbed Lia's hands, her eyes helpless. "Do not leave me here alone. You could be sick too."

Lia snatched her hands away. "If I am sick too, then other help will be sent here. Now moan."

"Moan?"

"Moan!"

Sowe let out a half-gurgling whimper.

"That was pathetic," Lia grumbled as she hurried down the ladder.

***

Those who cannot read the tomes of the ancients are typically confused by the meaning of "Medium" because of its multiple definitions. With their lack of education, this is understandable. In the simplest terms, I seek to teach them thus—that the term "Medium" was chosen precisely because it conveys multiple meanings. It is the means that connects two opposite sides, allowing a maston, for example, to bring fire from the core of the earth to the surface. It is the intervening substance through which any power, or the potential of power, is transmitted. It is also a means of communication. Engravings in stone or precious ore are a manifestation of the Medium for those who can read them, for its power can be conducted through the chisels and etchings and interpreted through the eyes of the reader. The Medium has power over all things, both living and dead, and can be the means of communicating between them. It is also the means by which the dead are revived. Even if their bones are dust and blown by the wind, the Medium could find the specks and restore them to life. It happened at the oldest Abbey in the realm, Muirwood they say, though only a few ever knew of it.

—Cuthbert Renowden of Billerbeck Abbey

CHAPTER FIVE

Reome Lavender

L ia usually had a small bit of time for washing, just after the morning meal was finished and the dough punched and set rising for the dinner bread. The learners of Muirwood would be at their studies in the cloisters, and with the storm still menacing the grounds, very few would be outdoors. Pasqua slipped out to use the garderobe at the manor—something she did about ten times a day, since there were only chamber pots in the kitchen and she loathed using them. Lia had waited for the moment, and after the door shut, she scurried up the ladder.

Sowe was asleep, despite her complaints, but there was no shirt. She searched for a moment, then stepped over the sleeping girl and climbed on a barrel. "I am going to the laundry. Let me have your shirt."

"No."

It was bright now, and sunlight streamed in from the window in the nook of the loft. Motes speckled the air. His face had color again, his skin was tanned and dark, his chin stubbly instead of smooth. The bandage at his eyebrow was soaked with blood—she would need to change it later.

"Ugh, you smell horrible. Here is some cheese." She handed it to him.

He took the cheese and started into it. "Bread?"

"The dough is rising. Now give me your shirt. Look at those stains. I am going to wash my dress now."

"It is not needed. I will not be staying here long."

"Three days is long enough with smelly clothes, and I will not steal you a shirt. That would be something I could not explain." She held out her hand and wrinkled her nose. "I can smell you from here."

He hesitated.

"Quickly! Pasqua will not be gone for long." She wiggled her fingers at him.

He gritted his teeth with anger. "Very well. Turn around."

For a moment, she thought he was utterly insane. That he, a knight—a squire, or whatever—was too timid around...around her? But then she noticed something she had not observed. A silver gleam beneath the collar.

"You wear a chaen shirt! You are a maston yourself?"

He closed his eyes, his face looking as if he'd bitten through lemonwort, peel and all. He trembled with anger, but he mastered it. Opening his eyes, he looked at her with disgust. "You are a wretched. How do you know these things?"

His reaction was silly considering their location. "Sir... this is Muirwood Abbey. We receive visits from mastons each fortnight. We have our own silversmith to make the shirts, for those learners who achieve it. Otherwise they are handed down..."

"From father to son. This was my father's."

"If you wear it, then he must be dead or very old."

He scowled at her again. "Do not mock the dead."

"Why not? Do you fear hurting their feelings? Can I have your shirt now? I will not tell anyone you are a maston, if that is what troubles you."

He untied the lacings on the front and pulled it over his head, then thrust it at her. The chaen shirt beneath was beautiful and more exquisite than ones crafted at Muirwood. The shimmering links extended to his forearms and draped down his neck. The border was treated with the symbol she had seen on the sword—interlocking square-stars along the fringe.

"Stop looking at me," he said gruffly. "Wash the stains and bring it back." He nestled back into the shadows, below the window where the light blinded her, and folded his arms gruffly. The chaen shirt did not jangle as he moved. It was quiet, like the whisper of silk. Mastons who wore them had proven skills at hearing the whispers through the Medium, and had passed the tests of knowledge required to enter the inner sanctuary of the Abbey.

Lia folded the shirt as she backed away, then turned back and looked at him. "Since you are a maston…you know you can claim sanctuary in the Abbey. No one could force you to leave, not even the king himself. It is the oldest privilege of the Abbey. You know that, do you not?"

Silence was his reply.

She turned and went to the ladder, wondering if she should add some woad to the wash and turn the shirt a different color out of spite. As she descended, she heard his voice, barely more than a mutter. But she did not make out the words.

Taking Sowe's extra dress from the chest beneath the loft, along with her own soiled one, the vomit stink was as bad as the squire's, she dropped them all into a wicker basket. After fetching her blue cloak from a peg and raising the hood to cover her mass of untidy hair, she hoisted the basket and headed into the rain.

Lia left the stone path leading to the manor. The lawns were squishy and wet, the air was chilly, the rain steady. She joined another paved path that would take her around toward the Cider Orchard, and she was a little muddy by the time she reached it. In the past, she had dreaded going to the laundry. But today, everything felt alive with excitement. A squire hiding in the Aldermaston's kitchen! The king's sheriff on his way! Clouds loomed over the grounds, painting even the flowers with somberness, but they could not quell her mood. She walked with bold strides, trying to reach the laundry before getting soaked. Inwardly, she was pleased with herself. Pasqua was wary, but that was normal. She knew the woman was incapable of climbing the loft ladder. Three days was not long at all. Feeding the squire would be easy as well. She wondered what she could expect from him for the food and shelter.

As she followed the path, she caught sight of the cloister in the haze of rain. The cloister was where the learners were locked away doing their lessons. It was offset from the Abbey walls—not a towering structure, just a series of four covered walkways that opened into a garden square in the middle. The doors in and out were always locked, and helpers were never permitted to enter because of the costly metals learners used in their craft. When the hours of study and engraving were complete, the learners were allowed out to wander the grounds, tease the helpers, and generally make life difficult for everyone.

Only in the cloister could a boy or girl learn the secrets of reading and engraving tomes. The secrets were fiercely guarded. Lia stared at the building. It was the only thing in her life that made her truly jealous. She longed to have her own tome, to choose which ancient passages to engrave, to listen to whispers from the past by reading their words.

The laundry of Muirwood was a small wooden structure protected from the rain by wooden shingles attached to a sloping roof held up by six sturdy posts. There were no walls, but the roof was broad enough to provide shelter, for it rained often at the Abbey, and overhung the little spillway where the water drained away toward the wetlands. At first Lia thought that no one else was there, but she heard humming and discovered, to her disappointment, that Reome was there.

Reome was seventeen and worked as a lavender. She was the kind of girl that Lia always distrusted because of the way she gossiped. She had a certain cruelty to her—a way she talked to others that showed how little she cared about their feelings. One moment she would praise a girl for a pretty embroidery, the next she would mock how her hair was braided.

Lia had witnessed this behavior firsthand on many occasions, though she had rarely been the victim of it, except the occasional jeer that she was taller than the other girls her age or that her hair was neither brown nor raven but pale as flax and too crinkled and wild—both attributes Lia could do nothing about. The best way to handle a person like Reome was to ignore her taunts and her praise and to desire neither. Lia arrived at the shelter of the laundry and set the basket down, then shook the droplets of water from her hood and let her cloak hang on a post hook to dry while she worked.

Reome scrubbed a soaked gown on the ribbed stone edge near the water, then dunked it again. Her hands were wrinkled and sudsy. She twisted the garment, wringing out the water as she would a hen's neck, loosened it, then twisted again. She had strong hands. Lia had seen her pinch a girl once, leaving a bruise and making the girl weep.

"Hello," Lia said, announcing herself to the other girl.

She received no answer, which did not surprise her.

Lia knelt at the other end, across from Reome, and drew the stained dress from the basket and dunked it into the water. Because of the rains, the stone trough was nearly full. During the summers, a Leering was used to summon water for the duty. A teacher might summon its power, or the Aldermaston himself. She had seen it done on occasion, followed by gasps from the other helpers who watched. She looked at the Leering, its cold stone eyes flat and life-less, no glow of light emanating from it visibly. But even kneeling a few paces from it, Lia could feel the power sleeping within the stone. She would not wake it, at least not in front of Reome.

Lia pulled a cake of soap from a wooden tub and smacked it against the fabric. She churned the garment with her hands, scrubbing it against the soap, then knelt down and scrubbed it against the stone. She worked quietly, ignoring Reome, wishing the other girl was gone already.

For some reason, the boys of the Abbey did not notice the same cruelty in Reome. It bothered Lia that so many would offer to carry a basket for her. They would leap over a well hole if they thought it would earn them a fickle smile. Last summer, Reome had taken to wearing a leather choker around her neck with a polished river stone dangling from it. No doubt she was mimick-ing, as only a wretched could, one of the learners who sometimes wore chokers fashioned of silver and glittering with a gem. One by one, the other lavenders started wearing them. Then the other kitchen help—not Lia and Sowe, of course—began fashioning them. The boys cured leather or searched for stones in the river. It was silly how desperate some of the girls were to have one, or the boys to assist.

After a short while, Lia heard Reome folding the wet clothes and stacking them in her basket. Rain pattered on the water in the trough and tapped on the shingles overhead. The air smelled like soap and purple mint. She continued to scrub her dress, wringing and rinsing it. Reome started to leave, then stopped.

"I know who is going to ask you to dance at the Whitsun Fair," she said.

Curse her, Lia thought blackly. "Hmmm?" She pretended not to care, but her stomach started to churn.

Reome's basket rested against her hip. "Everyone knows. The boring one. The one who is always reading, yet never misses the chance to bid a girl hello. Neesha says that he walks around the cloister, greeting only the girls. Never the boys. But he greets us too, even the wretcheds. His shirt is in your basket. Did he ask you to wash it for him? Will he pay you, or are you doing it to be nice?"

Lia wiped her forehead, trying to think quickly. Reome was teasing her about Duerden, one of the first-year learners. He was small for his age, in height and look he appeared to be about ten, instead of thirteen. He was the nicest young man at the Abbey, the most thoughtful and friendly, treating everyone the same way, whether wretched, teacher, or other learner. Lia liked him because he explained to her what words really meant. He would not teach her to read or engrave, of course, but he did not mind sharing knowledge with others.

"I would gladly dance with anyone who asked me," Lia said with a yawn. "Duerden is generous. I should not be ashamed to dance with a learner." She secretly hoped that Reome would not pull out the shirt, for she would learn very quickly that it was too large for the one she suspected to be its owner.

"Yes, but he is a boy. A very small boy. It makes me laugh. The two of you. He, in his noble shortness, standing near you, all stick and height. You are too tall, Lia. Boys do not like girls who are taller than them. Are you as tall as the Aldermaston yet? I should think so."

Lia wrung out the dress again and scrubbed a little harder. "If you know a good cure for being tall, I am glad to hear it."

"Since you are so tall, maybe one or two of the older boys will take pity on you. But they do not care to dance. The teachers force them to ask us. You could pass for sixteen if you were not so skinny. Does Pasqua feed you Gooseberry Fool every night? It must be hideous working for her."

"Pasqua is very patient with me." *Please go away, Reome. You are finished. Just go!*

"She scolds whenever she opens her mouth, which I do not need to say is often enough. Has she prepared you to dance at the maypole this year? Or has she been too busy plotting what to sell to teach you anything else?"

"I already know the maypole dance, Reome," Lia said, bristling, squeezing the water from her dress and wishing she was back in the kitchen.

"Really? Who taught you? Have you learned watching it while selling cakes? Did graceful Pasqua take your hand and teach you? I should love to see that."

Lia looked over her shoulder. She was furious inside. It was like being pecked at by a crow. Reome had a gift for making people feel clumsy and foolish. Lia did not say that Jon Hunter taught her the maypole dance when she was ten. Or that he had also taught her to string his bow and hit apples from targets in the orchard. Or that she could make Gooseberry Fool every bit as well as Pasqua could.

"Who taught you the maypole dance?" Lia asked, trying to divert the conversation.

Reome hugged the basket to her stomach. "Before Getmin was learning to be a smith, there was a boy. He is a smith in the village now. He taught me the dance." There was something in her look, some memory that she savored like treacle sugar. Then the sweetness was gone, and she gave Lia a naughty look. "Since you said you would dance with anyone, shall I ask Getmin to dance with you?"

It was a question meant to provoke her even more, for the whole Abbey knew how much she and Getmin hated each other.

"You had better not. I do not believe he has forgiven me for not being afraid of him." In her heart she thought, and I will never forgive him for how he bullies everyone.

Reome started to leave, but stopped again. She reached into her basket and plopped a bunch of purple mint into Lia's. "You smell strange. Like cardamom or vinegar mixed with smoke. Fold this with the shirt before you dry it, or hang it while you dry it. He may thank you for it. You may or may not want him to." A sly smile followed, and then she left into the rain.

After Reome was gone and Lia was alone, she reached in and withdrew the fragrant, purple flowers. She would have to warn Duerden in case Reome teased him. That meant she would need to tell another lie before the day was through. For a moment of embarrassed, frustrating rage, she nearly crumpled the flowers in her fist and cast them away. Instead, she placed them gently at the bottom of the basket and took her washed gown to the Leering.

Leering stones could do many things, depending on how they were carved. The ones in the kitchen summoned fire from their mouths. This one by the laundry could summon water while others summoned light. Though they were carved differently—some with faces of lions or horses, men or women, even suns or moons—they all had faces and expressions. Some ferocious, others timid. Some were meek, joyful, or tormented, and each showed an emotion.

She looked into the Leering's eyes, into the curiously bland expression carved into a woman's face in the stone. She never used them unless she was totally alone or with Sowe. Only learners or mastons could use the Medium to invoke their power. Staring at the eyes, she reached out to it with her mind. The eyes of the Leering flared red and water began gushing from its mouth. The water was scalding hot and steam rose up from the laundry like morning fog in the spring. It burned her hands as she scrubbed, but it cleaned the filthy clothes better and faster than the cold, sour-smelling water.

Only mastons and some learners could coax the Leerings of the Abbey to obey them.

And Lia.

CHAPTER SIX

Leering Stones

"Maybe that sore belly will remind you to think better next time," Pasqua said in her most scolding tone.

Sowe bowed her head to hide her blushing. "Yes, Pasqua," she whispered.

"Drink another cup of valerianum tea, and you will feel better tomorrow." Smugly, the cook cleaned her hands on her apron while looking around the preparation table. "Lia, grind some fresh nutmeg before you lie down. In the morning, make some topping with oats, treacle, sugar, and butter for the Aldermaston. I wish it were the season for apples, but we have some other fruit, so we will use what we have."

"Yes, Pasqua," Lia said with an exaggerated yawn.

"You should very well be tired. I hope you both learn to be wiser, or the Aldermaston will make you wait another year to dance around the maypole." She paused, glancing around the kitchen once more as if she'd forgotten a ladle or something. "Secure the door when I am gone. Now, Lia. No dawdling."

After snatching her cloak from the peg near the door, Pasqua went into the gloomy darkness, and the door thumped shut.

Lia dusted her hands and drew the crossbar in place and turned back to Sowe. "Complain if you must, but it did work."

The squire's voice ghosted from the loft. "Will she return?"

"Not tonight. She was fidgeting to use the garderobe again, so she will not walk back through the mud unless she sees the kitchen on fire."

"Where is my shirt?"

Lia walked to the basket beneath the loft poles and touched it. "Still damp. I could not dry it in front of Pasqua, but I can dry it now. It will not take long by the fire. Come down, if you can manage it."

A thin cord was already stretched taut on the corner wall by the bread oven, the wooden pins still fastened there. The dresses she had washed earlier were already dried and folded, so she withdrew and unfolded the shirt, taking aside the sprig of purple mint in the basket, and fastened both to the line. She stared at the Leering carved into the wall at the rear of the oven. The walls were caked with soot and smoke, the Leering's visage black, its mouth twisted open like a scream of pain. She stared into its eyes, waking it with a thought. The eyes blazed orange, and fire engulfed the oven from the Leering's mouth. The heat singed her cheeks, making her smile with satisfaction. With the Leering, the oven did not need wood to burn.

"What are you doing?" Sowe whispered after rushing over. She looked over her shoulder at the squire climbing down the ladder. "You never do that in front of people. Lia, he will see it!"

"And who is he going to tell?" Lia asked smugly. She ducked around the shirt and straightened the fabric.

He reached the bottom and stared at them both, his face twitching with anger. "How did you start a fire so quickly?"

She ignored the question but saw that he had noticed the bright flames. "It will dry your shirt faster," Lia said, but he walked past her and planted his hand on the stone above the fireplace, looking at it, then at her, then back at it again. The flames went out with a whoosh, the Leering tamed.

"Do it again," he ordered. He had a look on his face, a mixture of fear and anger.

She scratched the side of her neck, stared into the tortured eyes, and the flames flared up, even hotter this time. With a thought, she made them hot enough that he had to retreat or be burned. His chaen shirt glimmered in the firelight. As his eyes locked on hers, the flames went out again.

His gaze wandered down to her neck. "You wear a charm on your string. Let me see it."

She had worn the gold ring around her neck since the stormy night long ago. "It is just a trinket. Why?"

"Let me see it."

She pulled the ring from her bodice and let it hang in front of her gown. He squinted at it, his face filled with a terrible look. The blood was black against his eyebrow, the bandage askew. For a moment, a fish of fear wriggled inside her, and she thought he might try to snatch the ring from her.

"May I handle it?" he asked.

"I never take it off," she replied. "But you can see it." She held it up so that the firelight played off its smooth edge. Sowe gulped, her eyes wide.

The squire reached out tentatively, cocking his head as he examined it. "Just a ring? A gold band?"

She slid it on and off her small finger to demonstrate, then let it dangle. With a little thought, and without the Leering in her direct sight, she made the fire flare up again and he jumped, startled.

"How long have you practiced taming the Medium?" he asked her, turning around and staring into the flames.

"Now and then. It is not difficult for me."

He turned back and looked at her, his eyes blazing. "Many third-year learners cannot control it so effortlessly!"

"It is not my fault that they have trouble. I have told the Aldermaston that I want to be a learner, but he swears he will never let me."

"But how did you—I mean, how did you learn if no one—if you were not instructed? How can you do it?"

Lia shrugged and went over to the cook's table, the only heavy table in the kitchen. The others were trestle tables that could be cleared away easily and stacked. She dragged over the pestle and a stone bowl. "I saw the Aldermaston do it once one winter when I was little. So we could warm our hands when we were cold."

"You saw him do it once?"

Lia shrugged again. "Once." She had also seen him calm a storm, but did not mention that.

The flames were gold and orange, and waves of heat came from the oven, making the shirt rustle. Sowe quietly padded over and opened a crock and withdrew two nutmeg seeds, as large as walnuts. "I'll crush them," she said in a small voice.

Lia smiled at her then turned around to face the squire. "You need a new bandage then. Now sit on the stool near the fire. I will get some warm water."

He obeyed and sat on the stool while she fetched the kettle and some linen cloths to clean the wound. Standing over him, she

44

untied the knot of the bandage and gently peeled it away from the crusty skin. He winced once, but remained still, though his jaw muscles clenched.

"You seemed surprised that it was only a ring. Why?" Lia asked.

"Not surprised really. Perhaps the ring was left with you when you were abandoned here."

"Then why did you wish to see it?"

"You are too curious, girl."

"Life is curious, is it not? I like to ask questions. Now give me an answer. Why should it alarm you that I can use the Medium? Not because it is difficult. You were frightened that I could do it."

"Because there are only two ways to affect the Medium. One way is through inheritance and learning about your potential and letting it work through you. The other way…forces it—controls it. I wanted to be sure you were not doing the latter. Those who were not born into the power wear a medallion to force it to obey."

"What does the medallion look like? The one you fear?"

"I do not fear it. I am wary of it as I have been trained to be. Any way I could describe it to you would not be suitable, but I have seen its likeness. It resembles a braided rope, flat though, like leaves or the sashes on a maypole woven together into a circle."

"I see. So it does not look like a wedding band. Since you do not fear them, what if I had been wearing one?"

"I would have ripped it from your neck instantly." He looked up at her, his eyes deadly earnest. "With it, you may have sought to control me."

She pinched the ring between her fingers and looked at it again. "Then we are both grateful it is only a plain ring. You would not have enjoyed me scratching your face and leaving more scars."

Sowe coughed over at the table and dropped the mortar with a thud.

Lia pretended she did not care and continued to clean his wound. "You said most second- or third-year learners cannot summon fire," she said, dabbing his eyebrow with a soaked piece of linen. "When did you first do it?"

"By my first year," he answered.

"Why are you so surprised that I can? As I told you, I saw the Aldermaston do it."

"I could do it because my father had taught me for years before I even went to the Abbey in my Hundred to learn. My Family is strong in the Medium. That is important. As with his father and his father before him, my father started teaching me as a small boy. I had used the Medium before I became an armiger."

"What is an armiger?"

He closed his eyes, his mouth twisting into a snarl. "I bear the arms of the knight-maston I serve."

She sensed his discomfort and wondered at it. "I see. Since I cannot study the tomes, I like using Leering stones when no one is around to practice. They do so many different things." The scab was softened by the moist linen, but it did not start to bleed again. She sponged his forehead and cleaned away dried blood.

"I have always hated that your kind calls them that. It is not the proper name."

"It is a very proper name."

"I doubt you know what the word 'leering' means."

She bit the inside of her cheek. "It means a sly or cunning look." Bending closer, she squinted at the wound and patted it dry with a clean linen. She took the dirty ones and tossed them into the fire and watched them shrivel. "There is a learner here who tells me what words mean. Leering stones are faces carved in rock. Some are carved into suns. Some are carved into the moon at different degrees of fullness. Some seem to be carved out of stars. But they each have faces. And they always stare at us."

"Then why not name them Staring stones then? The word leering has other meanings."

"Such as?"

"I do not want to discuss it."

"Why? Are you too proud to tell me?"

"The connotation, what it represents, is not modest."

"What do you mean?"

He was getting even more impatient. His eyes blazed with anger. "Words have specific meanings, yet they can have multiple meanings. The word 'leer' is to stare at. But it also means to stare at someone in a certain way."

She looked at him pointedly, raising her eyebrows to ask the question.

His expression clouded over, as if he were nearly frantic with discomfort. His hands clenched in his lap. "I should not be discussing this with you like this."

She folded another linen into a padded square and pressed it against his wound. With a long length of linen, she secured it to his head and then tied off the knot.

"What a riddle you are," she said with contempt. "Most learners are. You study the true meaning of words and how to engrave them. How to use them. How to understand them. Yet you keep that knowledge to yourselves and then get proud when someone like me gets it wrong. Do you think that because I am a wretched, I cannot understand difficult things?"

"No, that is not it."

"Then why not tell me? If I do not understand, then you can mock me. But why withhold it?"

"Because I am not comfor…because it has to do with the way that some men look at women. A leer is not a flattering look. It is not a look of love." His hands were trembling. "It is not a look of respect. I have seen this look and when you see it, you will know it. I have seen it in wretcheds and I have seen it in knights." He stood, clenching and unclenching his hands, his thoughts visibly troubling him. "The stone carvings are merely emblems. Their proper name is *gargouelle*."

Lia shook her head, confused. "I do not know that word…"

"No, of course you do not. *Gargouelle* is from another language, the Dahomeyjan word for 'throat.' If you ponder it, maybe you will see why they are named such. Most wretcheds do not know the language of Dahomey exists, let alone how to pronounce it properly."

"You said they were 'emblems.' Explain that word."

"An emblem is used to represent something else. The carvings are an emblem of the power of the Medium inside us. They bear the face of man—or woman or beast—to show that the link to the power of the Medium is within us. In both of us. You are not bringing fire out of the stone. The stone helps you bring the fire out of yourself. They are powerful emblems, and should not be misunderstood, misused, or mispronounced."

Something in his words caused heat to rush through her. They were exciting words and thrilled her. A great deep thought brushed against her mind, so large she couldn't feel the edges of it. That somehow, the ability to cause fire, or water, or plague, or even life slept inside of *her*, not the stone.

"What you are saying," she said in a near whisper, "is that I do not really need the Leering to make fire."

"No, no. That is a twisted understanding. For you see, you have no control over that. It is the tragedy of your state. Your ability to use the Medium is an inheritance. It is a result of who your parents were, not you. Who your grandparents were, not you. Who your ancestors were back to the original fathers. Not you."

Lia glanced over at Sowe, who stared at them, her hands idle on the mortar and pestle. She lowered her gaze and started crushing the seeds again. "So even if I did become a learner, it does not mean that it would be easy to practice it. Someone born from a weak lineage would not…"

"Be able to warm a cup of water," he replied. "No matter how hard they studied. As a wretched, you will never know your full potential until you know your parentage. Learners spend a great deal of time learning who their forebearers are to understand how their gifts have mingled and been passed along to them."

Lia wanted to ask what it meant that she was able to do something that some learners could not, when a heavy knock sounded at the kitchen door, startling them.

The wounded young man started for the ladder to the loft, but Lia caught his wrist. "There are windows. You will be seen. There, behind the changing screen!"

He rushed to the wooden screen beneath the loft. She could see part of his boots in the gap beneath the screen and cursed herself. Another heavy knock sounded and she crossed the kitchen to the door.

"What will we do?" Sowe whispered fearfully.

Lia silenced her with a glare, then had an idea. "Take the kettle to the screen and rinse your hair. Tell him to hide in the tub."

"I am not going to bathe…"

The look Lia gave her must have been more frightening than a grim-visaged Leering, for Sowe snatched the kettle and rushed to the screen without a word. Lia watched the boots disappear and heard him settle into the small wooden tub they used for bathing.

She raised the crossbar and pulled the door open a bit, grateful that the glass was so smudged with soot. Light from the lamps spilled out on Jon Hunter's bearded face. His clothes were filthy, his shirt loose from the leather girdle, the collar open to a forest of gnarled hair.

"Oats, Lia," he said and started to push past her, but she held the door and put herself in the gap.

"Sowe is washing her hair. Go to Ailsa's kitchen for oats if you are hungry."

He sighed. "Lia, I am not walking to the other kitchen when I am here."

"Why not? Is she trying to kiss you or something? Or just being stingy with the honey ladle?"

Jon sighed, his eyes flashing. "You have been lingering around Reome too much. The oats are not for me."

"Who are they for?"

"I am not supposed to tell anyone. Another reason I came here."

"Very well. And you know Pasqua's rules about letting anyone into the kitchen but the Aldermaston after she is gone." She rested her head against the door and raised her eyebrows.

His voice was soft. "Does the Aldermaston know you stole one of the rings from the old cemetery?" he whispered, nodding down to the front of her dress.

Lia nearly lost her composure. She had forgotten to tuck it back inside her dress and now he had seen it. She said as calmly as she could, "The Aldermaston knows everything that happens at

Muirwood. Surely you know that. Why do you need the oats? You know I can keep secrets, Jon Hunter. You know that very well."

He sighed. "I will tell you, but remember it is a secret." She nodded eagerly. "I found a horse in the woods today."

"Really? Can I see it?"

He smirked. "If you do not tell anyone, Lia."

"Even Pasqua?"

"Of course not her, though you know the Aldermaston trusts her."

"I will fetch your oats then." She held the door a moment and then shouted, "Sowe, don't come out yet. It is Jon."

She quickly ascended the ladder and carried down a sack of oats. After shoving it into Jon's hands, she was about to close the door when he stopped it with his boot.

"Whose shirt is drying by the fire?"

For a moment, Lia's mind emptied of all ideas. Jon was trained as a hunter, and his watchful eyes noticed everything, first the ring and now the shirt. She stood for a moment, guilty, her ideas gone to the winds. Her mouth went dry. What could she say? What could she tell him?

"It is my secret," Lia said, blushing uncontrollably, and then she had the next idea. "I cannot share it, but you could ask Reome since she knows."

Jon gave her a confused look and withdrew into the night.

After she shut the door, she pressed her forehead against it. Hiding a man for three days would be more difficult than she thought.

***

The first commonly accepted reference to the term "Aldermaston" was engraved in the Third Tome of Soliven, one of the more tedious texts that learners struggle to translate during their first year. The passage can be read thus: "And he that is the Aldermaston among the brothers and sisters of the Family, upon whose head the anointing oil was poured, and is consecrated to put on the garments of chaen, shall not reveal his wisdom, nor rend his clothes; neither shall he go in to any dead body; neither shall he go out of the Abbey grounds, nor profane the Abbey grounds; for the crown of the anointing oil is upon him." The record goes on to speak about what wife he may take and what blemishes may disqualify him from the anointing.

This is the accepted origin of the term "Aldermaston" by most learners, and many hold mastons themselves to these high standards, excluding knights, armigers, or squires who fight in the service of their king, properly sanctioned, and thus visit death upon the bodies of their foes.

I am told there exists another translation of the Tome of Soliven, which mentions and describes the first use of the term "Aldermaston" in a different manner. It tells of King Zedakah, back in the day of the first Family. As a young boy, he was strong enough in the Medium to stop, as Soliven wrote it, the mouths of lions and quench the violence of fire. He instructed the ancestors of the first Family in the order of Aldermaston, telling them that they should have power, through the Medium and by their lineage, to break mountains, to divide the seas, to dry up waters, to turn them out of their course; to defy the armies of nations, to divide the earth, to stand in the midst of the sun; to do all things according to the will of the Medium, and at its command, subdue principalities and all powers.

I should think learners would prefer this account, if only the original could be found.

—Cuthbert Renowden of Billerbeck Abbey

CHAPTER SEVEN

The King's Men

Lia and Sowe both slept in the loft that night. The young man, who would not tell them his name, insisted on sleeping on rush-matting on the hard kitchen tiles. After complaining that he had dozed for much of the day and was not tired, he paced and skulked through the dark kitchen as if it were a prison. Lia watched him from the loft.

After Sowe fell asleep, which never took long, he took up a broom and practiced with it like a sword, swinging the pole around in a series of studied moves that would have been grace- ful except for the time he stumbled against a bucket, or when the makeshift blade clacked against a table during a down strike. He muttered to himself often. Lia watched for as long as she could keep her eyes open, then fell asleep out of pure exhaustion.

She awoke before dawn and discovered him sitting by the small oven, his face reflecting the hue of the fire, rubbing his mouth as he stared into the flames. His clean shirt covered the chaen, fitting him well at the shoulders. He glanced up at her as she started down the ladder, then looked back at the oven fires.

"Did you sleep?" Lia asked him, noticing the bandage over his eyebrow was missing, the scar red and swollen.

"Does it matter? I can do nothing but sleep during the day."

She determined he was in a sour mood again, and thought it best to prepare him something to eat before Pasqua arrived. Hunger made the calmest men cranky. After tying on an apron and fetching some oats, she started a pot boiling and gathered some spices to flavor it. The water bubbled quickly, and she added the oats. Then she cut into a loaf that had survived the day before and lathered some butter and honey on it, then set it by the oven to warm and melt the butter. He took it, without thanking her, and started to eat.

His sullen expression threatened to wilt her courage, which made her angry and determined. "The horse that Jon Hunter found must be yours," she said, handing him the steaming bowl she'd prepared and a wooden spoon.

"I am sure it is," he said sourly, taking it.

"I could help you get it back." She scooped some milled flour onto a mat and then cracked an egg into it. "He must be keeping it in the pens behind his lodge. It is on the other side of the grounds, but not far, and if the horse knows you, it probably would not make much noise."

"I am not afraid of your hunter."

"He has a bow and a gladius and you have nothing."

"What, a half-sword? And who trained him to use it?" He grunted with a chuckle and turned to look at her scathingly. "Do you ever stop talking?"

She wanted to strike the bowl of porridge out of his hand. Instead, she frowned with fury and kneaded the dough. "I have plenty of faults but would rather have mine than yours."

"It is not a fault to enjoy a respite from constant conversation. A respite is…"

"I know what *respite* means," she said, slamming the wad of dough and looking back at him fiercely. "Do you understand where you are? This is the Aldermaston's kitchen. He has eaten many meals in here. I see him every day and serve him his food. Do you think he changes the way he speaks to suit us? No! I have heard him use words that *you* may struggle with. When I do not understand something, I ask. He answers me for the most part—and when he will not, there are learners who do. I know what respite means."

"I have insulted you."

"You are very astute, Sir Armiger."

"Perhaps you will afford me now a moment to think quietly."

She was incensed. "You have had it quiet all night! What do you need to think so quietly about still, if I may ask?"

He turned back to his bowl and ate more of the steaming porridge, poking it angrily with his spoon. "I may not stop you from asking, it appears, even when I insult you. I am trying to determine your age."

It had flattered her that the knight-maston thought she was tall enough to be sixteen. "The man who dragged you to my doorstep was more polite than you. If you desire to know, then ask!"

He looked baffled. "It would not be proper to do so."

"Is it more proper to insult me instead? Why do you care how old I am?"

As Lia continued to punch the dough, adding the proper ingredients, she spied movement at the top of the loft and saw Sowe rubbing her eyes. That their argument was loud enough to have awakened her was surprising. Quietly, Sowe climbed down the ladder and disappeared behind the changing screen.

His eyebrows were knotted with anger, and he looked at Lia as if she were a fool, as if his every action should be obvious. "It is inconvenient knowing that my fate and my life are in the hands of a wretched who cannot keep quiet. Your friend is quiet. I find her courtesy and deference admirable. You talk too much for someone who says she keeps secrets."

Lia wanted to laugh and she did, under her breath. "Sowe is quiet because she is shy, especially around boys. She hardly says two words when the Aldermaston comes."

"I would say that is a proper token of respect."

"Then you fear that I will spill your secret? That I might stumble and it will come blurting out of my mouth? Is that it?"

His eyes were earnest, and something in his mouth was defiant. "I do not fear it, but yes."

Her fingers were thick with dough, and she scraped them clean on her apron. She scooped up the bud of dough and began shaping it. Part of her crinkly hair dropped in her face, and she brushed it away with the back of her hand.

"I am not like the girls that gossip in the laundry," she said. "Maybe that is what you are used to."

"It has been my experience that females in general cannot keep secrets. My life depends on your ability to keep mine."

"But I am not like that. You may believe me or not, but I have kept a secret of this Abbey for years. A secret that the Aldermaston has forbidden anyone to know. You could trust me with your name, and I would tell no one. Not even the Aldermaston."

His mouth tightened. Was he starting to believe her, or did he still doubt?

"I cannot trust anyone like that," he said softly. "Except my sister."

Lia shrugged. "At least you have a sister. You had better climb up to the loft. Pasqua will be here soon."

He nodded, scooping the last of the porridge with his spoon, and took the bread and honey with him. Pausing at the ladder, he looked at her.

"The shirt, thank you for troubling yourself to wash it."

"It was no trouble." She turned back to the dough and set it in a bowl, sprinkling flour on it. "I am thirteen. My nameday is a fortnight from now so I will soon be fourteen. So you do not have to wonder any more. Hopefully, if all goes well, your knight-maston friend will come for you tomorrow. " And then you will leave us, she thought with satisfaction. He truly was insufferable.

"I hope so," he said and climbed the ladder, disappearing into the tangle of vats, pumpkins, sacks, and jars.

"As do I," she whispered as she walked to the main door and raised the crossbar. Pasqua arrived shortly after.

***

Dawn was cold, bringing a soupy fog to the grounds. With Sowe working again, the chores were nearly done when the pear tart was finished baking. Pasqua asked Lia to carry it to the Alder-maston while it was still hot. Donning her cloak, she set off the short distance to the manor, tortured by the aroma from the tart. It smelled fragrantly of cinnamon and nutmeg, and she broke off a little crumb around the edge to taste it. She entered the manor from the rear, scuffing her shoes on the rush-matting to keep from tracking mud across the tiles, and went to the Aldermaston's study. Normally it was quiet there, but today it was abuzz with commotion.

Lia knocked on the door and opened it, spying the Aldermaston in conference with his elderly steward, Prestwich, who was bald except for a fringe of snowy white hair, and Jon Hunter, who was explaining something to them both.

"I was thorough. No markings on the bridle or on the saddle or saddlebags. No coat of arms, no signet. No maston symbols either, but that is not surprising considering the murders. The saddle was of such quality as you would expect from a knight… or squire."

The Aldermaston leaned back in his chair, motioning Lia to enter and directing her to the serving table. With his other hand, he gave a little motion that meant that Jon Hunter should stop talking. He was very good at that, Lia noticed. The Aldermaston's hands were gnarled with hard work, the skin purple with veins, but there was still strength in those hands, and a feeling of authority.

"Thank you, Lia. Come here, child."

She obeyed, trying not to look at Jon, or else she might start giggling. She was tempted to get him in trouble by saying she already knew about the horse and they could go on talking.

He squinted at her, then rubbed an earlobe that had several gray hairs poking from it. "I have a message for you to give to Pasqua. Please pay attention."

Lia stood still, listening.

"We are expecting guests. Emissaries from the king arrived in the village last night. They stayed at the Swan, not the Pilgrim. Pasqua will care about a detail like that, so do not leave it out. I have been told that they will come to the Abbey. I received no warning about this visit, so apologize to her that she was not given time to prepare."

Lia's heart fluttered. Her stomach went sour. She remembered the knight's warning. *If Almaguer comes, do your best to hide him.*

As innocently as she could, she asked, "How many shall we cook for, my lord?"

"Tell Pasqua that the retinue is at least twenty men."

"What does 'retinue' mean?" she asked.

"They are those who owe a noble lord their allegiance. They do his bidding and travel with him. There will be many mouths to feed. I know that Whitsunday is approaching, and she will be loath to relinquish her stores. If you must, send her to me to discuss it. They should be given our hospitality."

The sound of footsteps came running down the hall, and the page opened the door. His name was Astrid, and he delivered messages for the Aldermaston throughout the grounds. He was ten.

"Riders from the village, Aldermaston!" he gasped "We told them you would greet them in person in due time, but they... they would not wait. My lord, they are riding their mounts on the grounds instead of walking them! One of them asked me...he demanded to know where the kitchen was."

The Aldermaston surged to his feet, his face livid with anger. "Take me now."

Lia experienced a sudden bristling rush of panic. Her ears burned hot, her stomach twisting like one of Reome's wet garments. Her knees became shaky. She nearly dragged the hot pan off the serving table accidentally. It could only mean one thing.

The possibility was now real.

The king's men had come to search the Abbey. What if they were already at the kitchen doors? What if she was too late?

CHAPTER EIGHT

The Cider Orchard

Worries swirled through Lia's mind, and most of them ended up in her stomach. When she had decided to hide the young man, she had truly believed she would not be caught doing it. She had faith in her own cleverness, but events unfolded differently from how she had planned. A single thought blazed in her mind—she had to get the squire out of the kitchen. Pasqua might not be able to climb the loft ladder, but she had no doubt that soldiers could. No one would believe her if she pretended not to know that he was hiding in their midst. She could not begin to imagine the trouble that would hound her then. Where could she hide him, though?

Lia rushed. As she turned the corner of the squat, square building, she dreaded that she might have arrived too late.

No horses or soldiers could be seen, but she could hear them. The morning fog clouded her sight, but the whinnying of steeds, the jangle of spurs, and voices filled the void. Even the air had a strange smell to it—a coppery scent that clashed with the aroma of flower beds and grass.

Hurrying into the kitchen, Lia found Pasqua by the preparing table, mixing something for the midday meal. "Soldiers!" she said, gasping. Sowe's eyes blazed with fear at the words and her face became chalky.

Pasqua looked up irritably. "What nonsense are you talking about, child?"

Lia knew she had to get Pasqua out of the kitchen immediately. "Soldiers from the village. They just arrived. The...the Aldermaston said they are the king's men. I think one is a nobleman. He wants us to prepare a meal for them."

"A meal for... and they just arrived? I have a mind to let them eat uncooked fish. And with Whitsunday coming. Does he realize how long it takes for bread to rise? The nuisance."

Lia swallowed, straining to hear the sound of hooves approaching in the mist. "The Aldermaston wishes to speak with you, Pasqua. Right away. He just sent me."

"Right away? Of course right away. Right away and I will blister his ears. Right away and I will shake my spoon at him. Well, do not just stand there, girls, get working! Start some soup. That will feed more in a trice. We have some broth already, so cut up some vegetables. Quickly! Quickly!" She bustled out the main door, still grumbling to herself and wiping her hands on her apron as she left.

"Lia?" Sowe said desperately. She trembled with fear.

"Astrid said they were looking for the kitchen," she said in a loud voice. "We must hide you. Now! Come down."

"Where?" Sowe begged, clutching Lia's hands.

The young man emerged from the den of barrels and bags. His face was drawn with worry, but his reflexes were sharp. He bounded down the ladder in a blink. "How many?"

Lia looked him in the eye. "Twenty, I think. No one knows you are here. I have told no one. But if the entire Abbey hunts for you, then there is only one place we can hide you. The ruins of the old cemetery. No one is allowed to wander in that part of the grounds where the landslide happened. Only Sowe and I know what is there."

He nodded. "I will not risk your safety. How do I get there?"

"You will never find it in the fog. I will take you."

Sowe's fingers clenched around Lia's arm. "You cannot leave me here!"

Lia looked at her panic-stricken face. She only had an instant to decide. Sowe had to come with them. If the king's men came, she would never be able to keep the secret. One hard look and she would confess it all.

"You are coming too. Grab your cloak."

While Sowe rushed to get it, Lia crossed the kitchen to the rear doors and raised the crossbar. They did not open those doors as often, so she had to tug on the handles hard to get them moving, and they groaned from lack of use. Glancing outside, she spied no one else. Thank Idumea for the fog, she thought.

"Hurry, Sowe!"

She joined them, and the three left out the rear of the Abbey kitchen. Sowe wrung her hands, whimpering. The armiger looked each way, his neck muscles tense, his jaw clenched, his hands opening and tightening again and again as if craving a sword. But one man against twenty was madness even with a weapon. Lia led them across a soft patch of grass. The fog concealed everything except the squishy sound their shoes made and the swish of their cloaks against the green. There was noise and commotion on the grounds. Horses stamped and huffed. The noise of blades drawing from sheaths made Lia shiver. Voices rang out.

"Spread out. Surround all the doors. Don't be a fool, Brickolm— you two go the other way!"

Lia started to run and the others followed her example. From the swirl of fog appeared looming shapes, but Lia was expecting the quarter circle of oak trees ahead of them. The crooked limbs and stout trunks rose up like giants, but they would also provide cover. Would someone see them? Anxiously, she expected a cry of alarm. A warning to stop. They went past the oaks and into the Cider Orchard. It was not the season for fruit, or else she would have gathered a few apples that had dropped during the night. The trees were low and squat, which gave them excellent cover as they ran.

The Cider Orchard was a maze of apple trees. The branches were slender, the bark grayish and smooth compared with the scraggy oaks surrounding it. The apples were different in Muirwood from those of other Hundreds. They were famous for their cider. Lia led them through the willowy shapes, hearing Sowe gasp as she tripped, but the armiger caught her and kept her from sprawling facedown in the dirt. Threading through the trees, her heart racing as fast as her feet, Lia began to hope.

The orchard seemed as wide as the world that morning. In the spring, when the wind blew white blossoms from the branches, they looked like winter snow; only the smell was fragrant, the petals softer than roses. Each step brought them deeper into its domain. Ahead, the fog grew thicker, the air more moist and moldy. A smell rose before them, of bracken, scum, and fish, and she realized they had wandered astray and were approaching the fish pond.

"This way," she said, changing direction. They continued to cross the orchard, heading deeper once more. Past the orchard, a thick mass of oaks crowded around, and Lia knew they were near.

She slowed from a run to a walk because the ground became treacherous and they would drop suddenly off the hillside if they went too fast. Sowe panted, and even the armiger breathed heavily. Lia could hear them both behind her as she led them through the expanse of trees. Then the ground changed, becoming sturdy and hard as she stopped.

Turning around, she faced her friend and the young man. She stamped her foot on the ground. "Do you feel the stone beneath? It is a footpath, but grown over. No one in the Abbey is allowed here."

"Why?" he asked.

"This is the secret I told you about. Follow me." She led them down the crooked path between the oak trees. It was narrow enough that it did not really seem like a path at all. Clawlike branches grasped at her, forcing Lia and the others to duck and dart as they crossed. At last, the path ended at a startling drop. A Leering had been set at the end of the trail, its stern expression a warning to anyone not to wander farther. The eyes glowed a dull red. This was not an ancient stone—the carving was done by the Aldermaston himself. As a child, Lia had seen him work on it for months.

"When you climb down, use the roots as handholds," Lia said. "Sowe, stay up here and listen for the king's men. I will show him the cave."

Sowe nodded, hugging herself, and looked back the way they came. She shifted from foot to foot, shivering.

Lia led the way. The earth pitched forward suddenly, but she supported herself with exposed roots from the mighty oaks. The loamy smell of earth and trees was pleasant. She had never minded dirty hands. Positioning herself to a crouch, she gently lowered herself down and extended a foot first until she felt the firm stone.

"It is a little challenging because you cannot see what you are stepping on, but it will support you," she told him.

"How far down is it?" he asked, following her into the chasm.

She blocked his view, but that was probably a good thing. There was enough room for them both, but she gingerly scooted farther to make more. His boots came first and then he was standing on the rock next to her.

"For all that is holy!" he gasped when he realized he was standing on a boulder in the middle of the air. He started to back up, but she grabbed his shirt.

"There is a drop that way," she said. "The safe way is over here. See down? There is another stone lower. Then another one. These big stones are like steps. They go all the way down to the bottom of the hill, where you will find a little gully-brook and water. When the hillside washed away, it revealed them. The dirt went away, but not the stones. They just hang in the air. Partway down, there is a cave. There are Leerings for light and fire in there, so you will not be cold or unable to see. Sowe or I will bring food for you later today, if it is safe. Or after Pasqua sleeps, if it is not. If you search, you will find thickets with shrewberries, or mushrooms, or pods. But we will leave you food up by the waymarker above."

He looked nervously down at the next step. "How far...how far down is the cave?"

She sat on the rock and pushed herself off. "Not far. Some of the steps are taller than others. I have climbed them since the storm washed the hillside away. Sowe and I explore here all the time. I think we even left a blanket down there. We have to make sure no one sees us, though, or the Aldermaston will be... let us just say that he would be furious if anyone else learned of this place."

"Someone could get killed," he muttered, following her down some of the steps. A breeze kicked up, and he grabbed onto the rock to steady himself.

She led the way. "It proves the Medium is real. How else do stones float like this, with nothing holding them up? They must be ancient stones from another time or another earth. I think maybe the reason I can make Leerings work is because I know the Medium is real. I do not question it. Look, there is the entrance over there. Do you see it?"

After leaping to another rock, she maneuvered beneath one of the floating boulders and led him into a cavelike opening. With a thought, she made the sun-shaped Leering flare, filling the darkness with radiance. The room was carved into the hillside stone; the walls were smooth but speckled with black lichen. It was tiny compared to the kitchen, but the cave offered refuge from storms.

He touched a stone near the ceiling, tracing his finger along the maston symbols carved into the wall.

"The fire Leering is over there," she said, looking around, "And there is the blanket. Good. Sowe and I sit on it and eat the berries. I should get back. If we are missing much longer, Pasqua will get suspicious as well as angry."

"Do you need...do you need help climbing out?" he asked haltingly.

"You are frightened for me? You get used to the climb, but do not try it at night. It is dangerous unless the moon is out." She started to leave, but he stopped her.

"I will not forget that you did this," he told her. He shut his eyes. "For a moment, I thought they saw us. They would have killed me."

"The fog was a blessing. No one knows these grounds better than a wretched. If you lack a place to hide, go to the bottom of the hill. There are a heap of empty ossuaries down there. Big stone ossuaries. Are you surprised I know that word?"

He winced. "Not anymore."

"We used to hide in them, and Sowe and I would find each other."

"You hid among the bones?" His face looked sick with revulsion. He shuddered.

"No, you fool. The dead had already revived. They were empty of bones, except for grave linens." She fished in her bodice for the ring. "And these."

He stared at her. "I did not know they buried the dead with gold rings in this Hundred. And you…you took one?"

"If the dead left it behind, they obviously no longer needed it." She scooped it back into her dress, winked at him, giving a warning not to fall off the hillside, and hurried out of the makeshift cave, scrambling up the rock steps to the top. She was winded when she finished the climb.

Sowe was nearly frantic. "You were gone too long!"

"Stop acting like you are six. Back to the kitchen." They started walking quickly, holding hands so that Sowe could keep up.

"What if the soldiers are there?" Sowe whispered.

"Do not say anything. I will answer them."

"What if they ask me a question?"

"Pretend you are frightened of them."

"I *am* frightened of them!"

"Then it will not be difficult for you to show it, will it? If Pasqua asks where we went, I am going to say we went to sneak a look at the soldiers. Watch out for that branch." They both ducked.

Walking the rest of the way through the orchard in silence, they gripped each other's hands as the mist swirled around them. It was fading now that the sun was up, and they could make out the looming silhouette of the Abbey kitchen ahead past the screen of oaks. Lia's heart raced.

As they crossed the grass to the rear of the kitchen, two shapes emerged from the wall, stepping into their sight. Both held drawn swords.

"In the name of Almaguer, sheriff of Mendenhall, I bid you stand fast! Are you the missing kitchen help?"

"Yes," Lia said, her hand throbbing in pain from Sowe's clenching fingers.

The soldiers approached and grabbed each girl around the arm. "Then his lordship, the noble sheriff, desires to speak with you both. You will come with us!"

***

There was an Aldermaston long ago, over an Abbey that I will not mention, who allowed a wretched the privilege of reading and engraving. The wretched was a talented young man and strong with the Medium. The learners of the Abbey disdained him due to jealousy and his lack of rank. The Aldermaston encouraged his progress, however, convinced that his abilities would bring the Abbey great renown. But the wretched desired one thing above all else. By learning to read, he hoped to discover the identity of his forebearers. Instead of studying the words of the ancient mastons before him, he pored through the Abbey records, seeking the identity of his parentage. The clues were sufficient in the Abbey history, and he determined the identity of his mother, who had been a helper in the Abbey and a wretched herself. Abandoning his studies, he sought her at a neighboring village and forced her to reveal the identity of his father, who, he discovered, was a learner at the Abbey but never became a maston. He confronted the man who gave him his life, and he robbed him as vengeance. To this day, Aldermastons keep learners and helpers apart, and they refuse, completely and rightfully, to allow wretcheds of any circumstance the privileges.

—Cuthbert Renowden of Billerbeck Abbey

CHAPTER NINE

Almaguer

The sheriff of Mendenhall was balding. That was the first thing Lia noticed about him. What hair he had was short, spiky, and patchy across the dome of his head like a stretch of grass that had been trampled too many times. He was taller than the Aldermaston, but younger, his beard more steel than gray. As the soldiers gripping Lia and Sowe thrust open the rear doors of the kitchen, he turned from his conversation with the Aldermaston and Pasqua, a satisfied smile on his face. He looked pleasant, except for his eyes. His eyes were cunning, like those of a man used to counting silver.

"You see, Aldermaston, I knew my men would find them."

"We did not exactly find them," said the soldier holding Lia.

"They were sneaking in the mist," said the one holding Sowe.

"We were not sneaking," Lia said, yanking her arm free and glowering at the man. "We wanted to see the horses. I told you we should not have gone," she snapped at Sowe, whose complexion was paler than milk. The girl's knees were shaking.

There were four other soldiers in the kitchen too, searching every sack, looking around every barrel, and even poking their blades into the oven flues.

"In all likelihood, it was the older girl's suggestion to see the horses," the Aldermaston said. "Now, let us conclude this unseemly episode as quickly as possible. Ask the girls, sheriff, if they have seen a wounded knight, squire, or any other such person on the Abbey grounds and, more specifically, inside my kitchen. Your accusation has already caused an inordinate amount of commotion at Muirwood. I would prefer we end it."

The sheriff approached, his gait smooth and graceful despite his size. He approached Lia directly, and she met his quizzical expression with a look of defiance. The expression on his face was unexpected. He stared at her, at her face, with a strange look—a familiar look—a look that said much, but in a language she did not understand.

"I too would like to end this farce as soon as possible. If you would be so kind as to leave us, Aldermaston."

Lia swallowed. The man was demanding the Aldermaston leave?

"I will not," the Aldermaston said, his voice turning hard. "I will not allow you to threaten anyone in this Abbey."

"Threaten her?" said the sheriff, coming even closer to Lia. "You mistake me, Aldermaston. And you injure my tender feelings. If the report I heard is true, and if you are harboring a fugitive in your kitchen, my questioning would be best posed to the girl alone where you cannot influence her answers. I am sure she would say anything to protect you."

"This is nonsense and ingratitude," Pasqua said, bristling. She clenched a long spoon in her hand like a weapon. "This is my kitchen. The doors are locked every night. I will not hear another word of this nonsense. You are tearing this place asunder before my own eyes. Your soldiers are looting my stores. Now begone, you rascals! I'll not let you lay a hand on either of these children. Now let her go. Let her go!" Pasqua swatted at the one holding Sowe, and he hastily backed away from her. She stood between them.

"I wish to speak to the girls alone," the sheriff said, his voice calm, his eyes earnest.

"You will not," Pasqua said. "Ask what you will, but you will do so in my presence."

"Your cook has spirit, Aldermaston," the sheriff said.

"You will find that spirit throughout the Abbey," he replied. "Lia, child, if a wounded soldier were hiding in this kitchen, would you know of it?"

"Yes, Aldermaston," she replied, looking at him, not the sheriff. "There are only two doors to get in, and little room to hide as you can see, and we…"

"Lock both doors at night, yes," he said. "Your men have seen for themselves that there is no one hiding in either kitchen. Nor has any soldier, or maston, or fugitive sought sanctuary inside the Abbey itself. There are laws governing that, as you well know. As I told you before, Almaguer, I would like to conclude this rude interruption. The learners and helpers will gossip for months, if not years, over this incident. Not a single productive thing has happened in the Abbey since you arrived. It was an enthralling display of horsemanship, weapon mastery, and an unmitigated show of contempt for my authority here. Which, I feel impressed to remind you of once again, you have no authority here."

"I am sheriff at Mendenhall," the man replied angrily. "I am the king's man in this Hundred."

"A sheriff has authority over every place where the king's tax is collected. Muirwood Abbey does not owe the king's tax. It never has, not since its founding. I offer you my hospitality and the hospitality of our blacksmiths, our cider, our stores, even the hospitality of my own personal cook. If you wish to be invited to celebrate Whitsunday here this season or any season in the future, then accept my hospitality as a welcome guest. Otherwise, I will report your conduct to the king and tell him you defied my authority with no proof beyond the idle report of—what? A drunkard? Have I made myself clear on this point? To be sure, I will say it again. Come enjoy the rest of this day with us as our welcomed guests, or you will never step foot on the Abbey grounds again."

Lia watched the Aldermaston with amazement. A little smile crept to her mouth at his words. When she glanced at the sheriff, she saw that he was not looking at all at the Aldermaston. He had not taken his eyes from her.

Summoning a smile to wash away the anger brooding in his eyes, the sheriff said, "I accept your gracious hospitality, Aldermaston." He followed the Aldermaston a few steps, and then stopped, turning back and staring at Lia again. "When was she left on the Abbey steps—nearly fourteen years ago?"

The Aldermaston's eyes blazed with anger. His lips pressed together and his hands clenched at his sides. Lia's mouth went dry, as a hunger—a deep hunger—roared inside of her.

"It must have been fourteen years ago," the sheriff continued, seemingly oblivious to the Aldermaston's fury. Stroking his beard, he said softly to Lia, "I think I knew your father."

The Aldermaston's words were cold and short. "You have said more than enough, sheriff."

***

The day was a blur of activity. Both kitchens worked furiously to feed the sudden influx of mouths, but Pasqua's kitchen bore the brunt of it. The three worked slavishly, kneading dough, preparing sauces, and cutting meat. Wronen Butcher carved up a cow and had the pieces delivered to each kitchen. Additional help from the larger kitchen joined the fray, though they sent the younger ones to help scrub the pots and clean the wooden spoons.

"Was there truly a knight hiding here?" one asked.

"Did the Aldermaston use the Medium on the sheriff?" another said.

And it was usually after such a question that Pasqua would roar a new order and fill the kitchen with her hostility and insistence that no boy was or ever had hidden there. Lia watched to be sure the old cook wasn't adding salt instead of sugar to the countless sweet dishes they were preparing. That she had to prepare her best meals for soldiers who had spoiled her kitchen and run roughshod over the grounds brought out Pasqua's most colorful language.

Lia worked feverishly, but she also felt feverish. The sheriff's words haunted her. *I think I knew your father.*

Pasqua had told her to forget it as soon as the king's men had left the kitchen. The man was a sheriff, she had said, and they would use any trick or torture to get someone to confess a wrongdoing. Sowe, on the other hand, had seemed almost jealous. Her feelings were hurt because Lia had again blamed her for something she had not done—sneaking out to see the horses. Finding a man who may have known one's father was the fulfillment of every wretched's secret dreams, so jealousy was a natural response to it.

As Lia tasted some broth, she thought about the sheriff. As she climbed into the loft for a pumpkin to cook, she thought about the armiger. One cannot be a wretched without pondering deeply the reason for being abandoned, but Lia was not the kind of person who felt sorry for herself very often or resented knowledge she had not earned.

As a helper in the Abbey kitchen, it was one of her duties to serve the guests who stayed with the Aldermaston. The hall was nearly full with the sheriff and his retinue, along with all the learners and the teachers. It was a boisterous occasion, full of laughter and jesting. The learners were giddy with the change in routine. The teachers seemed cautious and reserved, surreptitiously looking at the Aldermaston who sat at the head of the hall, brooding.

Lia ladled stew into a learner's bowl, but a voice sounded on her other side.

"Hello, Lia."

It was Duerden. She almost had not seen him, since he sat so low in the chair. She turned and ladled soup into his dish.

"What have the king's men been talking about?" she asked him in a whisper.

"A silly thing. War. The king has summoned an army. A waste of taxes. Such a waste." He took a sip from his cup of cider.

"Where?" she asked, pausing by his chair, her eyes darting from face to face. Almaguer was talking to a teacher at the other end of the table. He had not seen her enter.

"Where what, Lia?"

"Where is the army gathering? Where are they going?"

"I am not sure 'gathering' is the right word to use. 'Assembling' or 'mustering' are good alternatives."

She wanted to sigh. "Where is the army mustering?" she asked patiently.

"They claim that rebels are gathering at Winterrowd, wherever that is. There may be a battle soon. A whole army—how expensive. What if the rumors are not true? Such an expense."

Lia swallowed. Winterrowd. She had never heard of it before, but that was not surprising since she had never left the Abbey in her life. Every time visitors came, so did news from the outside, and everyone gossiped about it for days. The learners were always the first to hear, and then scraps began to be tossed down to the helpers. She liked Duerden because he treated her like she was from Family.

"Do any of the learners have to go fight for the king?" she asked, giving him another helping of soup.

He took a slice of bread from beneath a linen wrap in the basket in front of him. He bit into it, thinking as he chewed. "I think only Reuven is old enough. This is very good bread."

Lia crossed to the other side of his chair and served the next learner, a girl named Aloia who had a jeweled choker and stared at her with anger for not having served the soup yet.

Lia bent down and whispered near Duerden's ear, "Tomorrow, tell me everything you hear about the war. Meet me by the duck pond after studies."

He looked at her, puzzled.

She gave him a pleading look. "Please, Duerden. I will dance with you on Whitsunday if you do."

His complexion went pink, and she hurried to the next learner and kept ladling soup. Glancing up, she saw the sheriff still talking to the teacher—except this time, he was staring at her. She did not know if he had spied her talking to Duerden.

When the crock was empty, she left the hall through the rear doors and started back to the kitchen to refill it.

"Lia," the Aldermaston called from behind.

It was just the two of them, alone in the corridor near his chamber. She stared at him, cradling the crock in her arms. "Yes?"

"Stay in the kitchen the rest of the evening."

She bit her lip and said nothing for a moment. "What did I do wrong?"

"The sheriff has taken an interest in you."

She looked at him coldly. "He said he knew my father."

The Aldermaston's face was composed, but his eyes started to churn with anger. "What would it matter if he did know?"

"What would it matter?" Lia said, clenching the crock tighter. "How can you ask that?"

He took a step closer. His voice was so low, she barely heard it. "You think that knowing would make your life easier? You forget, child, that I have dwelled at Muirwood a very long time. I have witnessed many wretcheds grow up and leave. Some come back to ply the skills they learn here. Some, only a few, have ever found the knowledge they sought. Not one of them was ever grateful that they did. Not one. They wished that they never knew. Do not be tempted by the sheriff's words. They were intended to harm you, whether or not you wish it so."

Lia trembled, but tried to calm herself. "So he was lying then?"

"It makes little difference whether he was or not. My instructions are clear. I want you to stay in the kitchen tonight. They leave at dawn. And that is the end of our conversation."

CHAPTER TEN

Garen Demont

The dream started gently with a kiss on her cheek, causing a flush of warmth inside her. Then it turned into a dark, all-surging quickness, and it was as if she were drowning in fear and shame. She awoke with a start, trembling with terror. She blinked, too frightened to breathe, and tried to calm herself. Feelings from dreams always lingered with her. Nothing could banish them quickly. There was an inky, oily feeling in the air, a murmur like a harsh whisper. The corner kitchen fire, the one with the Leering, was burning bright and hot, flooded with flames instead of winking with embers in the dark as it should have been that late at night. Lia sat up and scooted to the edge of the loft to get a better look. The sheriff knelt by the flames, staring into them, a hand on his chest. When he turned to look up at her, his eyes were glowing bright silver in the dark.

He cupped something in his hand that was threaded through a gold necklace. The shape was tarnished and circular, like interweaving leaves or flower petals, or the coil of a snail's shell. He tucked it back into his shirt, the firelight revealing a tattoo mark on his chest, which was blocked as he fastened his collar.

"There you are," he said, rising to his full height. The glow in his eyes began to dim as he approached.

"You are not"—she could barely talk and swallowed to clear her voice—"allowed to be here. The Aldermaston forbids it."

"You have your grandmother's famed beauty. The slope of your nose, your cheeks, they must be hers. The sons were handsome, to be sure. Your father was indeed a handsome man. Did he ever know about you, I wonder?"

Lia could not stop trembling. Breathing was an effort. "I do not believe you."

He stopped at the bottom of the loft ladder. "So young. So very young." And he gave her a look, a look that made her stomach sick, her head swim, and the floor feel like it was spinning.

"Go," she whispered. She wanted to scream, but there was something terrible in his dimly glowing eyes. Something warped and black, the color of shadows behind the gleaming silver.

"I was there when your grandfather and uncle died. I fought in that battle. That glorious battle when so many accursed men of your Family fell. I would never have dreamed it possible that one of them would leave a wretched behind. They were so sanctimonious! So full of pride and their own worth. You must be one of them. Your face…your sweet face. It is staring at me past the brink of death. Child, you are special."

He put a hand on the ladder and started up.

"Do you wish to know the name? Are you not curious why you were abandoned? The shame of it! Oh, the glorious shame they must have felt." Each step of his boots shook the ladder, doubling her fear. "How they must have choked on it, a cup of gall spilling over."

"Go," Lia whispered huskily again, her voice too dry to speak out loud or scream. Sowe was asleep near her, her back facing them. A spasm of fear went through Lia's heart as his face crested the loft floor.

"I can tell you all. I know where your father died. I know when he died. The blood of your Family is still on my sword. The moans have never rubbed clean. But I will tell you of them. Of their traitorous hearts. Of their punishment even after death. Your grandfather. Your uncle. Their heads spitted on spikes. How we played with their corpses. Oh, child, how we avenged you!"

His gloved hands gripped the top of the ladder poles, and his breath reeked of something fetid. His presence smothered her, like a bell jar encasing a candle and withering the flame. It was the Medium, and it was awful. She saw the thin gleaming chain around his throat.

Like a kitten struggling to survive in a raging river, she clawed at it. Her fingers tightened around the chain, and then she yanked as hard as she could. The medallion slipped loose from his shirt front and the sight of it nearly made her vomit. The misshapen twisting pattern looked unnatural, and it exuded darkness and fear so powerfully it made her insides shrivel. The chain snapped.

"Little!"

With the chain still in her fist, Lia shoved him hard, his weight sending the ladder backward. He was quick, so cruel and quick, and grabbed a fistful of her curly hair as the ladder tottered backward. He dragged both of them down, and she fell, landing atop the ladder—on him—and he flinched with pain and grunted as they slammed on the floor.

Lia was breathless, stunned, but the gloom had left. The feelings were gone. She clawed her nails into his face, then yanked her hair free. He shoved the ladder off, and she ran for the door. Already he was struggling to his feet, wasting no words on curses or threats. She raised the crossbar, yanked hard on the door, and fled into the night, only to run into one of his soldiers outside.

In a fury, she tried to rake his face with her nails, and only after he caught her wrist did his familiar leathery smell, scruffy beard, and tangled hair come together in her mind. It was Jon Hunter, gladius in his hand.

She had never felt more grateful to him than at that moment. The door opened again as the sheriff followed her out. Lia cringed, but Jon thrust her behind him. Looking up, she saw the Aldermaston closing the distance with a glowing orb in his hand. She recognized having seen the orb in his chambers, but had never witnessed it glowing with the Medium's power.

The sheriff's eyes blazed. Blood dripped from a scratch mark on his forehead, and he seethed silently, his hands opening and clenching. Jon's blade was up, the point aiming at the intruder's heart. His expression said, draw your blade man, and I will run you through, sheriff or not.

When the Aldermaston reached them, Lia felt another surge of relief and started to cry. He bent over her, taking her chin and forcing her face up. He looked ferocious and concerned. "Did he hurt you, Lia?"

Unable to speak, she shook her head no.

His gaze lingered on her face for several moments as a storm of fury built across his countenance. He was known for his fierce temper. Patting her cheek, he raised to his full height and faced the sheriff.

"Almaguer, you violated my hospitality. How dare you."

The light from the orb in his hand made the sheriff wince as it flashed brighter. "I was seeking answers from her, Aldermaston. Nothing more. That is my duty to our king."

"My duty is to protect the inhabitants of Muirwood Abbey. I cannot tolerate anyone polluting the protection these grounds provide. They shield every pilgrim soul from any kingdom. The king will learn how you have abrogated your duties. You will be sharply punished."

"You may tell him yourself when he arrives!" the sheriff said with a snarl. "It will not be long. The traitors are festering nearby. You can smell it in the air like a kill rotting in the sun. Anyone who has supported them in any fashion will feel the fullness of the king's wrath. Even you, Aldermaston. Even in this ancient place."

"We have survived many wars and many storms and many such threats. I care only for the proper instruction of the learners here and to preserve this place from the peevish intrigues you waggle at me. Be gone, Almaguer. Be gone at once! Your men with you. Either you or I will die before any unfortunate reunion between us must occur. I revoke your welcome. Jon, escort the sheriff to the gates. I warn you, sheriff, that he has been well trained. Defy him at your peril. Prestwich will evict the rest of your men. Then lock the gates."

"Yes, Aldermaston," Jon said, never lowering his blade until the Aldermaston motioned him to.

As Lia watched the sheriff go, he looked back at her one final time. But his eyes were no longer glowing. She could see him looking at the thin thread of chain clutched in her hand.

***

There was a loose tile in the kitchen floor, under which Lia hid all her treasures. So the next morning, she hid the sheriff's medallion and chain there during one of Pasqua's garderobe visits. She learned that, thankfully for her, Jon had prowled around the kitchen all through the night and had seen the sheriff intrude. He had rushed to warn the Aldermaston and arrived back at the moment of Lia's escape. She was so grateful for his timely rescue that she kissed his bearded cheek, which embarrassed him crimson and made Pasqua gasp and rush for a broom to shoo him out, but his exit was already hasty.

Sowe, on the other hand, needled Lia constantly about confessing their crime to the Aldermaston before something even more dreadful happened. Lia managed to convince her, after much persuading, that it would only do more harm than good. The Aldermaston could faithfully deny knowing a wounded stranger was being tended at the Abbey. It would be best to tell him later after the armiger was gone.

When the afternoon meal was over, Lia was surprised to learn that people were gossiping about the king's men who had departed in the middle of the night without a word. There was no mention of the attack against Lia in the kitchen. Sheriff Almaguer, it was said, had commanded his men to mount up and ride, which could only mean that their hunt for the wounded soldier continued.

Sowe said she did not feel well, so she stayed in the kitchen while Lia took a cloak to search for Duerden near the duck pond. The day was sunny, though damp. It was clear enough that even the crouch-backed hill known as the Tor was in full view. Many of the learners and helpers had doffed their cloaks, and all enjoyed the sunshine. A few children chased butterflies. Most of the learners and helpers used the field in front of the pond as a place to meet and wrestle or play games.

Lia found Duerden sitting beneath the largest oak with a tome in his lap. He carefully turned the thick metal pages, his finger tenderly tracing the etching as he read. All the learners had tomes made of precious aurichalcum, a metal made from blending copper and gold. The gleaming pages were held together by three sturdy rings mounted into a thick, flat base. She looked at it, jealously wishing for one of her own.

As she approached, he gave her a mock frown and carefully closed the record. "Treasa Lavender was churlish with me yesterday. For no reason I can name, she came up to me, poked me in the chest, and said that the next time I needed a shirt washed, I should ask her or one of the other lavenders and not you."

"She is right, you should," Lia said. The walk from the kitchen, combined with the sun, had made her very warm, so she unfastened her cloak and used it as a blanket to sit on. She had forgotten to warn him and silently cursed herself. "It is Reome's fault. She just assumed I was washing yours. I never told her that I was."

"What affronts me is that she does not think I, or any learner for that matter, ought to wash my own clothes."

"You are all highborn, Duerden. From a Family."

"That makes no difference. Aldermaston Willibald who wrote the *Hodoeporicon* planted his own crops, and served his people instead of himself, and I am quite convinced that he even did his own laundry. It is laziness, pure and simple."

"You do not bake your own bread," Lia reminded him. "Or forge your own tome."

"But laziness does not prevent me from learning any craft. Far from it, I arise the same hour that you do. Mundane tasks are equally relevant for controlling the Medium, and I enjoy fresh air before sunrise. Work has a way of cleansing the mind. One does not grow strong unless one works at where one is weakest."

Lia yawned. "What did you learn from the king's men yesterday?"

"Why do you care so much about it, Lia?"

"Because Sowe and I are always the last to hear and the war would be over before anyone decides to tell us anything."

Duerden laughed and leaned back on his elbows. "Gossip. Fair enough. You probably are still the last to know. Everyone has talked about nothing else all day. Traitors to the realm are gathering in Winterrowd. They seek those willing to join them in a revolt against the king. And they will be slaughtered. Even with Garen Demont leading them."

"Who is Garen Demont? Is that a Family name?"

"Only one of the more famous ones. Garen's father was Sevrin Demont."

"And who is that?"

"You do not know who Sevrin Demont is?"

"I would not be asking if I did." Sometimes he was feather-brained.

"How can that be? Everyone knows who he is!"

Lia shrugged, trying to tame her impatience. "I have never heard that name before. Who is he?"

"He used to be king in all but name. Never lost a battle, except his last. They say he was brilliant on campaign, knew no fear, yet he held true to his principles. He was a true knight-maston in every way that matters most, and though he was only an Earl, he was treated like the crown prince. Our last king, of course, hated him. That was our current king's father. Our good king, our cruel king, our crowned king was the man who defeated the Demonts in the battle of Maseve. It has been said, at court, the battle was between equal forces. But I was told it was five or six men to one. Usually the highborn of Family are imprisoned and ransomed. Not the Demont Family. They were brutally massacred. That was the end of chivalry in our kingdom, I think. There are few knight-mastons left in this generation. It is easier to serve the king, they say, if you are not a maston."

"And Garen Demont is the son?" Lia asked, sitting up straight and leaning in.

"He is one of the younger sons. Gravely wounded at Maseve and imprisoned instead of butchered, which one might attribute to many reasons, some of which may involve the Medium. He escaped after his injuries healed and fled to another country. Dahomey, I think." He sat up, his eyes twinkling. "There is one story about him that I particularly admire. After Maseve, he joined the service of some foreign king and won many battles. One summer, he was visiting an Abbey in a distant land and one of his cousins arrived, for they are cousins to our king through marriage. This cousin had fought against his Family at Maseve. Well, Garen drew his sword and nearly beheaded the man right then and there. Yes, in the middle of the Abbey grounds! Everyone gawked, expecting to see blood spilled. Then he paused, spat on the ground, and said, 'Though you had no mercy for my father and brother, I will grant mercy to you.'"

"That was very generous of him," Lia said, wide-eyed.

"An act of clemency that made him practically as famous as his father. Rumor has it, Lia, that he is back from fighting foreign wars, and that he has come to raise an army to topple the king who killed his father. The thought of Sevrin Demont's son, like his father revived, coming to our realm has the whole kingdom ablaze with a thousand different rumors. So this may be rumor only. He may still be leagues and leagues away serving a foreign king. But from what I heard the sheriff's men say, they are not treating it as an idle report. The full host of the king's army musters and marches on Winterrowd. As I told you before, there will be another slaughter."

Lia was desperate to see the armiger, tell him what she had learned. "Why will they be slaughtered?"

"No one has defeated the king in twenty years of battles since Maseve, although many have tried. His battle flags bring fear to his enemies, for he flaunts the flags of his foes amidst his own standard. No army who has faced him, not even Sevrin Demont himself, has won. From what the soldiers were muttering in their cups last night, only the younger knights and squires are joining Demont. The experienced ones, the ones who have fought for the king all these years, are paid and fed. They know his kind of war. Let me say again that there are but few, if any, knight-mastons among them."

"I need to go," Lia said, gathering up her cloak and shaking the grass off it.

"Lia," Duerden said, shifting awkwardly, then rose with her. "Can I ask you something first?"

"What is it?"

He fidgeted with his sleeve, tugging it taut. "When you said you would dance with me at the Whitsun Fair...I want you to know that...you realize that I would have told you all this anyway. You need not make me any promises. I would...I should like to dance with you...but I do not want you to feel coerced."

Lia stared at him for a moment. "That was not a question."

He swallowed. "I guess you are right."

"I have a question for you then. Why do you only greet the girls at the Abbey?"

"I...what...you mean...I greet everyone..."

"No you do not. I have seen you. We can be walking together and talking, and you will greet another girl who passes by, but never one of the boys. Why?"

He was flummoxed. His face turned red.

Lia clasped the cloak around her throat. She gave him a teasing smile and then hurried away.

What she really wanted to ask him, which she dared not, was about the twisted charm she had yanked from Almaguer's neck during the night. She would save that question for the armiger hidden in the forbidden grounds.

***

The power of the Medium should never be compelled. Its power must be coaxed, persuaded, allured, or invited. Throughout the generations of Family, a relationship with the Medium has formed. As each generation honors it, the union is strengthened until they gain access to the ultimate power of the Medium and free their line from the bands of death. But there are those who, because of anger, spite, jealousy, or domination, cannot engender even the briefest flicker of agreement with the Medium.

To them, the power is closed because they will not yield their thoughts, their desires, or their wills over to it. They think their own thoughts. They desire their own cravings. And they demand obedience to their own will. As with all things in nature, there is opposition. Sun and dark. Sweet and bitter. Courage and fear. And like the Medium, there is a means by which one can force power to obey. A fellow can compel another to serve him. It is my experience, and has always proven to be the case, that when humans give in to their baser instincts, they discover ways to forge a link to the Medium that is unnatural. This forging is not only figurative but literal. Those who do parade the emblem of this union from a chain around their necks.

—Cuthbert Renowden of Billerbeck Abbey

CHAPTER ELEVEN

Getmin's Scorn

The face on the waymarker frowned at her, a reminder that the Aldermaston would be angry if he knew she was creeping down into the ruins again. But despite the scowl, she went down anyway. The warmth of the sun on her face and arms calmed her, but her heart was aflutter with thoughts and ideas. Was she a Demont? Was that what the sheriff had hinted? Not just any family, but a famous Family? Did that explain why she could use the Medium so easily?

She ventured into the gorge and jumped down to the floating stone, gripping a linen full of foodstuffs in one hand. Clambering down each step, she hurried until her breath was harsh in her ears. The wind carried earthy smells of fragrant wild grasses, woods, moss, and dirt.

Darting inside, she found him sitting on a stone, a golden tome in his hands, his face eagerly reading each word.

"Where did you find that?" Lia asked, startling him.

He nearly dropped the tome, but steadied himself, his eyes wide with wonder. "I did not hear you come down. This is…this is

beyond belief. This place you found. It is singular. I have heard…
but I did not know there was one like this at Muirwood."

"Where did you find that tome?" she demanded with a surge
of jealousy, for she had searched the ruins for years and found no
such treasures.

"Over there," he said, pointing to the far wall. Except it
wasn't a wall; it was open now. The door was made of stone. Lia
approached eagerly and discovered that it opened up to a deeper
cave. There were stone tables, and on the tables, tome after tome
with no dust. Scriving tools of all shapes and sizes, tubs of wax,
a bone stylus, parchment maps in long, leathery rolls, and coins
from many realms crowded around and beneath the tables. Just
inside the door was an oil cruse, a barrel full of milled grain, and
a basket of apples—which was absurd since it was not the right
season for ripe apples.

"This was here all along?" Lia asked, staring in wonder.

"Yes, but you never would have found it," he replied, carefully setting down the tome he was reading on the stone table. His
face was expressive, his eyes alight. "Only a maston can open that
door. It requires more than just affinity with the Medium. You
need to know the right words to say."

"Can you teach me?"

He shook his head. "No. That is forbidden. This is the secret
place, hidden from the eyes of the world. A Wayfarer lives here
or stops here when he is in this country. Someone who has been
writing the history of the land. The record on the table has a final
entry—it seems to have last been written a dozen or so years ago.
I do not think anyone has been here in at least that long. But there
are other records, things I have never seen before. Earlier ver-
sions of the Tomes of Soliven, for example." He shook his head.

"There are passages missing from the version I studied when I was a learner."

She looked him in the eye and watched for a reaction. "Is your name Garen Demont?"

His enthusiasm guttered out as if a bucket of water dousing a candle. Wariness replaced it. "Why do you ask that?"

Whether or not he was the man, she could see that he knew the name. "Because the sheriff's men are looking for anyone rallying to Garen Demont. And you would not tell me your name, so I was suspicious."

He stared at her, squinting slightly.

She wanted to throw something at him out of pure frustration. "If I was going to betray you, I would have last night, when the sheriff came sneaking into the kitchen with his black amulet and tried to force me to tell him our secret. Can you not trust me still? Who are you?"

"Where is the sheriff now?"

"The Aldermaston sent him away. His men left in the night."

"And he wore an amulet? Like the kind I warned you of?"

Lia nodded, then folded her arms and stared at him hard. She was not going to tell him that she had stolen it from the sheriff during their scuffle. Not yet anyway, especially if he was determined to keep secrets. "Please tell me."

"This is madness," he muttered to himself. "I do not know why I am even considering it." He rounded on her. "For your own good, you should not know. It can only harm you and this Abbey. You know too much already." He ran his hand through his hair, clenching his jaw. The scab on his temple was black.

Lia dropped her shoulders. "I told you that I keep secrets. I will keep yours. I promise."

He sighed, deep and heavy, his eyes closing. "Even if they kill you for it? You are nearly as old as my sister. I could not even trust her with what I was doing, and yet you ask it of me?"

"I am not your sister. I am only a wretched. Yet maybe, just maybe, I can help you." She squeezed her hands in frustration. Why wouldn't he believe her? "The Aldermaston will not let them kill me. He is not that vicious."

"I do not even know where I am going. So how can you help me get there?"

"I may know where you are going. If what I have heard is true, Garen Demont is mustering at Winterrowd."

His eyes blazed, his expression frantic. "This you learned from the sheriff's men? They know the gathering place?"

"How else would I have heard it? Do you know where Winterrowd is? If you are not Garen Demont, then you are loyal to him?"

He clenched his teeth even tighter, fighting to master himself and his frustration. Then he sighed heavily. A haggard look crossed his face. Lia knew she had won.

"I am not Demont. Demont was the Earl of Liester. My father is the Earl of Forshee. Their earldoms border each other. In a few months, I reach my majority where I may be invested with the earldom. Right now, my uncle holds it for me." He sighed again, twitching with dread. "My name is Colvin Price. The king is my cousin."

Lia gave him a satisfied smile, but kept her arms folded imperiously. "It took you long enough to tell me. So. You are joining the rebellion?"

"I am."

"Where is Winterrowd?"

"I do not know. It is a coastal town, west of here. It is somewhere in this Hundred. Demont landed in the country of Pry-Ree a fortnight ago. Do you know of it?"

She shook her head.

"It borders our realm to the north, separated by a little water, but there are ports on the south side not far from this Hundred. Not far to cross if you have enough boats. Much faster than traveling by land. When I learned about the summons, he had already set sail. His agent, a knight-maston, was to meet me at the outskirts of Muirwood Abbey and lead me there."

"The knight-maston that brought you here?" Lia asked.

"I do not know. I never met the man."

"He seemed to know you."

"I would not doubt it. Perhaps he was told. Perhaps I misjudged him. When I came, I went to the village first, but did not feel safe there, even with a storm blowing. There were too many questions, too many suspicions. So rather than sleeping at one of the inns, I rode south, and then circled back toward the Abbey another way. Someone followed me from the village. I thought I escaped him into the woods during the storm, but I remember hearing a noise, turning around, and something struck my head. I thought I had been captured. When I awoke, I was in the kitchen, sick to my stomach."

"Yes, I had almost forgotten that part," she replied, wincing at the memory. "A knight-maston brought you to the kitchen. You may have been running from him without knowing he was there to guide you."

"Indeed. And yet I worry. I have been thinking on it, and it makes sense. That when the sheriff arrived in the village, whoever it was who saved me was captured himself."

"He seemed a clever enough man to me. Why would you fear his capture?"

He walked back through the stone doorway and stood facing the sky. "Because they were searching for me at the Abbey yesterday." He turned and looked at her. "How else would they have known I was here? How would they have known to search the kitchen?"

Lia swallowed. That made sense. Hope wilted. "Then the knight-maston…is not coming back for you tonight. Is he?"

Colvin—she now knew that was his name—looked troubled. "I fear he will not, and I do not know the way to Winterrowd."

"If the sheriff's men are still looking for you, the road will be watched."

"If I stay at Muirwood under the Aldermaston's protection, then I have risked everything in vain. That is why I do not claim the protection of sanctuary. The Abbey may protect my life, but it can easily become a prison with the Aldermaston my keeper. There is too much to risk trusting him with my identity. I have come this far. I must go on. Demont needs to know that the king's men are on the hunt and know about Winterrowd."

Lia swallowed, feeling worse. "The sheriff said last night that the king was coming. The king himself."

"Then it is even more urgent that I leave," he said darkly. "My horse, where is he? You can help me get him? I could leave tonight."

Lia bit her lip, thinking quickly. Then she remembered the orb in the Aldermaston's study. The one she had seen him holding in the night that shone like a lamp. "I can lead you to your horse. Maybe I can also help you find the way to Winterrowd."

"But you said you did not…"

"I do not know where it is. But the day is not done yet. I may be able to discover it."

He leaned forward. "Can you? How?"

"If I can, I will find the way. Here, some food for your supper." She handed him the linen, remembering she had been holding it the whole time. "And where did you get those apples? It is not even the season for Muirwood apples."

He looked over his shoulder. "They were already there. Same with the grain."

"Out of season?"

He shrugged. "Season or not, the apples are good."

Lia went to the basket and knelt. The fruit was round and firm, the skin pinkish, red, and yellow. Just like the Cider Orchard. Muirwood apples were famous throughout the kingdom.

"I doubt you know this, but there is a secret to finding the best ones," she said. "Look at the skin. If it looks a bit rough, a little worn, with little splotches—those have the sweetest flavor. The ones that are perfect on the outside tend to be a bit more bland. That is true about many things in life. I always hunt for the best one before I take the first bite."

Gingerly, she lifted one out that had the telltale signs around the stem and brought it up to her nose to smell it. Closing her eyes, she inhaled the scent. Most apples just smelled like wood. But a ripe Muirwood apple had a subtle scent. She cherished the time when the harvest was done, when bushels of apples were stored up in the loft, and she could sleep amidst the tender smell.

"Whatever are you doing?" he asked her, his voice a bit amused.

"You never just eat a Muirwood apple, Colvin. You must always smell it first."

"It is fruit. The coloring is a bit odd. At first I thought they weren't ripe until I tasted one."

She gave him a mockingly stern look. "Never just eat them. Smell them. Savor them first." She closed her eyes and let its glorious scent fill her again. "Then you can eat it." She took a bite and it was tart and sweet at the same time, juicy and crisp. "There are many ways to bake, boil, mash, spice, and fry them, but they are perfect alone." She relished the flavor, the texture in her mouth. After swallowing, she looked up at him. "It was a Muirwood apple that tempted the first parents, you know."

He gave her an exasperated look, but did not reply. His expression indicated that she was being discourteous to the dead again.

She straightened and brushed some dirt off her dress while she enjoyed the fruit. "I will see if I can learn the way to Winterrowd. Watch for Sowe and me at sunrise at the waymarker." She took another bite. "Leaving tonight would be dangerous anyway. Dawn will give you a full day to ride tomorrow."

He nodded, saying nothing in farewell as he was eating ravenously from the food she brought. She finished the apple after climbing back up the ancient steps. To get back to the kitchen, she crossed the orchard. It would be a while before the orchard filled with blossoms and heavy fruit. Having been raised at the Abbey, she knew everything about apples. That they each had five seeds, and if cut a certain way, they were shaped like a star. They were useful in many dishes, including soup. Lia knew dozens of ways of preparing them.

"Where have you been hiding, Lia?" came a voice behind her as she crossed the ring of oaks bordering the kitchen.

She glanced back at Getmin Smith with annoyance and kept walking. "I have not been hiding anywhere."

He caught up with her and grabbed her arm. "Hold a moment. Where were you?"

She tried to yank her arm free, but his grip was strong. Some of the boys said he was stronger than Jon Hunter, though she doubted it.

"You are hurting my arm." She gritted her teeth to keep back the pain.

"Tell me where you were."

"Why does it matter where I was?"

He squeezed even harder which nearly made her cry, but she sucked it down and glared at him. "Because they say you know where the wounded soldier is. Is it true? Do you, Lia? The one the sheriff was looking for?"

She wanted to slap him across the face, but she dared not. She had seen him thrash someone for daring to scowl at him. "Do not be a fool, Getmin. They already searched the kitchens. Both of them. You are wrong…" His fingers dug into her arm even farther, and she nearly went wild with pain. "Stop it, Getmin!"

"If they had found him, we all would have known. Do not be a fool, Lia. Do not think I am a fool. The Aldermaston visits your kitchen all the time. You hear things that none of us do. Is the Aldermaston hiding him?"

"You are daft!" Lia shouted at him. "The old man does not tell us anything interesting." She finally managed to jerk her arm free.

His face scrunched up with anger. "If you have lied to me, I swear by Idumea you will regret it. The sheriff's men offered a reward to the one who finds the soldier. I am getting that reward. You remember that. The Aldermaston is a fool if he is risking hiding him. A true fool."

Lia held her tears back until she made it inside the kitchen.

CHAPTER TWELVE

Winterrowd

Pasqua ground some peppers with the pestle with vigorous strokes. "Carry the meal to the Aldermaston, Sowe, before the old niffler starts grumbling again. He has been in high dudgeon since that sheriff left."

"I will do it," Lia offered. Sowe pouted, and Pasqua noticed her frown.

"Both of you go then. The looks you give each other lately are wont to bring an early winter. Quickly now. Do not dawdle at the manor. Whitsunday is near enough. There is much to prepare, and we need to count the stores to be sure there is enough. Laziness from either of you and I will be tempted to bring back the switch."

"We are not lazy," Lia said under her breath as she hefted the tray. Sowe opened the door for her and followed her out.

"You never like carrying food to the Aldermaston," Lia said to Sowe. "Why do you care if I should do it twice?"

"We should tell the Aldermaston," Sowe said softly.

"You are thinking like a goose. The king is coming. The Aldermaston would be in trouble if he knew."

"Then why are we helping him get in trouble by hiding… that man?"

"He has a name," Lia said with a smug feeling.

"Which he has only shared with you."

"And you are jealous that he did?"

"I am not jealous. I am worried."

"You are always worried, Sowe."

"You should be worried too! The trouble is that you are not worried enough. If the Aldermaston finds out that we lied to him, he will punish us. I do not want to be sent to the village."

"He will not send us away," Lia said, though not totally sure of herself. She was about to tell Sowe to open the door to the manor, but Sowe did it on her own. They walked in uncomfortable silence to the Aldermaston's chamber, and Sowe knocked timidly.

"Knock harder," Lia said with frustration. "You knock too softly."

Sowe knocked a little harder, then pulled the handle and opened it, and Lia entered first.

"Thank you both," the Aldermaston said. "It has been a calmer day for all of us. Ah, the soup smells wonderful. Very fragrant. Give my compliments to Pasqua."

"We will," Lia said and Sowe turned to go, but Lia lingered.

The Aldermaston paused before the steamy bowl and gave Lia a quizzical look. "Yes?"

Lia swallowed. "They say that the king's army is coming. That there may be war."

"There may be. Do not be concerned about it." He raised his spoon to sip.

"But if there are soldiers, they may come to the Abbey. The sheriff said…"

The Aldermaston interrupted, "I would not regard anything the sheriff told you."

Lia clenched her teeth, tried not to frown, and glanced at the chimneypiece on the side wall. It was a quick look, the slightest glance, just to be sure the orb was still on the mantle. It was.

***

Lia, with Sowe fidgeting alongside her, returned for the tray and dishes after sunset. She knew the Aldermaston would be discussing the events of the day with the teachers. His personal chamber was usually empty at that time.

"What are you doing?" Sowe asked as Lia approached the chimneypiece. "You are not supposed to touch…Lia, what are you…Lia!"

On the mantle, beneath a leather wrap, was the shiny metal orb, its rim decorated with intricate markings. The bottom half was made out of solid gold or aurichalcum. Two spindles were suspended on a round inset. The top half of the sphere was made from gold stays that joined at the top in a sculpted design. It reminded Lia of the kitchen roof and how the beams arched upward and supported the weight of bricks and shingles. The orb was heavy, but not unexpectedly so, about the size of a large apple.

"Put that away!" Sowe whispered, looking back at the door. "If the Aldermaston saw you…"

"If you are so nervous, then listen at the door instead of whining at me. I need to see if it will work for me."

"Work for you? That is more valuable than the ring you stole, Lia. Do not tell me you are going to steal it. Put it down, please!"

Lia held the orb in her hand and looked at the spindles, at the rim. Years before, a child had wandered from the nursery and was lost in the swampland surrounding the rear of the Abbey. Every helper spent hours trying to find the little boy, and since Jon

Hunter had not returned from a neighboring abbey, no one else had the abilities to locate the missing boy. As sunset threatened nightfall, the Aldermaston used the orb. The spindles had spun dizzyingly and then directed them on the right course. The boy was found just after sunset in the woods surrounding the grounds.

The weight of the orb against her palm was reassuring and warm. In her heart, she believed it would work. If the Leerings obeyed her, she knew this would too. Taking a deep breath, she sent her thoughts inside it—*show me the way to Winterrowd.*

"Lia, please…oh!"

The orb came to life, the inner ring whirring faster than a waterwheel. The spindles on the top joined together and pointed west. Writing appeared on the lower half the orb, as if an invisible hand with a stylus etched them there in the blink of an eye.

"Lia…how did you do that?" Sowe whispered in awe.

Lia stared at it, a broad smile on her face. She was very pleased with herself. "I just asked it to show me the direction of Winter-rowd. Let me try it again. Show me the Aldermaston."

The spindles whirred again, the points going apart before coming together again, pointing in the direction of the cloister.

"Where is Pasqua?" Lia said, and again the spindles parted and then joined, pointing exactly in the direction of the Abbey kitchen. She looked into Sowe's eyes and saw fear and respect blazing there.

"Bring me the mug from the tray."

Sowe shook her head no. "You cannot steal this, Lia. If you are caught…"

"I am not going to steal it. I just need to borrow it. If it will point the way to Winterrowd, then all is done. We can send our friend on his way, and I can return it tomorrow."

"But the Aldermaston, what if he…?"

Lia wanted to shake her. "Yes, if he misses it, he will be furious. But there is a life at risk. Do not be so heartless. We have helped him this far. We cannot abandon him to the sheriff to be murdered."

"No, Lia. You are stealing from the Aldermaston's private chamber. This is worse than the ring, for those did not truly belong to him anyway. If he finds out, do you understand the risk? If he finds out you did this…"

Lia stamped her foot. "What is the likelihood that tonight, of all nights, a disaster will happen that will require him to use it? We can sneak it back tomorrow the same way we are taking it tonight. He will not even know we touched it."

"But if something did happen, he would know. Who else would he blame? Astrid?"

"Sowe, a life is in danger! I know you are afraid, but we can do this."

"Where would we hide it? How would we sneak it past Pasqua?"

Lia grinned, glad she had convinced Sowe at last. "Those questions are better, and I have already figured them out. I will take the blame for this, not you. Bring me the mug to take its place on the chimneypiece. Hurry!"

And so, despite Sowe's protests and hand-wringing, Lia stole the orb. For even though she had said it was borrowing, in the deeper part of her, she knew the truth.

***

His name is Colvin Price, and he will become the Earl of Forshee, Lia thought as she nestled against the wall near the low-burning flames from the bread ovens. The Leering eyes were dull. The bricks smelled of yeast and milled flour. She thought about Colvin and the first night he had ended up in the kitchen, bewildered, sick, and wounded. His distrust was understandable now. His very life depended on people not knowing who he truly was. The king did not suffer traitors to live. In fact, the penalty for treason was a harsh death. It made her sick inside thinking what the king's men would do to him before killing him. Only the bravest of knight-mastons would risk that fate. And Colvin was not even a knight yet.

She looked up at the loft. Even down by the fire, she could hear Sowe breathing. It amazed her how long Sowe could sleep. She prized it greater than snitches of treacle or stolen edges of crust. Lia could not sleep. She was too excited about the dawn and what the daylight would bring. And she was conflicted—especially by the thought that she might never see Colvin again.

The thought caused a little pinprick of regret which she tried to squash, but it still poked her.

Lia stood, setting the orb down near the flagstones, and then tied up the linen stuffed with food. Stolen cuts of meat stuffed into husks of bread, along with carrots, turnips, two kinds of cheeses, nuts, and a flask. She and Sowe had wrapped it in several sheets of linen to preserve it and would carry it down to the waymarker before dawn.

A firm knock sounded on the rear kitchen door, making Lia jump with fright. She rushed to the door, expecting to see Colvin. Hurryingly, she raised the crossbar and pulled the door handle.

But it was not the armiger. It was not the sheriff.

It was the knight-maston who had brought Colvin to the Abbey days ago, still haggard and mud-splattered and wearing the magnificent sword belted to his waist.

"Look at you, lass. You seem surprised I came back. Why is that?"

"You came," Lia nearly gasped. "I did not think...the sheriff's men...I thought they had captured you."

"The sheriff's men? Unimaginable. They do not have enough brains among them to fill the husk of a nut, but that is neither here nor there. From what I heard in the village yesterday, you have done your part with great cleverness. He is safe?"

Lia nodded triumphantly.

He smiled broadly at her. "There is a good lass. I knew you were a clever girl. So young to be so clever." He nudged the door with the tip of his boot. "He is not hiding in here, is he?"

"No, the sheriff ransacked the place looking for him. Sowe and I—she is my companion you know—we took him to a safe place."

"Is he far?"

"Not very. I was going to fetch him at dawn and steal his horse back and..."

"His horse? It wandered here too?"

"Yes, days ago. We are trying to help him find Winterrowd. But now that you are here, you can take him with you."

He shook his head, his eyes darting from shadow to shadow. "No, it is nearly dawn. I must flee before the other helpers awaken. Tell him to meet me at the Pilgrim Inn. I will be waiting for him. The sheriff's men are leagues from here by now."

"The Pilgrim," Lia echoed. "It is nearby. I will tell him. You are a brave knight. Garen Demont is lucky to have you. Do you suspect the sheriff is watching the road?"

He smiled, appearing flattered. "It is you who are brave. Oh, I am sure the road is being watched. Sheriff Almaguer is not as clever as you, but he is still a fearful man. Did you see him when he came to the Abbey?"

"He came to the kitchen looking for…" She almost said his name and stopped herself, not knowing if the knight-maston already knew who he was escorting. "For him."

"That must have frightened you."

"He is a frightful man. But the Aldermaston sent him away."

"Brave lass. I am proud of you. Here, for your bravery and for the risks you have taken." He reached into his pocket and withdrew a coin pouch that jingled when he shook it. "I would do more, and I will after he is delivered safely to the Pilgrim. Perhaps it will be of use to you when you are eighteen and ready to make your way in this harsh world. Hide it where you put your other treasures." He handed it to her. As she tentatively took it, he clasped his other hand on top of hers, warm and rough—a soldier's hand. "I will not forget. Thank you, lass. Now hurry, hide it before the cook comes and ruins our plan. You remember the name of the inn?"

"The Pilgrim," Lia said, bursting with pleasure inside.

He let her hand go after a gentle pat. "First the Pilgrim. Then to Winterrowd. We may have a chance yet, with him on our side."

***

Learners question why faces are carved into stone as a means of preserving the magic of the Medium. There are many levels of symbolism involved that can be shared openly. Stone symbolizes permanence. The faces represent mankind's ultimate and eventual dominion over the elements of nature and even time itself. Nature continues on its course, a continuing cycle of birth, death, and rebirth. But one, acting under the proper authority of the Medium, can alter that course. The likeness of the sun, moon, and stars symbolizes that great power exists beyond this world that can control this one. We are, after all, living on only one of the worlds inhabited by the Family. Any deeper meaning of the symbolism, along with instruction for creating them—the uninitiated mockingly call them 'leering stones'—can only be had through the rites of the Abbey. All mastons know this, and they do not share it outside their order.

—Cuthbert Renowden of Billerbeck Abbey

CHAPTER THIRTEEN

The Cruciger Orb

Fog shrouded the Abbey grounds with fleecy wisps and dew. Lia and Sowe wore their cloaks and hugged themselves for warmth as they crossed the Cider Orchard toward the way-marker near the rock cleft. In one hand, Lia clutched the metal orb and used it to point the way in the mist. She kept in her mind the image of the armiger, his brow mottled with a scab, his cheeks and chin scruffy with whiskers. Sowe said nothing as she carried the linen bundle with the foodstuffs. Ahead, in the gloom, they spied the burning eyes of the Leering.

Colvin must have heard them approach, for he appeared out of the gloom, his hair damp with dewdrops. He met them in their approach, his face eager, intense, worried. His arms were folded tightly, as if he were very cold.

"What is that?" he asked Lia, staring at the sphere as the spindles pointed directly at him. He looked at it, his eyes widening with recognition. "I cannot believe it. Where did you get that? From the Aldermaston?"

"Yes," Lia answered. "You know what it is?"

"I do, but I have never handled one before. They are rare." He examined it, squinting in the darkness. "I cannot see it well. Bring it to the waymarker." They did and the eyes suddenly shone more brightly, revealing the surface of the beautiful implement. "I cannot believe it. A Cruciger orb. But then I should not be surprised. Muirwood is the oldest abbey in the realm. May I?"

Lia extended it to him and the spindles spun around once and then stopped.

He held it in his hand and stared at it. Nothing happened.

"You think about where you want to go," Lia suggested.

"I know that," he snapped. "It is precisely what I am trying to do." His brow furrowed. Nothing.

Lia wanted to laugh. A soon-to-be earl from a Family could not work it. But *she* could. The fiery feeling of triumph blazed inside her. "Like this," she offered and took it from him. "Show me the way to Winterrowd." The spindles spun, the inner circle whirring deftly, and the way was made clear—westbound though slightly north. Writing appeared on the lower half of the orb. "What does the writing mean?"

She brought it closer to the light emanating from the waymarker's eyes, and he squinted again. He stopped, swallowed, and shook his head. "I cannot read it. I do not know this language. It is an older text…an ancient text. It may even be Idumean. I have never seen this style of script before."

Lia was deeply disappointed. "I thought all mastons knew how to read and scribe. I want to know what it says."

He shook his head, looking at the curving, elliptical markings. "I cannot make it out without knowing the language. I do not know all languages. I certainly do not know Idumean. I am not even sure my own Aldermaston knows it. Let me hold it again." He held out his hand.

As she gave it to him the second time, the spindles behaved the same way, returning to their idle state and refused him. The writing vanished as well, as the groove etchings filled in. He paused, he scowled, he waited, but nothing happened. "What is wrong with me?" he grumbled.

"Thankfully, this is not the only news we brought," Lia said. "I should have said it first. The knight-maston who brought you to Muirwood came back. He knocked on the kitchen doors not long ago, looking for you."

He straightened, his expression shocked. "I am all amazement. Did he?"

Lia nodded, giving him a smile. "He eluded the sheriff's men."

"Where is he now? At the kitchen?"

"He said he would wait for you in the village. At the Pilgrim Inn—it is the biggest one in town, on the main way not far from the Abbey walls. He will be watching for you and will take you to Demont."

Sowe held out the bundle. "We bundled some food for you," she said in a voice so small a mouse might have whispered it.

Colvin accepted it and smoothed the top of the linen. "There is no doubt you will both earn a scolding for helping me. Were it possible, I would forbid Pasqua to scold either of you ever again. I heard enough of it, hiding in the loft. I pity you." He let out a pent-up breath. "My gratitude, though, exceeds my words. Think of what reward you desire. If it is within my power, I will grant it. You are both so very young, but before long, you will have repaid your debt to Muirwood. I will and shall honor my debt to you."

Sowe blushed furiously and looked at her feet. Lia was not so shy.

"I know what I would ask for," she said, squeezing the orb tightly.

"What is it?"

Lia could not help a blushing smile. "Sowe already knows what I want. Beyond any gift or treasure, I desire to learn to read." She swallowed, building her courage, nurturing hope like sparks from drowsy ashes. "When I saw you…reading from the tomes… I was so jealous. I am always jealous of that craft. The Aldermaston refuses to let me learn. He has said…he has said more than once, that as long as he is the Aldermaston of Muirwood, he will not let me. Please, sir—I want it more than anything else."

He studied her, his eyes deep with shadows, his face dispassionate. It was a heavy expression, as if he were weighing in his mind how much it would cost—and whether her service to him truly deserved such a princely sum. She held her breath. She held back her fears. She hoped in her heart, she yearned with her being, and she stared at his face, wishing to scald him with her need.

He was silent. It was not an easy answer to give. Had he tossed out an answer with less than a thought, she would have doubted the sincerity of it. He was brooding over his answer, brooding over the request. It was not given lightly. Silence fell on the woods. For a moment, it seemed as if the world stood still and held its breath with her.

"You shall have it," he whispered. "Even if I must teach you myself."

Sowe gasped at the immensity of the promise.

It was the best day, the best moment, the best instant in Lia's life. She would remember it all the rest of her days. Lia wanted to throw her arms around his neck and kiss his cheek, but she knew from her previous demonstrations of friendliness that he would shun it and detest her. The surge and storm of gratitude in her heart brought tears to her eyes, but she willed them not to fall. She must not cry in front of him. She must not show how much she was indebted to his kindness. He could have asked anything from her, and she would have done it, without flinching.

Barely able to get the words out, she whispered, "Thank you, sir. I thank you."

He stood motionless and hard, like a waymarker himself. His mouth was terse, his expression grave. Then he dropped his hand to his belt and hooked his thumb there. He looked at Sowe and said somberly, "Leave us a moment."

Sowe, nervous, backed down the road toward the Cider Orchard.

Lia drew closer, worried now that he had changed his mind.

"I pray I have not made a vain promise. I did not make it lightly, nor do I seek to cheapen it with excuses." He stared down at his boots, then met her gaze. "As you know, I go to war. Should I fall," he paused, choking for a moment, "seek my steward. His name is Theobald. Tell him of the promise I made to you. If I do not live to fulfill it in person, he will do so on my behalf. Does that satisfy you?"

Shocked, Lia swallowed and nodded. Then she saw it, she saw through the facade and into his soul. It had happened to her before on a stormy night when she was nine. That night she had read the Aldermaston's thoughts. Today, she saw a stiff lip, a scowl, a rigid demeanor. And she recognized it for what it truly was. Colvin was afraid. He feared what would happen to him at Winterrowd as much as his honor compelled him on that road. They were tangled feelings. Since he had left on his journey, he had been worrying about his death and its effect on his sister, his uncle, and those who loved him. Now he was beholden to yet another creature, a lowly wretched. The thought of disappointing them all was almost too much for him to bear.

The insight came in a moment, a blink. At that moment, she knew him better than anyone else did. He was afraid of dying at Winterrowd, his blood-spattered body twisted and bent, crumpled with others older and more war-wise than himself. Of his sister and how she would worry and grieve, for he had not told her what he was going to do. Yet despite the guilty fear of what would happen if they failed to depose the ruthless king, he forced every footstep on the path leading to the fate that terrified him. In that moment of clarity, in that breach into his soul, she learned a little of the true meaning of courage.

In that moment, as she blinked back fresh tears, she knew that who she danced with at the Whitsun Fair would be the least of her worries. She would worry about him, Colvin, since even his own sister could not.

"Your horse is penned up at Jon Hunter's lodge," she said thickly, struggling to speak through a clenched throat. "We will take you there."

She did not know any other way to say goodbye at such a moment.

CHAPTER FOURTEEN

Thievery

Sowe waited for her in the mist, shivering. Sometimes it took hours before the sun chased the morning fog away. As they began their long walk back to the kitchen, in the distance, they heard the thudding of hooves.

"Was Jon away?" Sowe asked nervously.

"He is always gone before the sun rises. I swear the man never sleeps in that filthy hovel. He is more likely than not bedding down in a bush each night. At least he cared for the horse. It looked rested and brushed and there were oats for it still."

"So are we going to tell the Aldermaston now?"

"Before we put the orb back in his chamber? You are daft, Sowe, truly. I am glad we did not need it."

"So when will we tell him? Tonight?"

"Quit worrying, Sowe. Now that he is gone, you should feel more easy. Why worry the Aldermaston about it at all?"

"I should not, but I do worry. I am nervous about what will happen. We should tell him, Lia."

"And make him angry? He does not know—he did not find out. We did it, Sowe. Why not be happy about that?"

"Happy? I have been sick to my stomach for days. If I had a bucket, I could retch in it right now."

"Retch in the flower beds instead, thank you kindly. Just do not retch on me. I cannot help it if you are always nervous about everything."

Sowe was silent after that, and they both walked, their shoes sodden from the dewy grass, and approached the kitchen from the rear. They could hear the pots clanging like bells, and Lia could tell Pasqua was furious. She had a way of making the whole kitchen mime her moods.

Lia pulled open the door and gusts of warm, yeasty air engulfed them. Pasqua was laboring over a huge bowl, and she turned with iron in her eyes.

"Here they arrive at last, all damp and tired. I ought to take a switch to both of your skinny legs as I promised last night. Leaving the kitchen together! Letting some pack of hungry-eyed learners sneak in here and steal from the Aldermaston's stores. I have a mind to make you churn butter all day long so that your arms are sore for a week. Cheeky little waifs. Off you were, flitting about in the morning when you were supposed to be at your chores, and now someone has come in and made off with things they would be ashamed to confess."

Lia rolled her eyes and shut the door. Sowe took their cloaks and hung them from two pegs to dry out. Lia hid the Cruciger orb behind a barrel beneath the loft.

"Were we gone that long?" Lia said with a yawn. "It did not feel like it. Did it feel like it to you, Sowe? On a misty morning like this, it is hard to tell how late it is."

Pasqua jammed a wooden spoon into the huge bowl and gave it furiously circular strokes. "Have you been gone long? Gone long? Why if that is not a sooty lie…look over there at the Aldermaston's breakfast, which I made myself, and now it is nearly cold to the touch. Look at your hems, deep in mud. You will be at the laundry scrubbing them clean, for I will not have you tracking in filth. I am sorely vexed with both of you, especially because the gingerbread we made yesterday is gone. Whitsunday will soon be here, and I have a mind to insist that the Aldermaston forbid you to dance around the maypole."

Lia stopped. "What about the gingerbread?" she asked, confused, for they had not snitched even a crumb of it.

Pasqua's eyes were nearly bulging, and she thumped the spoon as she thundered, "Have you not been listening to what I told you? Someone has been in the kitchen while you were gone, stealing up scraps and taking this and that. It is shameful, it really is. Here, at Muirwood, that someone can feel justified in stealing what others labored to make. I am only glad there is none of the Gooseberry Fool done, or it would be missing too."

Lia tied on her apron, her mind dancing with thoughts, her stomach starting to wrestle with queasiness. She looked around the kitchen, and it did have a different feel. There were the stools, the brooms, the pans, the sieves, the sacks, the smells—but an underlying sense of wrongness as well. Fluttering memories darted here and there, and she snatched at them. Stolen things. Missing victuals. When the knight-maston brought Colvin that first evening, he had freely taken victuals for the road. Without asking, he had sliced off a piece of meat. He had swiped a tub of treacle. In fact, as she thought back on it, his actions had been deliberately subtle. He made excuses when she noticed, but it was as if he was trying to steal them without her knowing it. Why would a knight-maston steal?

She cinched the knot of the apron behind her, her thoughts spinning so fast that they blurred Pasqua's words into gibberish.

Why would a knight-maston steal? Would not a knight-maston, a true one, ask for victuals? Be grateful for what he was given instead of sneaking it? But the knight had not entered the kitchen—Lia had not let him in. Was someone else to blame? A learner, perhaps? Getmin stealing the gingerbread to get her into trouble?

Her mind filled with other possibilities. Maybe the knight had entered after she and Sowe had left. Without someone to stay behind, there was no way to secure the crossbar over the door.

"Why are you standing there paler than milk? Get to work, girls! There are messes plenty to tidy. Sowe, take the Aldermaston his meal. Lia, fetch the broom and sweep up that spill over there. Now, girls, before I fetch a hazel switch in earnest!"

Lia walked, dreamlike, to the broom, trying to put the pieces together in her head. She clutched it and walked over to the corner and began sweeping. Had the knight-maston entered the kitchen after they left to get Colvin and stolen the food? Was that all he had stolen? A sick feeling washed over her. She swept and stepped over to the corner beneath the loft, by the loose stone where she hid her treasures. When Pasqua's back was turned, she pried at the edge with her fingers until it budged. Lifting it, she stared into the hole.

Gone. Every coin she had ever saved. The bag of treasure the knight had brought her. And even worse, the sheriff's medallion. They were gone. She reached into the hole, confirming the emptiness with her own fingers.

The thought sent a spear of disbelief through her. Pain and shock linked arms. It was the worst feeling of her life. Worse than fear or sorrow or the dread of impending punishment. It hurt with a frenzy when she realized what she had done. She had sent Colvin to the Pilgrim and into a trap.

***

The man that brought Colvin to the Abbey kitchen was not a knight or a maston. He was, in fact, a wretched himself—a wretched who had also been raised at Muirwood but fled before his obligation to serve was fulfilled. He knew the Abbey grounds as well as Lia and could walk in the mist without getting turned around or lost. That was a key reason why his services were so valuable to the sheriff of Mendenhall. Lia would not have remembered him, for she had been very young when he abandoned his debt and the Abbey. But others would have recognized his expression, the tilt of his head, and the way he smoothed people's feelings with clever words.

They would also remember his inability to resist thieving. With a little bit of skill and flexibility, he could climb part of the rounded stone bulwarks near the doorway on either side of the kitchen doors, and from that vantage point, see inside the kitchen through the glass panels embedded into the door. From there, he had watched where Lia kept her treasures. Not only did it cost him nothing to win back the sheriff's amulet, but he had also laid claim to the rest of her coins. It panged what little shreds of conscience he had left, but in the larger context, he felt he was doing her a favor. A harsh lesson would teach her for the rest of her life not to trust the strangers of the world. It was a lesson he had learned in a thousand cruel ways.

He glanced down at the twisting vines and leaves that made up the shape of the amulet. There was something about it that attracted him. It was unique. It was a secret worth a great deal to the right people, he was sure. Did he really want to tell Almaguer he had found it after the sheriff had lost it to the girl? After all, the girl could have given it to the Aldermaston—or even better—she could be wearing it herself. Had he not noticed a bit of twine around her neck? Was there another path he could take, a way to turn the situation around yet again and earn even more profit? The nameless squire had carried embarrassingly few coins, though his knight-maston sword would fetch a good price in the local market, especially if it was sold while he was put to death in the village square for treason. Some fool would pay handsomely for it in the frenzy of passion that accompanied executions. Was there a way to get more coins from the lad prior to his punishment? Perhaps an offer to deliver words to a loved one after the sheriff seized him? The sound of clinking coins stoked his imagination. There had to be a way. And since the lad had never seen his face, he would not know who was dealing so treacherously with him.

He slipped the amulet into a secret pocket and patted it lightly.

He wondered how much the Aldermaston's good name would be tarnished. Would Muirwood Abbey be shamed with the unraveling of the Winterrowd plot? If that happened, it was worth all the treasure in his bag. Unable to help it, he started to chuckle. It had the makings of a merry day.

***

It was hard for Lia to breathe. She was harrowed by the feelings inside her; they were too much to bear. Guilt—she felt such a horrible guilt for her unwitting betrayal. Fury—her searing, scalding, ravaging fury burned toward the thief who had deceived her. How glibly he had done it. His words had achieved their every intention. By making her think that he was trusting her, she had unknowingly trusted him all the more. It was all so very clear. She hated herself for being fooled so easily. She was a fool. No matter that the thief was older than her and cunning as a serpent. Her own cunning had probably surprised him. He was the one who had sent the sheriff to the Muirwood kitchens, and only blind luck had prevented Almaguer from reaching the Aldermaston's kitchen first instead of the learner kitchen. If that had happened, Colvin would have been caught in their midst—and she would have been caught as his accomplice.

She had been so sure of herself, so sure that she would be able to outwit them all. With trembling hands and with tears dangling from her lashes, she whisked the dirt and spilled seeds into a pile. Truth was painful. Her own greed had hastened the deception. The desire to read had driven her for as long as she could remember. She stopped, seeing the look in Colvin's eyes as he promised to help her achieve that dream. The memory caused so much pain, she had to stop and cough loudly to keep Pasqua ignorant of the sobs that threatened to completely break open. How could she have been so blind? What was there to do? Colvin was on horseback. The village lay beyond the Abbey walls. He was probably at the inn already.

The kitchen door burst open and Astrid Page ran in. His tousled black hair settled as he came in breathlessly. He went to Pasqua. "The Aldermaston...desires to see Lia. He says she must come straightaway."

Pasqua scowled at the boy. "What is this nonsense? We have much work to do. There are other helpers he can call on."

"No, Pasqua, he requested her. She must come right now."

Lia's heart shuddered in her chest, and she clenched the broom handle until her arms trembled. Looking about, she noticed that Sowe had not returned yet from bringing the Aldermaston's meal. *Oh, no.* For the second time that morning, she understood the complicated and vicious feelings of betrayal. As clear as the noonday sun, she knew Sowe had told all. Gripping the broom handle angrily, she nearly snapped it over her knee.

Everything in her life was unraveling around her, but she was determined to stop it and mend it. There was little time to think—she needed to act rather than be acted upon.

"Let me fetch my cloak first," she said impatiently, walking to the pegs, drying her eyes.

"You hardly need a cloak," Pasqua scolded. "If the Aldermaston begs for your audience, then you move. No trifling here. You obey. That is always what is best where he is concerned. Did Sowe spill something? What is this about?"

"I do not know, mum. She was there in his chamber, crying. There were no spills that I could tell."

Lia fastened the cloak and walked to the loft ladder, ducked quickly behind a barrel, and grasped the Cruciger orb. She licked her lips, giving less than a second thought to what she was about to do. If she thought about it much, she would lose her courage. Her choices were dwindling like water through her fingers.

"What are you fiddling with, child?" Pasqua demanded, one hand on her hip, a bowl in her other hand. "What have you there? In your hand?"

"I know what the Aldermaston wants. It will not take long. Go on, Astrid. I will be right there," she lied.

"What is that in your hand, child?"

Lia rushed past her, where the page boy was already pulling open the door. As soon as she felt the cold misty air on her face, she took a deep final breath. The smell of the kitchen, the luxurious scent of breads, cheeses, roasting meat—she breathed it in one last time.

"Lia!" Pasqua called after her. "You come back here! When I call you, you come! Lia!"

Lia started to run, away from the manor house. In her mind she said the words, *find the Pilgrim Inn*. The spindles within the orb began to whirl.

***

Those who have not been initiated into the order of the mastons may wonder why these beautiful abbeys are built. The fact that each one takes nearly a generation to construct is a reminder of their great importance and sense of permanence. They are built from stone that may endure through the ages like the mountains. The walls, joints, arches, trim, flowerbeds, and even the unspoiled trees nearby are rich with meaning and symbolism. I shall not divulge the rites that take place inside, but instead draw your mind to the fact that learners must study for years before they are allowed within the precincts. Within, each dungeon, room, screen, and veil speaks of our progression in this life as we toil to draw ever closer in unity with the Medium. There are some whispers now and then, spoken in hushed tones when they do not think they are heard, that these grand abbeys are not just buildings of learning and reflection. Rather, they are gateways to other worlds, and when those living who listen for the utterances of the Medium truly hearken, in all ages and across all time, they will build themselves structures of chiseled stone and polished pewter. Then they can travel beyond to other worlds—even to Idumea itself. I will not say whether or not these rumors are true. Only this—that the reverence and humility given to these magnificent structures are unequivocally deserved.

—Cuthbert Renowden of Billerbeck Abbey

CHAPTER FIFTEEN

The Pilgrim

The days of the Whitsun Fair were the only times Lia ever walked beyond the walls of the Abbey. Those who lived within, especially the wretcheds, never left until their time of service was complete. If something was needed from the village, it was brought to the Abbey and handed through the gate. For the most part, both worlds existed as separately as possible. Lia had an idea where the Pilgrim was, on High Street just beyond the northernmost walls of the Abbey grounds, and that was the direction the pointers of the Cruciger orb led as she ran through the mist.

But as she drew closer to the enormous sanctuary, the pointers swung directly at it instead of where she expected. Her shoes squished in the grass and her breath came in quick gasps as she stopped running. Behind her, in the mist, lay the manor where the Aldermaston waited for her. She stared at the orb, confused. The walls of the grounds were somewhere in front of her, but the pointers were fixed on the Abbey itself. She started walking again, and the pointers swung even more prominently back, directing her toward the Abbey. Strange writing appeared on the lower half of the orb, but there was no way of understanding what it meant.

She stopped again, wondering what to do. In her mind, she thought the words, *Find the Pilgrim Inn*. The spindles did not move. The pointers did not waver. She thought again. *Take me to Colvin*. More engraving appeared, its beautiful curving text shimmering against the surface of the orb. The pointers did not change. Though confused, she decided to trust it. Was Colvin at the Abbey? Had he managed to escape the sheriff somehow?

As she looked up at the Abbey, fear began to churn inside her. It was not built like a fortress, with battlement walls and looming parapets with drapes dangling from poles. Its looming presence was a sight she had witnessed all of her life, yet she looked at it with new eyes. The stone structure was enormous, rising well above the heights of the towering oaks. The windows were all veiled with mottled glass, so thick that it was impossible to see inside, and even if that were not so, there were heavy curtains within.

Wretcheds never went inside. Only learners who had completed their studies and the rites would emerge wearing a shirt of chaen beneath their clothes. She had no idea what happened, how it happened, or what mysterious things the learners were taught inside. It was whispered that those who entered had to demonstrate their mastery of the Medium in order to receive their chaen shirt. Since it took four years of intense learning to acquire the skills necessary even to enter, the trials experienced within must be beyond comprehension.

Lia had walked the grounds since she was old enough to get into mischief. She had run her hand across each surface and crevice around the entire structure. Sometimes she and Sowe had lain in the grass and imagined what it looked like inside. What gruesome Leerings were there? Scrollwork and carvings decorated the entire facade, with repeating themes like arches that overlapped.

The front end of the Abbey was shorter than the rear side, two levels high compared to three and four farther back as it rose like a mountain. Lia had already passed the main doors, which were always locked. No one ever entered through the main doors. But along the lower levels, there were several other entry points that had been carved into the design.

The pointers of the orb shifted as she approached, directing her along the north face of the Abbey. In fact, the orb directed her to a beautifully crafted doorway. It was made of three connected archways. Each one fit within the one before it, shrinking slowly to the door itself, which was made of solid wood and gleaming with pewter. The sinking feeling in her stomach grew more intense. Foreboding seethed inside her soul. Wretcheds were not allowed in the sanctuary. It was totally, absolutely, strictly forbidden. Why was the orb showing her the door?

She stopped at the threshold, shivering. Sweat popped up on her forehead. The pointers on the orb did not change—they pointed directly to the doors. What if she were caught? What if the Aldermaston found out? Did that really matter anymore? Had she sinned enough by stealing the orb that he would cast her out of the Abbey forever anyway? If that was so, then this would be her last chance to see the inside, maybe her only chance.

She took a step forward and the foreboding darkened her thoughts even more, nearly making her cry. It was so big, so vast, so hugely important—and she, a wretched, was nothing. Then she noticed them. Her eyes were drawn to them, and their subtly glowing eyes stared at her. There were small Leerings carved into the base of the arches. One a man. One a woman. One a lion. One a sun. She realized that they were all exuding their power, warning her to back away. If they were Leerings, she might be able to control them. With a thought, she silenced them, and the sense of foreboding vanished. The oppression and heavy feeling fled, leaving her gasping with relief. Somewhere in the mist, a bird whistled its song, startling her.

It was only the Medium. The feelings were not real.

Lia mounted the steps and approached the pewter doors. Reaching out, she gripped the huge door-pull and tugged. It opened smoothly with the sound of a breathless sigh as the outside air was sucked in.

Holding her breath, she entered.

When the door shut behind her, all was dark until the Cruciger orb flared alive, shining like a lamp as it had for the Aldermaston in the night. The scene took her breath away. A sharp ceiling rose up, supported by giant stone buttresses. The walls were adorned with colorful tapestries. Small tables stood here and there, their bases of solid onyx or marble carved into Leerings, and on the tabletops were pots of flowers in bloom, rich and vibrant, as if fresh sunlight fed them daily. Blooming flowers—in the dark!

Taking a step in wonderment, she stopped as soon as her toe left the woven mat and touched the polished, perfect, square tiles. Her shoes were dirty and wet, and not only would they leave marks on the polished floors, it did not feel right to be wearing them. Kneeling, she removed her shoes and wiped her feet on the hem of her cloak. Clutching the shoes, she stepped onto the cool tiles and followed the direction the pointers led her.

The hall was vast, the illumination of the orb chasing the shadows only so far. Each step she took sounded in her ears, her bare feet padding over the smooth stone. Sowe would never have gone this far, she thought with a little throb of smugness.

The pointers turned sharply, and she noticed that she'd nearly passed an interior doorway. After crossing to it, she pulled on the handle and saw a set of stairs leading down into the gloom. The tunnel was dark, but there was no dirt, nor did she see a single insect hiding in the corners. The steps curved down and around, depositing her in another room.

She was below ground level in a room where the roof was supported by many thick arches. The floor tiles were a different color from the ones above. These were slate gray, in thick squares that tiled the entire area. Rows of wooden benches were arranged facing the head of the room, with an aisle separating them. The benches were waxed and polished, made from dark-stained oak that could seat several people across. She walked down the center aisle, stopping to feel the wood as she passed each one, and the light from the orb illuminated the head of the room.

In the center of a small cove at the head of the room stood a stone table, with a flat, squarish surface. It was built atop several layers of stone blocks. It was long enough that a single body could lie on top of the surface, and the sight of it transfixed her. A rushing, soothing, excited feeling came over her when she saw it. What was this strange table? What did it mean?

Reverently, she approached it, running her hand along the edge, careful not to let her muddy shoes touch it. There was something familiar about it, something that whispered inside her heart, calling to her. She glanced down at the orb and saw the pointers aiming to an alcove to the right.

Lia hesitated, not wanting to leave the peculiar room and its enigmatic stone table. Biting her lip, she rested the heel of her hand against the table one more time, trying to understand the source of the feelings inside her. Then she followed the pointers into the alcove that appeared to go nowhere. The alcove was raised slightly up a thin stone step. There was no other way to go.

What was wrong? The alcove led nowhere. Confused, she stepped back off and looked at the pointers again, but they were still pointing into the dead space. New writing appeared in the lower half of the orb, but it was not helpful to her. When she went back to the table, the pointers directed her again to the alcove.

At the alcove, she looked for carvings or Leerings that might give her a clue what she was to do next. The walls were polished stone, like the rest of the room. The workmanship exquisite—no—dazzling. She touched the walls and pushed, but they were firm. Then she stepped back off into the room and looked down at the lip of the step. It had a small gap between it and the floor. She knelt and ran her finger along the edge, and it was cold to the touch. After setting down the orb and her shoes, she pried her fingers beneath it and lifted.

The entire floor of the alcove, stone and all, rose effortlessly, exposing steep stairs down. Breathless with excitement, Lia descended carefully, and the lid of the alcove floor swung down above her. With the orb as her only light, her toes scraping against rough stone, she made her way into the bowels of the shaft until it ended in a jagged room that was not pristine or sculptured or scented with fresh flowers. The den was harsh and gloomy and smelled of earth, moisture, and worms. Beneath her feet, the ground was hard and cobbled, and she slipped her shoes back on. Three tunnels diverted in three different directions. Each one was low enough that Lia had to stoop. Without the orb, she never would have known which one to take. It pointed clearly to one of them.

An ancient feeling stifled the air. Above her the full weight of the Abbey oppressed her, and the wonder of it startled her and made her a little fearful. Until Colvin had come to Muirwood, she had no idea there were secret rooms beneath the grounds.

Perhaps one of the tunnels led to the room where he had discovered the tomes? How many more tunnels were there? What other secrets did the Aldermaston guard so silently?

Clutching the orb, Lia ducked low and started down the tunnel.

***

The Leering in her way was carved into the likeness of a man with a sad face. It was fixed inside a stone wall that completely blocked the tunnel. The journey through the tunnel felt as if she had walked at least a league, but it could not have been that far, for the Pilgrim was just beyond the outer walls of the Abbey grounds, across High Street. Walking with a crouched back and a halting pace did not lend itself well for speed. The Leering seemed subdued, and she looked at it, wondering what kind of power it held. In her mind, she invoked it. Nothing happened. No fire or water or any other such manifestation responded to her. The orb, glowing as brightly and smokelessly as it ever had, continued to point to the wall.

Reaching out, Lia pushed against it, but it did not budge. Then she pulled at it, but could not work it loose. The ground was soft and made entirely of dirt, the air stale and putrid. She worked at it for a while, trying to find a way beyond the barrier.

A sound behind the stone wall startled her. A voice, muffled by the stone, was speaking. Then the stone began to open.

"Sorry it took a while, but I am here. So much commotion upstairs. One of the children had to tell me you arrived. There we are, and you already have a lamp I see and...and who are you?"

As the wall swung open toward her, spilling light and smells, it also revealed the face of a middling man, with pasty skin and reddish-brown thinning hair, staring at her in surprise. The smells that struck her were familiar to one who had been raised in the kitchen. Sacks and kegs and milled grain and the sweetly sour smell of a cellar surrounded her.

"Who are you?" he repeated, looking at her crossly. He had a lamp in his other hand. The doorway beyond opened into a cellar—the cellar of the Pilgrim, if she was guessing right—and there were a boy and a girl, about her own age, staring at her with interest, and another little girl, not older than eight, looking at her with wonder and licking dough off a wooden spoon.

Lia had no idea what to say.

CHAPTER SIXTEEN

Valerianum

The older girl leaned and whispered to her brother, "Who is she?"

"I have not seen her. Must be a learner," came the brother's reply, and in that moment of questioning, Lia had her answer. If they thought she was a learner, and if she acted like one instead of a wretched, she could fool them into helping her.

Looking at the father, or so she presumed, she gave him a snobby look and said, "It would be better if you did not know my name." The words and disdain were Colvin's, but they worked. She passed the barrier, brushing against the man who was a little shorter than her, and entered the cellar. The children scrambled backward to give her room, their eyes shining with curiosity.

She straightened, relieving the ache in her back and shoulders from stooping so far, and then looked down at the Cruciger orb. The spindles pointed to the ladder. Her mind scrambled quickly for words. Whirling, she faced the man as he latched the door and shoved a heavy barrel in front of it.

"Have the sheriff's men arrived?" she asked with a superior tone.

The boy, who was probably her age, answered first. "During the night. Some just left for the Abbey not long ago, but a few are still in the common room." He looked at her eagerly. "One wears a maston sword, but I do not think he is a maston. I would love to have a maston sword!"

His sister swatted his arm, and the father seemed to gasp like a fish for words.

The older fellow fidgeted. "I was not expecting...the Alder-maston usually sends Jon...it is just that with the sheriff...and they are looking...children, be still! Go to your mother."

"Father, can I sing for her?" asked the littlest one with the spoon.

"Not now. Please, all of you. Upstairs now. Get your mother."

The boy looked pained, and he gave Lia a look that nearly exploded with information. The girl and the boy seemed about the same age—perhaps twins? The girl was obedient, but her expression was full of mischief and excitement. She rushed to obey first, taking the younger one by the hand.

The boy lingered at the ladder, obviously struggling with the urge to disobey. Then his expression changed. "I will find out how many are guarding the prisoner!" he gasped, and then scooted up the ladder.

"Brant, you will not! Stay in the kitchen. Do you...I mean..." he turned, flustered, back to Lia. "Wait here a moment."

He hurried up the ladder, said some warning things to the young man, then scampered back down again, his face flushed and sweaty.

"I am sorry...it is just that...well you see...It is awkward. Most of the sheriff's men are banging on the Abbey gates right now, threatening to burst through. What would the Aldermaston... what are his orders?"

It made sense to Lia that any tunnel leaving the Abbey grounds would be guarded by someone loyal to the Aldermaston. How many tunnels honeycombed the grounds? She had never imagined it before, and the possibilities spread before her like stars in a dusky sky. Of course the man would think that she was serving the Aldermaston as well, especially since he had seen her holding the orb and had not demanded where she got it.

"Tell me what you know of the situation," Lia said, wearing her most distrusting look.

"Well, it is awkward, you see. And well...it happened very fast. The stranger—the one the sheriff was looking for—arrived this morning. I believe he is a squire. But that does not make sense." He stopped and wrung his hands, pacing a bit. "First, the sheriff's men rode in at first light and entered through the rear doors. They waited until the squire's horse was tied, and he was inside before they arrested him. He was unarmed and outnumbered." He wrung his hands again. "There was no way to warn him or we would have. The sheriff's men were watching us the whole time. One of the soldiers even went with Brant to tie up the horse in the stables and unsaddle him."

Lia's insides twisted and churned, but she clung to hope. "Where is he now?"

"The sheriff? As I said, he went to the..."

"No, the prisoner. Where is he?"

He wiped sweat from his lip, and started pacing in the cellar. "Well...it is hard to say...but they took him up upstairs. Under guard."

Lia shut her eyes.

"What does the Aldermaston want us...what should we do? I did not think he would have had time to send anyone... you understand...to send someone so quickly. Usually it is Jon

Hunter, as I said. This squire must be important or he is worried about violence if the gates burst. But can the Aldermaston save him outside the walls?"

"He is more important than you know," Lia said, thinking furiously. "Where is Almaguer?"

"The sheriff…yes…well, after the arrest, he was alone with the prisoner for a time. Then he came out and took most of his men to the Abbey. You can almost hear the shouting from the windows. There are horses and swords and it is a frightful affair. They are saying the king's army is coming today or tomorrow. Do you think they will spare the village?"

Lia's heart lurched at the thought. Shoving it aside, she pondered the imminent danger. There would not be much time to free Colvin. She went to the ladder and started up. "We must hurry." As she entered the kitchen, she saw the littlest with the spoon sitting by a cradle, teasing the baby inside with the gooey end. The oldest daughter was rushing about, but she stopped when Lia emerged and looked at Lia eagerly. The boy was perched on a stool by the door, and he came near, pushing up his sleeves. The cook, the mother, Lia recognized. She had seen only glimpses of her before, at the Whitsun Fairs, selling meats and cheeses and bread to the passersby, while Pasqua delighted the crowds with her famous treats. What if the woman recognized her?

She looked up from her kneading bowl, glanced at Lia, and a strange expression came over her face.

Lia chose to act. "How many of the sheriff's men are still here?"

Brant nodded vigorously. "I will find out." And he flew from the kitchen like an arrow.

"I need a pouch—or a linen—some way to hide this," she said next, cradling the orb in her palm.

The older sister rushed over to a coffer and knelt by it, sorting through the contents.

How was she going to get Colvin out of the Pilgrim? Some of the sheriff's men would possibly recognize her. What could she do? She was only a wretched. What could she possibly do to save him? Frantic, fearing she would be too late, she quickly searched the kitchen, casting her gaze at the cauldrons in the pits, and the spoons and pans dangling from hooks in a ceiling sconce. Breathing in through her nose, she inhaled the familiar smells, and suddenly tears threatened her. After this, she would never be allowed back in Muirwood again. Anger and longing wrestled inside her chest.

"What can we do?" the man asked, his face quivering with fear. "If there was a way…I am not seeing it. My family—I cannot risk my family. The sheriff's…don't you see? The king is coming, they say. What can we…really then, what can we do?"

Lia turned away from him, searching the walls, searching her memories for a thought, a suggestion, a way to solve the dilemma. Then it came—a pure clear thought like a rope thrown down to someone trapped in a well. What could a wretched do? What could someone who had grown up in an abbey kitchen all her life do? What knowledge did she have that could save Colvin?

She knew it instantly. It would work. The Medium was helping her.

Turning, she faced the cook and her husband. "Soldiers are always hungry. If they rode in early, as you say, they are probably starving. Prepare a tray for them. Fill it. Bread, eggs, cheese, nuts, fruit, beans. You have a fatling roasting on a spit. Feed it to them."

Her words caused action.

The cook was still gazing at Lia, but she said in a hurried voice, "Bryn, start on it. Hurry, girl, there is not much time. Use the bread over there—it is fresher. Don't be sparing on the butter. I will cut the meat."

Lia turned to the man. "Do you have any cider in the cellar? You do? Get a keg, quickly!"

Food and drink aplenty would show honor to soldiers who represented the king's sheriff. Lia approached the cook, hoping the woman did not recognize her yet. The tall woman turned, looking at her. Her eyes were worn and puffy, her hair long and dark with strands of silver interspersed. Part of her belly bulged, and Lia remembered seeing the baby in the crib and wondered how new and fresh it was to the world. The tray of food was the distraction. What she needed she knew the Pilgrim must have in its stores.

"Where is your valerianum?" Lia asked in a soft voice. It was an herb Pasqua used when she could not fall asleep, or when someone else needed the remedy. Too much of it in her tea, and she overslept the next morning. Sometimes Lia wondered if she did it like that on purpose.

The cook started, her eyes widening as she realized what Lia had in mind. "Yes…but it is pungent…like cheese…they would taste it…"

"The cider," Lia said, "is sweet and strong."

"You are right," the cook said, nodding. She gave Lia a hard look, her mouth tightening into a small, tense frown. Then she went to her stock of herbs and quickly found the sealed pot from the upper shelf.

"Cider," the man said, coming up with a cask under his arm. He nearly tripped over the littlest girl, who had wandered over as he climbed up the ladder. "Careful there. Guard your little sister's crib, Aimee. Over there, go." He juggled the small barrel a moment and then brought them to the table and fished around for a tap to pound into the keystone.

The oldest daughter approached Lia, holding forth a leather pouch with strings to cinch it closed.

"Your name is Bryn?" Lia asked.

"Yes," the girl whispered, then smiled. She wore the same kind of dress and girdle as Lia, though hers was brown instead of woad blue. Her arms were dark and she was nearly as tall as Lia.

Lia slid the orb into the pouch and tied it to her girdle belt. She caught the girl's hand as she was about to go back. "When you take the tray upstairs, Bryn, look at everything in the room. Listen carefully. The prisoner has a scar on his eyebrow. If you can, tell the soldiers you will fetch a healer, and then I will come with you when you return for the tray. Can you remember all that?"

"I remember very well. Mother taught me."

For a moment, Lia was jealous of her. They were working together in the kitchen, each doing a part, even the littlest daughter. A father. A mother. Several children. Each part of something that Lia had never had—a family.

The kitchen door shoved open, and Brant rushed in. "Three upstairs with the soldier. I brought some coals for the brazier. Three in the common room. The rest are at the Abbey causing a ruckus, including the ugly sheriff." His eyes gleamed. "That means there are only six. If I get my friends, we can..."

The father snorted viciously. "You will do nothing more than get your head split open, Brant. Grab me the mallet over there. Over there...by the grain bag."

"I will get the mallet," Lia said, joining the bustle. "Brant—you need to do something else. Saddle a horse and have it waiting in the back."

The grin that met her was glorious.

The good man turned to her. "If the sheriff's men return..."

Lia smirked. "The Aldermaston will keep them talking. He is very capable of being long-winded in his tongue lashings." She snapped her fingers and pointed to Brant. "But your father is right. We need to be cautious. If you are found out, say you were given four pence to saddle it up. No one else would question you twice about that kind of excuse." Then another idea. The image of the thief shone in her mind. "If they ask you who paid you, then say a man with a maston sword, nearly a beard, dirty boots and who reeked of mutton. A plain shirt, with a brown collar, mud-spattered and…"

Brant looked at her in shock. "With a quirky eyebrow that twitches a bit? And he talks very fast?"

Lia was stunned. "He looks like a vagrant, but he is…"

Brant interrupted her again, "…in the common room right now with the sheriff's men. He's the one who tricked the prisoner into coming here and claimed the reward. A mound of coins, I swear it!"

Lia balled her hand into a fist.

***

It is difficult to explain how touching the Medium actually occurs. Communion with it always begins with a thought. Thoughts are powerful things. Thoughts fed by strong emotions can become real. At Crowland Abbey, there is an Aldermaston who has a very faithful steward. Their love and respect for each other is well known. I have myself heard of how this steward finishes the sentences of his master. He is so in harmony with the Medium and his master's thoughts that he can hear them before they are spoken. Distance has no effect whatsoever on its efficacy. This steward can stand before the king, speaking in the Aldermaston's name. Their thoughts are perfectly entwined. Those who are strong in the Medium can often read the thoughts of others, friends or enemies. We are each of us sending thoughts into the aether. Most are undisciplined and vanish into nothingness. But consider this carefully. Some thoughts are powerful enough to forge new kingdoms.

—*Cuthbert Renowden of Billerbeck Abbey*

CHAPTER SEVENTEEN

Befallen

By the time Bryn returned, Lia's heart and anger had scarcely calmed down. More than anything, she wanted to go to the common room, seize the thief by his hair, and claw his face with her nails or bash a pot against his head. Or maybe crush his fingers with a mallet. The commotion of the inn did not stop, but no one else ventured into the kitchen but the family. Most of the patrons, it was said, had gathered around the Abbey gates to watch the confrontation between the Aldermaston and the sheriff. Lia chafed her hands, wondering how long it would last. All eyes were fixed on that scene. It was the perfect moment to rescue Colvin. In her mind, she wished the Aldermaston would refuse entrance even longer. The delay benefited her, if only he realized it.

Bryn was too excited to sit. She brushed back her hair as she talked quickly to the others. "The squire…you know, the prisoner…he has a cross look. His scowl is truly frightening. He does not seem frightened, only angry."

"You have described him well," Lia said. "Where do they have him? Tell me of the room."

"In a corner, on the floor, like a dog. I am so sad for him. They have him chained at the wrists, they do. His face is bloodied…"

"Did they ask for a healer?" Lia asked, pleading.

"Yes, they said we should fetch one. One of them said they ought to clean him up so when the king comes, he will be recognized. They were grateful for the food and the cider. I have seen hungry men before, but they were more like wolves."

The chains would be difficult. Then an idea struck Lia, and she turned to the good woman. "A tub of fat. Grease. Anything slippery. That will help with the chains." Brant was still gone, saddling up the horse, at the rear of the Pilgrim.

"Take me to him," Lia said, her stomach twisting into knots. What if one of the sheriff's men recognized her? She had to worry about that. It would ruin everything. She would have to pretend to be someone else, someone they would never care to notice.

The good woman shook her head. "Valerianum does not work that quickly. Give them time to eat the meal first. Do not be hasty."

Lia bit her lip, then shook her head. "I must. If the sheriff returns, we have lost our chance."

Her expression darkened. "You should not have been sent," she muttered. "This is wrong." She rose. "You will not go up there. Silar—do not let her go. She is a child."

Lia turned to the good man, who gawked at her and then at his wife. "But what am I to do about it? If the Aldermaston sent her…"

"It is wrong to send a child to do this sort of work." She looked at Lia fiercely. "Sending up a tray of food will not arouse suspicion. But you are a girl still. Those soldiers are men. I will not let you do this. I will go instead."

The father gawked again. "You cannot go, let alone mount the steps. Now that is enough foolishness. If the Aldermaston sent her to save the young man's life, then we save him."

"It is wrong. He should not have sent a child."

"It is not our choice that he did. What you are asking me to do is defy the Aldermaston."

The good woman closed her eyes, shaking her head. "It is wrong."

Lia rose to her feet. "No one has sent me against my will. Please believe that. The young man's life is at stake. The king will not show him mercy."

"If the king finds out that we helped..." the good woman whispered.

Her husband took her shoulders. "The Aldermaston will protect us, as he always has. Have confidence in him. He would not have sent her if it was not the right way."

"She is only a child, Silar. And so is our Bryn. This is wrong!"

Standing tall, the good man confronted his wife. "Should the Aldermaston ask me to wear a noose, I would do it." His voice trembled with emotion. "For him, I would. He took us in when no one else would. Can you forget that? We were wretcheds. Now we are considered Family." He shook his head. "Your heart is fearful for our children. For this child. But I tell you, the Aldermaston will shield us as he always has." He turned to Lia, tears in his eyes. "Go now, child. You show your courage this day. The Aldermaston will shield you as well."

Lia stared at him, wondering and amazed at the depth of his feelings toward the Aldermaston. While Bryn was upstairs, Lia and the good woman had prepared a tray for healing—woad, broth, linen, warm water. She crossed to the table where the tray was and carefully lifted it. Glancing back at the family, she nodded to them, and then followed Bryn out into the hall.

"Mother is like that," Bryn whispered with a mischievous grin. "She worries overmuch. This way. There are the stairs. The common room is over there. Watch that floor board, it can trip you."

Lia was grateful for the warning and followed her up the steep steps that rose into the higher levels of the inn. She was careful not to jostle the tray and spill any of the contents.

"How old is this inn?"

"It's been here since Muirwood was built. When the royalty visit and send their children to learn, there is not room on the grounds for everyone. The Pilgrim is the closest, so we prosper from their visits. I have even served the king's cousins before."

In her mind Lia thought, *You are serving another of his cousins today as well.*

"How long has your family been in the village?" They walked up the final flight to the top floor and then started down the hall. Her stomach twisted tighter with each step. What would Colvin do when he saw her? Accuse her? Gasp with shock? She had to remedy that.

"I was born here," Bryn said. "We all were—here in the village. Sometimes I wish I was born a wretched and could live in the Abbey. It is comforting being so near to its walls…its protection. But I wish we were not living on this side."

"You cannot wish you were a wretched," Lia said darkly. "No one would wish that."

"My brother almost was. Brant is not my real brother. Well, he is now. But he was not born to my parents. But the Aldermaston made him so. He is my brother, and now his blood is the same as ours. People think we are twins, but we are not. How big is your family?"

Lia bit her lip. "I cannot say. Is that the door? Be ready."

Bryn opened it for her.

She did not recognize any of the sheriff's men and thanked the Medium for the mercy.

"Brickolm, that was a meal. I cannot finish this helping, do you want it?"

"I will take it."

"You are always hungry."

"And why? Because they do not feed us well on the saddle. Our hunger is shameful. Shameful."

Lia glanced at the three soldiers and quickly assumed the manners of Sowe. She did not meet any of their gazes. She slouched her shoulders. She summoned up all her fatigue and wore it like a cloak.

One of the sheriff's men, a heavyset man with a scraggy beard and very little hair, approached them and looked at the items on the tray, one by one. He paused at one item. "And what is this? Smells like fat."

"Goose grease," Lia mumbled. "A salve." She swallowed and looked down at her shoes, trembling.

"Goose grease?"

"Shame it were not Gooseberry Fool, eh?" chortled one of the others. "Now there is a fine dish if you can get it. I swear, Moise, if you keep yawning, I am going to kick you. Stop it!"

"I cannot…h-h-help it," the other said, yawning midword. "I cannot half keep my eyes open today."

"If we were outside, it would be far easier." The sheriff's man went to the window and ducked his head out. "Sweet Idumea, the entire village is out there." He came back in and shook his head.

"If Almaguer forces the gate, they might riot. I swear, I think they just might."

"Then they are fools," spat another, scratching his throat with a meaty hand. He spit on the floor. "Fools if they do, with the king's army so near. Go on lass, do your work. Do not just stand there like a stump. Clean up the little braggart and mend his ails so we can kill him properly, a traitor's death. Stop listening in on your betters."

That spurred Lia forward, the tray rattling with pretended nervousness as she walked cautiously over to the corner. On the far side was the tall four-post bed, draped with velvet curtains, stuffed and stuffed with feathers, and crowded with pillows and blankets. It looked twice the size of Pasqua's bed, luxurious even for a king, and Lia felt the very real desire to drop the tray and pounce up on it herself. Every night of her life she had slept in the loft or on a mat on the kitchen tiles. Near the foot of that spacious bed, Colvin sat on the floor defiantly. His shackled wrists rested atop his knees, his filthy, matted hair hung in lumps down his brow, his back against the wall. Blood stained his shirt, leaking from the cut on his eyebrow, which had reopened, as well as his nose and lip. As she set the tray down by his feet, he looked up at her face. His eyes widened with shock.

"Say nothing," she whispered as she bent over the supplies, opening the lid with the broth.

Glancing back at the soldiers, she saw one yawning so wide it looked like his jaw would break.

"I said stop yawning, you dolt! It makes me…y-y-yawn too. Bridges and ruts! Now you have me doing it! I swear, the next man who yawns gets a fist."

Lia dipped a linen in the broth and pressed it against Colvin's brow. He said nothing, but his lips and jaw trembled and clenched, as if he were about to speak or shout or rave and only iron determination prevented it. She pressed the linen against his injury and then wrung it out, dipping it again, then squeezed it against his brow until the juices trickled down his face.

What was he thinking at that moment? Were his eyes accusing her of betraying him? Were they warning her to run? Gratitude was certainly not the look. While she held the linen to his head with one hand, her other opened the tub of grease, and she scooped some of it up and began smoothing it on his wrists. He winced and stiffened, and she saw the blood there as well. He had been working to slip free of the iron cuffs and the chain had worn his skin raw in the works. Liberally, she applied more of the grease to his wrists and hands.

Behind her, Bryn gathered the tray with scraps of uneaten food, and collected the empty goblets of cider. One of the soldiers was already sleeping at the table.

"Brickolm? Are you daft, lad? Brickolm! Look at the fool, asleep on the table!"

Lia looked back, barely able to stop a smile from betraying her joy, then turned and scooped up more grease. Colvin nodded slowly and began twisting his wrists, twisting and pulling and straining against the cuffs. His frown was fearsome. His muscles tightened, his fingers pressing together to shorten the gap as much as possible. Then with a fluid slip, one hand came free of the cuff.

Lia mopped the blood from his face with a clean linen, remembering the night on the kitchen floor when she had bathed his face of sweat and blood.

"It is bad enough that we have to stay behind, but it tortures me to see a bed just sitting there. Have you ever slept in a real bed like that, Moise? A real bed, not one stuffed with straw and rats, but a *real* one."

"Not like that one. I am sure it costs a pretty crown for a room like this. Brickolm, get up, you fool. If Almaguer catches you napping…do you hear me? Oh, the daft, daft fool."

"Maid. Fetch us more food. I need something…I need to eat something…to stay awake. Fetch it, I tell you!" He waved his hand at Bryn and she nodded with the tray and left. The door thumped softly behind her, but the smell of the feast lingered in the air like candle smoke.

Colvin strained with the other wrist, twisting it, sliding it, pulling it against the iron cuff. He bit his lip, his neck muscles bulging. Blood dripped from his hand to the floor. Then it came loose.

Lia peeked back at the sheriff's men. Another sat in the chair, head back, mouth open—eyes closed. One left.

She took the crushed woad petals and dabbed the mixture into his wound again. The pink and scabby flesh looked painful and sore. She hoped the woad would work on it a second time.

The third man ventured to the window and gazed outside. He rubbed his eyes, swearing under his breath. He fought against the powerful force compelling him to sleep. Lia stared at him, willing the valerianum to work faster. He lurched away from the window, planting his hand on the table to steady himself. Slowly, he sank to his knees, his eyelids fluttering, his face going slack. He looked across the room at her, but there was no recognition as he fought a weary battle to stay awake. A battle he was losing.

Lie down, she told him in her mind.

And he did.

CHAPTER EIGHTEEN

Chalkwell

Colvin flinched with pain as she wiped the grease and blood from his wrists with a rag. Lia hefted the tray, whispering, "Follow me out."

Noise from outside the Pilgrim grew louder, but the sheriff's men did not awaken. Lia crossed to the door and opened it softly. Still they slept. Outside in the hall, they started toward the stairs.

She looked at him, at the conflicted, angry expression. "You have nothing to say?"

"What would you like me to say?" he answered tightly.

Angrily, she thought about shoving the tray into his stomach. "You could start with something resembling gratitude. That you realize I did not betray you deliberately. I was tricked by one of the sheriff's men. I wanted to make it right..."

"Do not justify yourself. I know you did not betray me. But we are far from being safe or free. Did the Aldermaston send you?"

"No."

"Then do you have a way out?"

"Your horse is being saddled."

"But then where? Is there shelter other than the Abbey for me?"

"I have the orb."

"What?"

"I said I have the orb."

"It is useless to me. I cannot work it."

"I know," she answered, wondering why he was being thick-headed. "But I can. I am coming with you."

He halted and grabbed her arm, stopping her as well, sloshing broth onto the tray. "What?"

She looked at him fiercely in return. "I stole the orb. Do you think I will ever be welcome at the Abbey again? I am coming with you."

"You would go with me to the battlefield? And then what will you do?" He shook his head, muttering darkly. "This sheriff will hunt us. He wants you. *You.* I do not know why, but he is deter-mined to have you. He hardly seemed to care that he arrested me. It is you he wants. A wretched. He kept asking about you. He is arguing with the Aldermaston to turn you over to him."

Lia's stomach, which had just begun to untwist as they left the room, coiled again. "Why would he...?"

"Several reasons I can think of, and I have had nothing to do but think since I was arrested. You should be hiding. And yet, here you are, in the lion's maw. When you came into the room, I swear..." He shut his eyes, looking more furious than ever.

"I came to help you!" she scolded. "I promised you I would. I keep my promises. If the king is coming to kill you, I will not let that happen, not if I can stop it." She tugged her arm free, but he let her go. "We are wasting words. When we get away, then we can talk it over." Her feelings were hurt—she had hoped he would offer to protect her and offer her sanctuary in his earldom. He had not.

"Agreed."

At the end of the hall there were steps descending. As they started down, the sound of others coming up met them. Men's voices. One of them, Lia recognized.

"A mob, I tell you. By Idumea's hand, the fools. Better ride out while we still can. Who cares about the girl when we have the other prize."

"You tell Almaguer I will stay behind and find the wretched. I know this Abbey. She cannot hide from me for long."

"Tell the sheriff yourself, Scarseth. Let us fetch the stripling and ride back to Shefton and meet the king. I do not think it matters which village the boy dies in."

Lia froze in the stairwell. She recognized the thief's voice. Now she knew his name. She had been so sure—so sure she would have enough time to get Colvin out of the Pilgrim. Three sets of boots came up the stairs, and they were almost at the top.

There were three sleeping men in the room at the end of the hall. Three men down below but coming up quickly. There was no more time to think. It was time to act, but she had no ideas, and Colvin had no sword. Helplessly, frantically, she froze as their heads appeared from the stairs below.

"I am telling you, if the mob riots, we will not make it out of town unscathed. The Aldermaston has all the power here. These villagers count on him, not Mendenhall. I told Almaguer not to confront him over the girl."

"Well, you are wasting breath with me. There are twenty of us with swords and hauberks, and if we leave a river of blood, then it is the Medium's fault. No one challenges Almaguer's authority in this Hundred. Aldermaston or no."

Lia saw their faces. It was over. She had done her best, but it had only made things worse. Now both she and Colvin would be captured by the sheriff's...

It happened so quickly, she nearly shrieked with surprise. Colvin yanked the tray from her hands and threw it at the sheriff's men below. Warm broth and water splashed, the crockery shattered, and the tray itself struck like a catapult stone, toppling one of them back into another in the narrow stairwell. Colvin leapt down the full flight of stairs, and Lia clutched the rail and watched.

Curses, shrieks, grunts, crunches. The sheriff's men fought back, fighting for their lives. There was no room or time to draw swords—the stairwell was all a tumble of arms and legs, of fists and chins and red-specked spittle. The force of Colvin's attack toppled the two men and Scarseth. Blood gushed from one man's nose, and Lia thought she saw a tooth fly from his mouth and rattle and drop down the stairwell like a pebble.

"Brickolm! Brickolm!" the other screamed, but Colvin grabbed his arm, pulling him closer, and silenced his cries by encircling his neck and throat with his arm. With a twirl, the man went head first into the wall and dropped like a sack.

Scarseth, dripping with broth and looking horror-struck, scrambled down the steps. Lia started after him, but Colvin was already there, jumping and grappling him as he wriggled to free himself, and both tumbled down the stairs.

The thief cried out in pain, then, "I swear it, I can help you! Do not kill me! I can help you!"

Scarseth raised his hands up, palms open, trembling like a shiver in winter, his eyes wild and fearful, blood dripping from his lip. "Almaguer is coming back now. A dozen men. You will not get free if you waste time on me. Please, for the love of Idumea, you are Demont's sworn man. I know you are. Not even he murdered. Please, for the love of Idumea, spare me!"

Lia reached them both, staring into the thief's blazing eyes. He looked up at her, recognized her, then closed his eyes shut as if he knew he was going to die.

"This belongs to *my* family," Colvin said with revulsion and fury mingling in his expression. His eyes blazed with hatred. He drew the maston sword from Scarseth's scabbard, the blade that Lia had admired. She stood there, helpless again, seeing the flesh at the thief's throat constrict as he swallowed.

The tip of the blade aimed at that point. Lia blinked quickly, quivering, believing she would see a man die in front of her. Colvin's eyes burned with passion. Part of her hungered to see it happen. Part of her knew she would never forget it if she watched.

"You betrayed me to die," Colvin said huskily. "But in this thing only, you do not lie. I am Demont's man. And I cannot end a man's life who lacks the spleen to fight me."

"I saved your life," Scarseth whispered hoarsely, his eyes opening again. "I could have left you to bleed to death by that tree. I carried you to Muirwood in a rainstorm. I carried you. She will tell you. I did save your life."

Colvin coughed with contempt. "Your greed saved me, not you. Your cowardice saves you now." He paused, raising the sword, staring down at the shivering man. Their eyes locked. Then kneeling down, Colvin clutched Scarseth's throat with his free hand, sword poised above, ready to fall. "You are a liar. You will always be a liar. But you will betray her again."

"I swear I will not!" he squeaked, his voice choking.

"By the Medium, I take your power of speech. You will not utter another word."

Lia felt it, as if a gust of wind had suddenly swept up the stairwell. She had sensed it that night long ago when a great storm had raged and the Aldermaston calmed the squall. The Medium was there.

Colvin released Scarseth's throat, and the thief's own fingers replaced Colvin's. His eyes bulged. His lips moved but no sound came out. Tears ran down his cheeks. Grabbing the man's belt, Colvin hoisted him up off the floor, then severed the belt in the middle, spilling him back to the floor. Colvin grabbed the scabbard, tugged it free, then motioned for Lia to follow him.

They escaped out the rear of the Pilgrim Inn on a horse held by a grinning Brant.

They did not make it far. The sheriff and his men rounded the corner.

"The girl!" Almaguer shouted.

Colvin stamped the horse's flanks. "Hold on to me. Tightly! Squeeze as hard as you can. No, even harder! Lock your fingers together or you will bounce off! Quickly now—before we start to gallop!"

At first Lia thought the horse was already galloping, but when it started, the entire feel of the animal changed. The sensation in her stomach went from nausea and fearfulness to glee. Her wild hair whipped behind her, the cowl of her cloak bouncing against her back.

Behind them, against the rush of the wind in her ears, she could hear the sheriff's men shouting. But running men, thronged by villagers, could not catch the surging rush of a galloping stallion. The motion jarred Lia, and she feared she might tumble off the back.

"I am slipping!" she shouted.

One of Colvin's arms tightened against hers, pressing her arm painfully, but steadying her.

"Use your legs. Squeeze them against the flanks. Press against me tightly!"

A voice in the crowd shouted out her name. She turned to look, but the movement nearly made her lose her balance the other way.

"Stop twisting like that!" Colvin growled. "Press against me!" He kicked the stallion again, and it felt as if they had left the rutted street completely—as if they were now flying.

Lia wondered who had called her name. She pressed her cheek against the sweat-dampend fabric of his shirt and held on until her muscles ached. So many times in her life she had mixed dough, churned butter, and used her arms and fingers as her tools. They did not fail her. Her grip was hard, and she managed to cling to him despite the bouncing, the speed, and the rush of wind. They rode down Chalkwell Street, along the Abbey's eastern walls. The tall spire of Muirwood rose sharply into the sky, but it was getting smaller with each hoofbeat.

She watched the Abbey, her home, fade away into the distance. Her entire life had been spent inside the grounds. Her nights, for as far back as memory spun its webs, she had spent in the kitchen. The face of Pasqua came into her mind, and it brought such a stab of pain and heartsickness that tears came to her eyes. Lia had not said goodbye. The huge oaks of the Abbey grounds could be seen above the wall. The branches of the younger ones swayed, as if waving farewell to her. She would never see Muirwood again. The grief was crushing her heart.

Turning her face the other way, to shut out the sight that would haunt her days, she saw the Tor rising ahead to the east. The Tor was a nearby hill, the highest point in any direction—a bald, crouch-backed hill with a few rings of trees along the lower fringes of its steep green slopes. As a child, it had always tempted her. But it seemed so far from the Abbey walls that she knew she and Sowe would never be able to make it there, climb it, and return before dark. The best she had been able to do was get Jon

Hunter's description of it. He had been to the top many times. *It is nothing but a bald, crouch-backed hill, Lia. It is a lonely hill. There are other hills in this Hundred with better views than it has.* But that made Lia love it even more, even if she believed she would never be able to climb it.

How long before the sheriff and his men would have their horses saddled? How long before their pursuers came after them? She did not know the land very well, but she imagined the road was not safe, not with the king's army on the way. Being a wretched, she only knew the names of the streets that bordered the Abbey on two sides—High Street and Chalkwell.

Looking up at the Tor again, she had a thought. If they needed a place to hide—or a direction to ride—the Cruciger orb would guide them.

"Stop the horse," Lia said.

"Are you sick?" he asked over his shoulder.

"No, remember the king's army. The orb! I have the orb to guide us."

Colvin sharply pulled on the reins and the mount fought him. He tugged harder, several jerking motions, and tamped the flanks with his boots, even though he did not have spurs. The stallion snorted and huffed, still giddy with the thrill of the run. Colvin calmed it with his voice as it finally came to a stop and thrashed its mane. He patted its neck soothingly, while Lia opened the pouch at her waist and, with trembling hands, withdrew the Cruciger orb. Her arms shook from holding on to Colvin so tightly, and the orb wobbled in her hand.

In her mind, she thought the words, *Show us a safe path to Winterrowd.*

Again the amazing spindles went to work, spinning deftly and quickly, pointing due east, directly at the Tor.

Colvin looked back at the direction. "It is pointing east. Winterrowd is the other way. The last time you asked it, it pointed west. This makes no sense."

Lia looked at it sternly. "Show me Winterrowd."

The spindles swung around and pointed west.

"Why is it showing us both?"

"Show us the safe way to Winterrowd," she answered, and the spindles pointed back to the Tor. Writing appeared on the lower half of the orb.

"How can Winterrowd be in both directions?" Colvin asked.

But Lia understood. "Because it knows things that we do not. It knows the way to Winterrowd, but it also knows other things. Like what is down this road. The safe way to Winterrowd brings us to the Tor. Guide us there and if it changes directions, I will tell you."

"Should we trust it?"

"Do you think you can find the way yourself?" she answered sternly.

Colvin made a clicking sound and tugged gently on the reins, leading the stallion off the road and into the trees. A quick tap and the horse plunged up ahead into the nest of towering silver birch. The branches were twisted and gnarled, trunks warped and bent and writhing in the breeze. Twigs and leaves churned under the hooves. The shade brought a chill and Lia felt a shiver tear through her. She was exhausted from the sheer terror of their escape.

Past the screen of trees, a gentle hill sloped downward to the base of the Tor. And there, before their eyes, was a walled garden nestled at the base of the hill a short distance away. Jon Hunter had never mentioned its existence before. Lia knew instinctively that it was their destination.

Colvin looked over his shoulder at her. A drop of sweat trickled down his cheek.

She nodded and they started down the slope toward a doorway set into the stone wall. In the air behind them, the sound of charging hooves drifted in from a distance. Colvin kicked the stallion hard, and Lia clutched him with one arm and pressed the orb against her queasy stomach.

***

There is but one way to truly gain mastery over the Medium, and that is to realize you cannot truly master it at all. It masters you. When one attempts to force it, compel it, command it, or otherwise exercise dominion over it—the power flees like a timid bird. This is because the Medium knows our innermost thoughts. It knows how we intend to use it. Man may deceive other men. But one simply does not deceive the Medium. If its will is sought, it will come. If we emulate the principles by which it thrives, it flourishes in us. Pride is poison to it. In reality, there is perhaps not one of our natural passions so hard to subdue as our pride. Disguise it, struggle with it, beat it down, stifle it, mortify it as much as you please. It is still alive, and will every now and then peep out and show itself. You will see it, perhaps, even within the abbeys of the realm. For even if I, an Aldermaston, could conceive that I had completely overcome it, I should probably be proud of my humility.

—Cuthbert Renowden of Billerbeck Abbey

CHAPTER NINETEEN

Blood Spring

The wall of the garden was too high. There was no seeing over it, even while seated on the saddle. Tangled vines and bright green moss marred the wall's surface. The air was fresh with the scent of the grass and flowers growing within. Snorts from the stallion came between the churn of earth beneath its hooves, but the wind still threatened with the thunder of horses coming down Chalkwell Street. The orb directed them to the door of the garden—a tall door, bound with rusted iron. Locked.

Colvin slipped off of the saddle and handed the reins up to Lia. There was a handle, and he pulled on it, but it did not open. He put his shoulder to it, but it did not give.

"There is a crossbar," he muttered. Stepping back a pace, he stared up at the wall's height. "We do not have much time. This is where the orb directed us?"

"Clearly," she replied, anxious to get out of sight. The sound of hooves drew nearer. "The wall is tall, but I think we can make it over."

"The horse is not going to climb, and we need it for our journey. I am not leaving it behind."

"I did not suggest that," she answered crossly. "Lift me higher and I will raise the bar from the other side."

He looked at her, his brow furrowing.

"I could probably reach it from the saddle. Here, guide the horse closer." She offered him the reins back, and he took them, guiding the stallion up to the wall.

It stamped and snorted as Lia set her feet on the saddle. She tucked the orb into the pouch dangling from her girdle and cinched it closed. Then carefully, she started to stand, struggling to keep her balance and using the wall to help keep from falling. Standing, she could see into the garden, which was divided into several areas with thick hedges, trees, and pools. Just beyond the wall, some wide stone steps led down, but she did not think the horse would have difficulty descending them. She had always enjoyed climbing trees.

"They are getting closer!" Colvin warned.

He steadied the horse, and she planted her hands on the rough vines and then hoisted herself up. The ivy vines scratched at her as she swung her legs to the other side, twisted around on her belly, and then hung from her fingertips. She was grateful to land gracefully on the other side, and quickly raised the crossbar and pushed the door open. Yanking the tether, Colvin pulled the stallion after them, secured the door again, and then they both led the horse down the broad steps.

The sound of the sheriff's men passed from the roadside, heading farther away.

Colvin looked around, warily. "What is this place?"

"I have never been here," she replied.

At the base of the stairs, the path was blocked by several hedges, but it opened up to a view of beautiful pools, flower beds, and shade trees. Ahead and above, the Tor rose up in its majesty, dominating the view.

"Which way?" Colvin asked.

Lia checked the orb and it pointed to another set of steps, leading up, across the garden.

Colvin rubbed the bristles on his cheek. "Where is the groundskeeper? Who lives here?"

"How am I supposed to know that? At least you have the sword. To think, all along, I thought it was his sword. Not yours. I feel such a fool. We go that way."

The stallion managed the steps without trouble, and they walked, looking at the sights. Birds with bright plumage went from tree to tree, looking at them quizzically. The pools and fountains were charming and secluded. As they reached the top of the steps, the path went two ways. The orb pointed to a thick maze of hedges, but across a short lawn there was a low stone wall with a Leering set into it in the shape of a lion's head.

"A well," Colvin said, tugging the stallion. "Let us water the horse and ourselves. This is a maston's garden. Even the hedges are shaped with our emblem." She had not noticed it until he pointed it out—the eight-pointed star in the stone and hedges.

He led the way to the Leering, which overlooked a stone trough. The stone was mottled in color but dry of water. A gentle rush filled the air, making Lia shiver, and the lion's mouth began to gush water and fill the basin. The water was clear, but had a pinkish blush coloring it. Colvin led the stallion to the other side and it dropped its head to the pool and began to drink. Holding his hands to the stream, Colvin washed them clean and then cupped some water into his mouth several times.

"It has a metal taste," he said. "Strange. It is not offensive, though. Drink while we still have fresh water."

Lia joined him and also washed her hands. She tasted it—the waters were a little sour with the hint of metal. The stone beneath the Leering had worn away from the constant lapping of the waters, brownish red in color. The water was cold, almost icy, so she thought about warmth as she did at the laundry at Muirwood, and suddenly the water came out gushing with steam. She bathed her arms in the stinging waters, when the flow stopped suddenly.

"What did you do?" Colvin demanded of her, his face angry.

"It was too cold. I wanted it warm."

"How did you...you cannot do that to a *gargouelle*. This one summons water. That is all. You are not supposed to bring anything else to the summoning."

"I do it at the laundry all the time," she said, wondering why he was so upset. "Hot water cleans better than cold, dirty water."

"You are not supposed to be able to...that is something that few learners even think of...what I mean is...it is just not possible. This one summons water. You are mixing fire with it."

"How else do you heat water then?"

He looked at her sternly. "It is just not done. There are ones for fire and ones for water. Not both."

She met his stern look with one of her own. "Do you object because *you* cannot do it?"

He stood silently, as if chewing his words behind his clenched teeth so that he would not speak them. "I will not argue with you any longer. If you have drunk enough, let us go."

His hard words had wounded her, but she tried not to let it show and motioned toward the other path. Colvin was utterly infuriating sometimes. Checking with the orb, she followed it over to a maze of hedges, with him pulling the stallion after them. Past those, the pointers guided them to a secluded area not far from it. The view was shielded by beautiful yew trees which formed a boundary around it, and the perimeter was offset with a low stone wall, leading to a circular well. Another Leering, like the waymarker near the ruins at the Abbey, stood at the head of the well. It was tall and narrow and carved with the face of a man, a weeping man.

Lia looked down at the Cruciger orb, and it showed the way toward the well.

Colvin wrapped the reins around a branch, tightened it, and then stepped down three short steps, looking curious and confused. She followed him, running her hand over the green foliage of a bush. The sun was nearly overhead, and there was no wind, so the shadows lay flat and still.

Lia looked into the eyes of the Leering carved into the waymarker, wondering what purpose it was built for. It seemed ancient, the features rubbed away by countless years. She joined Colvin by the edge of the well and they both stared down into the black depths. The throat of the well made a sound, as if it were alive but merely asleep and breathing softly.

"Here?" Colvin said, staring into the dark.

A man's huskily accented voice came from the trees. "Only a Cruciger orb would have brought you here." He stepped from the shadows, his dark eyes flashing with intensity. He was taller than Colvin, fat around the middle with skinny legs showing beneath his tunic hem, his black hair just starting to go white above his ears.

Colvin grabbed for his sword, and the man charged forward, waving a twisting staff.

"You reach first for a weapon! In my home? In this sacred place?" He was there by the time Colvin's sword left its sheath and aimed at the man's chest. His eyes blazed. "And what are you going to do with it, you miserable little *pethet*! Eh? Are you going to thrust me through? Eh? You are so brave with a teeny sliver of steel. Braver than the sheriff's men, even. Go ahead! Spill my entrails to the stones. Let my blood wail to the Medium for vengeance upon you. You little *pethet*! A limping man's crutch has made you so fearful? Eh?" He pushed his chest against the tip of Colvin's sword. "Eh? I cannot hear you. Eh? Why not kill me now and be done? Eh!"

Lia stared at the crazed eyes, sickened by the reek of his foul breath. Reaching out, she put her hand on Colvin's arm. "Put it away," she whispered.

His arm remained firm, his eyes distrustful. His jaw muscles throbbed from clenching his teeth.

"Put it away," she repeated, pushing gently.

"Sound advice, *pethet*! The wisdom of youth! Listen to the child. Listen to the one who holds the Cruciger orb and makes it spin. Eh! You wish to fight me still? Very well. Then I will fight you. I do not like to fight. But you do not show me proper respect. If I must shame you in front of this little sister, then I must. *Vancrola, pethet! Simoin!*"

"Put it down," Lia said more firmly. Then she whispered, "He will not harm us. He is a maston." She knew it to be true, even though he wore no markings.

Colvin wavered, his arm trembling slightly, then he swept the sword point down.

"I am disappointed in you, *pethet*. I would have relished shaming you in front of her. Defeated by a cripple!" He struck the staff down in front of him, then leaned on it. "Eh! Well, if you do not wish to fight, then we can talk. Talk is useful sometimes. For that is why you are here. Eh? I did not hear you. You were going to tell me why did you come to the gardens. Eh?"

"We sought shelter from the sheriff's men," Lia said, stepping in front of Colvin. "The orb led us here."

"Of course it did!" he bellowed, waggling the crutch at her. "Because it can hear the blood still screaming. As I can hear it. *Shaolic.*"

A shiver went down Lia's back at the word.

"Who are you?" Colvin asked warily.

"I am Maderos. I do not want your names, so do not tell me. They would be filthy to me, since you are not of my country. Filthy to speak. Bah! I do not like the names from this country. And I do not want your blood also on these stones. Besides, I already know why you are here."

"How do you know that?" Lia asked.

Maderos gave her a crooked smile. "Because you came with a maston, little sister. They always bury their own."

Lia swallowed. "There is another maston here?"

"Only a part of him, child. His blood has already been spilt. So the spring weeps again. It weeps with his blood."

Colvin slid the sword back into its scabbard. Anger stormed across his face. "Where? Where is the body?"

"You stand on it, *pethet*. I hid it in the well where they would not find it again to carve it like butchers. He did not name you, for he did not know your name. That saved you, I think. But he did name Demont. Gack! A horrid name to pronounce. Like speaking with worms on my tongue. Demont's man. He came looking for you. But he found one who cannot be trusted. Who betrayed him to the sheriff's men. He was a *pethet* too. Demont's man did not know your name. But he knew enough. He knew the name of Winterrowd. Now the king's army comes, and all the mastons gathering there will spill their blood in the fields. If you were a faithful maston, like the Aldermaston of Muirwood, you could stop them." His eyes widened with laughter. "You could lift up the Tor! Then drop it down on them!" He laughed, a sickening booming laugh. "But you are not a faithful maston yet. You are a *pethet*."

All the while the crazy man spoke, Lia realized something. His accent was foreign. If he was not from their country, perhaps he knew the language written on the orb. Perhaps he was the one who could read it. Not only did the orb bring them to a place of safety, it brought them to someone who could help them.

"You can read?" Lia asked him.

"Of a truth, I can!" he said, looking offended. "I read many languages. And speak them. And engrave them. I visit many lands and write their stories."

Lia and Colvin looked at each other. She could see it in his eyes—they were both thinking the same thing. Maderos was the one who had lived in the caves where the old cemetery had been. He was the one writing the record and recording the history in the tome.

"Can you read the writing on the orb?" Lia asked him, holding it up in her hand.

"Let the *pethet* read it," he sneered.

Colvin swallowed. "I cannot."

"Eh?"

"I cannot."

"You cannot? Because you think your language is the best language? That because you were born and your parents babbled to you in this tongue, that it is the best language to speak? How small is your mind, *pethet*. So very tiny. Little ideas. Puny ideas. Let me see it, child. Show it to me."

Lia held up the orb and he squinted, looking at the whorl of letters scribed in the lower half.

He pursed his lips. "Yes...yes...and then what...oh, then I see...I see...very well. Yes, there. I see. Yes."

"You can read it?" Lia said, hope welling up in her stomach.

"No," he said, shaking his head.

"You cannot?"

"No, for it is written in the language of the Pry-rian. A fallen people. But it is a good tongue. They had noble ideas in Pry-Ree."

"But…but you cannot read it?" Lia said, disappointed.

He looked up from the orb and angrily into her eyes. "No, no—none of that, child! You make it dark again. No…you must not do that!"

"What do you mean?" she said, biting her lip, confused by his erratic words.

"Doubt. Do not doubt. Never doubt. I cannot read Pry-rian. It is a language forgotten by many. Though I cannot read the words, I *was* understanding what it said, little sister. The Medium whispers it to me as it does many ancient languages. Some have the gift of speaking languages. I have the gift of reading them."

"How?" she asked, frightened and excited.

"You already know! I heard you whisper it. Because I am a maston, and because I believe I can. This is what it said so far. Or what it meant to say, but could not tell you because you cannot hear the whispers very well yet. I must give you the sword, the tunic, and the chaen of the maston who died here. These must be taken to the maston's brother. He is at Winterrowd now. You must go there. *You* must go there," he said to Lia, looking deeply into her eyes. "And he must go there. Yes, the *pethet*. He must go too. Let me read the rest…yes…yes…I can see it. Very well. Very well. The meaning is clear."

Gripping his crutch, he turned and started hobbling briskly. "Come, come. When we receive the will of the Medium, we obey it. Obey it *prontis*. Never delay. Come, to the sword and to the chaen. And the tunic. The *pethet* will wear the tunic into battle, I think. A battle that will soon rage near Winterrowd." He grunted as he started up the shallow stone steps. "Then we climb the Tor, for I must show you the safe path. The road is too treacherous. You will not make it on the road. You must go through the Bearden Muir."

CHAPTER TWENTY

Summit

The staff in Maderos's hand was a crooked, twisting thing. It was heavy at the top, with a flat mushroomlike head, its stout length gnarled, bent, and tapered at the end. Lia did not recognize the wood, all knobby and veined. He planted his hand on its neck near the crown, and he was off walking at a pace that defied Colvin and Lia to keep up. One of his legs was crooked, but with the staff, it did not seem to slow him at all. In fact, they both had to hurry to keep up with him.

"This way, this way!" Maderos hissed over his shoulder, bounding down the path. "Hurry along. Always obey, when the Medium asks us. *Prontis!* The Cruciger speaks to her in Pry-rian. In Pry-rian. Eh! I should have known."

The hedge opened up to a meadow, and husky sheep grazed beyond on the grass at the base of the Tor. Several looked up at them as they advanced. Colvin clenched his jaw again; his eyes narrowed into slits. His very posture spoke of distrust and wariness as he yanked the reins to pull the stallion after him.

Sweat trickled down Lia's cheek and she wiped it away. Maderos ambled up a small hillock to where a lone tree stood. It was an apple tree, but it looked nothing like ones from the orchard in Muirwood. The width of the trunk and the massive branches whispered of centuries. In fact, to Lia's eyes, the sturdy branches seemed the same color as Maderos's staff. As she entered the shade, she nearly stumbled over a stone. Only it was not a stone, she realized as she reached down and lifted a Muirwood apple.

Maderos looked back at her and their eyes met. "Wise, child. Gather more for the horse. More for you. You will need food where you are going. The fruit will sustain you."

An apple so out of season should have been mush—or desiccated. This one was firm and ripe, its yellowish, pinkish skin gleaming. She caught sight of a Leering near the trunk of the ancient tree, but she had felt it before she had seen it. Power emanated from it. If it were fire, she would have been able to warm her hands from the stone. The face carved into it was so old, that it was scarcely more than a few wrinkled crags in the nearly smooth surface. A bearded face. She approached it, drawn in by its eyes. She reached out her hand, but Colvin caught her wrist. He shook his head no, his eyes angry.

Maderos went around the trunk. "There we are. Right where I left them. Here, *pethet*. Treasures for you to carry. Gather the apples, sister. There will be more around the base in the grass. There will not be any in the branches. It is not the season yet."

As Lia searched and gathered apples, she brought them to the saddlebag of the horse, but paused long enough to feed the beast one first.

"Ah, the sword," Maderos told Colvin as she searched the grass. "It belonged to the father. A knight-maston's sword like yours. Bring it to the brother. And this…this is the chaen. You already wear one, so it is not for you. The lad is almost old enough to be a maston himself. It will be his. You are his father now. And his brother. No, no, that will not do. Do not scowl at this, *pethet*. This is your trust. Your duty. Now the tunic. Yes, you see the blood. But you do not hear its screams. No, you cannot hear that. Thank the Medium you do not. Take it away from here, that the blood spilled on it does not avenge here at this hill but elsewhere. Wear it, *pethet*. Yes, you must. Wear it. It is Demont's. You must!"

Lia dumped another armful of apples into the saddlebag. The stallion swung its head, its mane grazing her face. She smiled at its nuzzling and watched from the corner of her eye as Colvin released his sword belt, pulled on the tunic, and then belted it again over it. The tunic was a dark fabric, but she could see the slits and stains from a dozen sword wounds. In her mind, she heard the sheriff speaking. *The blood of your Family is still on my sword. The moans have never rubbed clean. But I will tell you of them. Of their traitorous hearts. Of their punishment even after death. Your grandfather. Your uncle. Their heads spitted on spikes. How we played with their corpses...*

An ill feeling churned inside her. Looking at the bloodied tunic, seeing the evidence of violence, made her stomach lurch. Dizziness and anger washed through her. She nearly vomited, but clenching her hands around the saddle horn, she waited until the urge subsided. Somewhere deep in her mind, it was as if she could hear the screams, though no more than whispers.

***

"Come, sister. Up the Tor. To the crest! Come!"

Lia did not know how Maderos could speak while climbing so fast, but he did. Her chest was burning, her legs were burning, and without gripping the saddle stirrup, she was sure she would have stumbled with exhaustion already. Colvin's tattered tunic was soaked with sweat, but he kept up without murmuring.

"Do you want to ride?" he asked her in a low tone, seeing her face.

She shook her head no, for she could not speak. Holding the saddle was enough. As long as the horse kept chuffing along, she would make it.

"You can see the Tor from Kennot Knoll. You can even see it from Haunton, on a clear day. Notice the trees lower down, but not higher up. It is bald. A bald hill. That is because this hill is new. It is new, I tell you! Have you heard how the Tor came to be here? Eh? Have you heard? You cannot speak, so I will speak. This was after the first abbey was built, many years ago. Hundreds of years ago. When all the land you can see there was flooded." He waved his free arm expansively. "Some soldiers in long boats came. They were from another land, ready to pillage. They had their own tongue, but greed is a language common to all men. When they saw Muirwood, their hearts were full of greed. The long boats came up the river. They destroyed the village folk by the lake. Murdered them. Their blood did sing to the Aldermaston of the Abbey. He heard their deaths." He looked back at them, his eyes gleaming. "Do you know what the Aldermaston did? Can you guess, *pethet*? No?"

Maderos stopped talking, for they had crested the summit at last. Lia would have sagged to her knees, but she held herself up, gulping air. Her heartbeat was thunder in her ears. Even Colvin looked winded, and he stopped, bending over to struggle for breath.

"Bah! You are young. Young legs. Young feet. You have no stamina. I have no horse. I must walk where the Medium takes me. Across this country. Across that country. Look at the horizon! Do you see it? Ah, the glory! I never tire of it."

Sweat dripped from the tip of Lia's nose. Her strength began to return.

"What did...what did the Aldermaston do?" she panted.

"Eh? What do you say, little sister?"

"When the soldiers came," she said.

"The rest of the tale? It is a grand story. The long boats came, and the soldiers charged toward the Abbey. Easy prey, just like the villagers." He snapped his fingers, then held one up to his lips. "But they did not know of the Medium. No, they could not guess at its power. How strong the Aldermaston was. He looked east and saw hills. He looked west and saw hills." His arms gestured broadly, mimicking the action of his words. "So with the Medium compelling him, he raised his arms high into the air. He had kept the trust to invoke its power thus. A hill from far away rose with his hands. Yes! A hill far away rose with his hands. It came. And it crushed the soldiers and their boats." He slammed a fist down into his palm. "Now the hill is called the Tor. When you are away from here, when you look back at the Tor, you will see that I speak truth. It does not belong here. One day, another Aldermaston will set it back where it came from. We do not live in such times now. Long ago. So very long ago." His gaze sharpened. "Show us the Cruciger orb, child. Show us where you would go."

Lia straightened. She believed every word he had said. The story was fantastic, but no more than a storm causing a landslide, exposing stone ossuaries that were empty save of grave clothes and wedding bands, or stones that hung suspended in the air.

Reaching into her pouch, she withdrew the orb and brought it to Maderos. His eyes narrowed as he looked at it.

"Believe," he whispered. "Believe and it will show you the way you seek. Always."

In her mind, she thought the words, *Show us the safe road to Winterrowd.*

The spindles spun, the inside of the orb whirred to life and it pointed again, away from the Tor, toward the western horizon.

She looked up to where it was pointing, and her heart leapt with what she saw. From the summit, she could see for leagues in every direction. The sight was breathtaking. She saw groves and glens, mirrored pools, and distant hills. Looking down, she saw the Abbey and her eyes filled with tears at how small it was. There was the kitchen cupola rising above a ring of oaks. She thought of Pasqua, and it went straight to her heart and brought out a cough and a sob together. The Cider Orchard. The fish pond. She could even see the laundry and, staring hard, she could see people walking the grounds.

"You weep, child?" he asked her gently. "Why?"

"I didn't think I would miss it so," Lia whispered, tears blurring the image.

"There is wisdom in climbing mountains," Maderos said softly. "For they teach us how truly small we are. This is just a pebble within one kingdom. There are higher mountains you must climb, child. Greater views you will yet see."

"Idumea's hand, it is the king's army!" Colvin said, his voice throbbing with awe. "I...I cannot discern its size for all the dust. Look at the pennants though, and the columns. They are coming. Look at it!"

Lia mopped her eyes on her sleeve and turned to see as well. Colvin stood on a short outcropping, gazing south, the wind tousling his hair and his tunic. In the distance, like a black snake, the army stretched along the road, a cloud of haze rising up from its back.

"Yes, the king's army, *pethet*! And that is only a part, from the king's city itself. Another marches from the south. They join at Bridgewater in three days. Three."

"You know this?" Colvin asked.

"The orb tells many things. Others the Medium whispers to me. Hearken to my words. If you take the road, you will be captured. And so will the girl. The road is not safe. The befallen king summons his full strength. He leaves no portion of his mind open for doubt that he will crush Demont's army. His thoughts are very strong. Always, he tempers his thoughts."

"How many?" Colvin asked.

"Eh, *pethet*?"

"How many does Demont have?"

Maderos smiled wickedly. "A tenth, if that. A tithing of the king's men. Does it weaken your will, *pethet*? To know you cannot win?"

"No," Colvin answered angrily. "Demont must be warned."

"Yes! You must warn him. Fill his mind with doubt. Yes, that will be helpful, *pethet*. Choke his confidence. Strangle his hope. Let it cease gasping and then die like a fish!"

"I did not say that!"

"You mistrust so easily. You do not even see it before you. Bah! Why should I linger? The road is barred before you. There is no safe road. The safe way to Winterrowd, the only safe way, is through the Bearden Muir. There! See the glistening waters? There—to the south—that is the town of Bridgewater. The hill to the north of the waters, that is Kennot Knoll. The water is the Bearden Muir. It floods when the rains come. Every year. There are few towns or villages, because few can survive its moods. They are the lowlands. The marshes. The Bearden Muir. Winterrowd lies beyond it. Look at the spindles. They show you the way. Fix your eyes on the course. It will lead you to Demont's camp.

Stray from it, and you will be taken by the king's men. I have warned you."

Colvin stepped closer. "What land do you hail from, Maderos? Are you from Hautland?"

There was a twinkle in Maderos's eyes. "I hail from many lands, *pethet*. I have walked as far as Idumea perhaps. From thence came the seeds…and thus the tree. It is a good tree. Tasty fruit."

"What Family are you?" Colvin asked.

Again, a cunning smile. "Aye, Family I do have."

"This girl led me to a cave near the Abbey. I have seen the tomes you are keeping. I have read them."

"Have you? And what think you of those tomes?"

"I should like to read more."

"How bold are your words! How proud to think you will survive even a fortnight hence! You must survive first the slaughter at Winterrowd. That may yet be, if sister holds vigil that night for you. A vigil, do you hear?"

Colvin's face twitched. He clenched his fists. "Sister?" he asked, nearly choking.

"Aye, sister indeed. You are a *pethet*. I mourn you. You will get no more counsel from me." He turned to Lia and put his heavy, callused hand on her forehead, then brushed a finger down her cheek. "When you have learned to read, child, I will show you the Abbey tomes."

Her heart was full to bursting. He did not say if she learned to read. He had said *when*.

"Thank you, Maderos," she whispered, bowing her head to him. Impulsively, she gave him a kiss on the cheek.

He smiled at her, a warm smile. "Bah, it is hardly a thing beseeching such a gift. You have set it in your heart to read. Many who serve the Medium wish it. That which you fix your heart to, believing with all your desire you will get, you will. 'Tis not a prophecy. It is the way the Medium delivers to us the very things we think on. It brought you both together. I see that plainly. Now let the Medium take you hence. Trouble will shadow your steps. See below! Those are the sheriff's men on the road. The murderers. They will ride back to Muirwood when they realize you are not fools to run headlong into the king's army. They hunt you still, little sister. But the Bearden Muir will help hide you from them."

***

Youth who come to the Abbeys of the realm come with training already in hand and fixed solidly in their minds. Some have exceptional Gifts already with the Medium when they arrive. Some can already summon fire or water or cause a stone to lift and tremble over their palm. But whatever Gifts they bring to the Abbey, we expect more from them. If they bring six, we expect twelve when they leave. If they come with but one talent, we test and try and prove them until we wring two or three more from them. But whether they come with but one or six, a few lose what they have. The rigorous training of the Abbey begins to take its toll on them. Or they submit their thoughts to the subtle poison of doubt. Not even an Aldermaston's power can cure it, for these students do harm to themselves. The mind, like the body, can be moved from sunshine into shade.

—Cuthbert Renowden of Billerbeck Abbey

CHAPTER
TWENTY-ONE

Bearden Muir

The Bearden Muir was a lair of mossy rocks, ravens, green reeds, and stunted skeletal oaks sagging on the occasional lumps of higher ground standing amidst a swamp that flooded every year. Its air was cloudy with gnats and mosquitoes and the smell of rotting earth. Ghostly noises wandered by like lost echoes. Every bit of ground was saturated with muck and mud and treacherous pools. There was no road through the Bearden Muir—it changed too often to construct them. The land was raw, savage, and eerily beautiful, like a damp gray moth with flecks of color in its wings.

Several murky rivers slit through the middle of the Bearden Muir, formed by three tributaries that tried in vain to drain the lowlands. One of the tributaries now barred the path to Winter-rowd. The Cruciger orb led them south, along its sluggish flank. The other side was choked with reeds, and the throaty growls of bullfrogs were warnings not to cross.

"What did Maderos mean about having a vigil?" Lia asked, while batting another insect away from her face.

"I do not know," Colvin answered sullenly, scanning the trees. The mud was slippery for the stallion's hooves, and his full attention was brought to bear on guiding it.

"I have heard of vigils before," Lia said. "They happen at the Abbey. Learners abandon sleep for something they treasure— something they desire. It is common before taking the maston test."

"You no longer shock me with your knowledge of the mastons' customs," he said over his shoulder.

"But surely you have an idea what Maderos meant?"

"He was talking about my sister, Marciana, in Forshee, who does not know I am here. Or he was speaking of you. By all that is…does this river never end? Can we not cross it yet?"

"If he was talking about me, then you need to teach me how," Lia said. "I have never done one before. I have gone without eating. And some nights I am restless and cannot sleep. But I do not think that is the same as a vigil."

"It is not."

"Then will you tell me?"

"Not yet."

"Why not?"

His voice was rude and annoyed. "Because I am struggling to keep the stallion from faltering! It requires concentration, which you ruin with your persistent questions. Can you never be quiet?"

Anger surged inside Lia again, and she was glad to be seated behind him so as not to see the impatience stamped on his face. That would have made her angrier still. Did he not think she noticed the sucking mud and its exhausting effect on the weary stallion? Her own stomach was in knots. Maderos's words whispered back and forth in her mind. She wanted to talk about them, to better understand what they were about. Half of what he had said were riddles.

Looking down at the orb, she saw that it had stopped working. For a moment, there was panic in her heart. True, perfect, helpless panic. *Show us the safe way to Winterrowd,* she pleaded with it. The spindles whirred and moved back, pointing south, following the river. She closed her eyes, grateful.

"I am sorry for distracting you," she mumbled. In her mind, she added *pethet.* "The spindles are turning. Hold a moment!"

"Are they? Let me see." He turned in the saddle and they both watched as the spindles turned and pointed into the river. "Here?" Colvin said warily.

The river was smooth, not choppy, but the depths were indeterminable. A sharp, clacking sound came from upstream, startling them. Then it was gone.

"Hold on tightly," he said. "If the horse starts to swim, it may throw us off. You hold me, and I will keep hold of the bridle. Tighter—good. Clutch the orb tightly as well. Do not drop it. We may never find it again. Can you swim?"

"No," Lia said, her stomach fluttering.

"There is a first, something I can do that you cannot. If we go under, do not panic. Do not cling to me too hard. I can bring you to the other side. If you squeeze me too hard, I will not be able to swim myself. Do you understand?"

She nodded, biting her lip.

"Then we cross," he said, tapping the stallion's flanks and nudging it into the water. It balked, snorting warily at the scum-flecked pool. Colvin tsked with his tongue and stamped harder, guiding the stallion off the riverbank. The mud was loose and slick and Lia felt her insides churn like butter as the horse began thrashing. With a splash and heave, her legs were soaked, then up to her waist. The gritty dress clung to her, the weight of the water crushed against her hips. She squeezed Colvin in a panic.

"It is all right!" he shouted. "Just hold the orb! Hold it tight!"

"Can horses swim?" she said, nearly choking with fear. The saddle was slippery, and she felt herself going off the back.

"Of course they can! Hold tighter, you are slipping. Slipping!"

He caught her arm as the motion and lapping waves swept her. His fingers dug into her bones, and it hurt, but he managed to pull her back up on the saddle.

"Just do not drop the orb! Do you have it? Good. The water is cold. It is all right. There we are; it is not that deep after all. Do you feel steady?"

"I am," Lia whispered, feeling ashamed of her fear. The stallion bucked a little, but the river was not deep at that point, and the horse was soon churning through the muddy gap without swimming. After crossing the midpoint of the river, the stallion lunged up the far bank, and again Lia had to hold tight or fall off. The reeds slapped at them as they advanced up the slope to slightly more stable ground.

Colvin sighed with relief. "We will rest here a moment. Climb down." He followed and landed in the squishy mud. His pants and tunic were soaked as well. "Let us walk a ways and let the horse rest," he said, patting the stallion's neck. "He will need his strength if the sheriff's men catch up to us. Though how they would find us in this swamp is beyond me. Are you all right?" he said, noticing her scowl finally.

Lia looked down at her skirt. The lower half was no longer blue, nor was her cloak, but dark with brownish, grayish sludge, and clung to her uncomfortably. Part of her sleeve was torn, probably when he grabbed her arm to keep her from sliding off. Her shoes were filling with ooze. Looking back, she could no longer see Muirwood, though she thought she could see the Tor saluting them in the distance.

"Well enough," she said with as much tartness as she could muster and stamped past him.

***

Lia was exhausted, cold, miserable, and above all, thirsty. There was no clean water to drink, nothing but brackish, cloudy pools that even the stallion avoided. In her mind, she thought of the lion's head Leering and wished she had drunk more from it. The thought of the clear, cool water tormented her. The sun was setting, and they had reached a small hillock to pass the night above the ankle-deep waters permeating the Bearden Muir. The vast swamp stretched in every direction. The land looked inhospitable. There were no signs of human life, other than their own. The hillock had three gnarled and diseased oaks crowning it, and the turf was thick with sharp-pointed, desiccated leaves lying beyond the reach of the foul waters.

Colvin huffed as he pulled the saddle off the stallion and carried it up the hillock, straining with the weight of it. Lia would have helped, but she was sitting against the trunk of one of the oaks, hugging her knees and trying not to cry again. She hated crying, and she had already succumbed to tears during the day as they rode. She had not let him know, though. Silently, her loneliness and grief had dropped from her lashes unnoticed on Colvin's shirt. He might die at Winterrowd, and then where would she go? Not back to the Abbey. Never to Muirwood. She had stolen the Cruciger orb. The Aldermaston would never forgive her.

"You can use this," he said with a grunt, plopping the saddle next to her. "As a pillow tonight." He breathed heavily and bent over, planting his hands on his knees, and gulping air.

"My arm is the only pillow I have ever known," she said sullenly. "I am a wretched. We sleep on rush-matting on the floor."

He nodded brusquely and then opened the saddlebags and withdrew three apples. His hands were filthy, but he extended them to her first. "Which one do you wish to eat? This one is the most scarred. It will be the sweetest then, by your measure?"

"Then let the horse have it," she said. "It labored the most to carry us this far."

He gave her a disdainful look. "As you wish it then," he said with a snort, tossing her one of the other ones and starting down the hillock. She wiped the apple clean, as well as she could on her sleeve, and held it to her nose. The smell of the swamp over-ruled most of her senses, but there it was—the hint of its scent, still clinging to the skin. She took a bite. The moment the juice touched her tongue and the flesh crushed in her mouth, an even deeper sadness filled her and spread as she swallowed. She gazed at the deepening gloom, knowing soon it would be darker than any other night of her life. The flavor was Muirwood. She pressed some of its unblemished skin against her nose again and inhaled, choking back sobs as she tried to eat it. Her throat was so parched, the juice only tantalized it. As tears dripped from her lashes again, she watched Colvin stroking the horse's mane while it fed on the apple. Why could he not understand what was torturing her?

All her life she had been raised at Muirwood. She had never realized how much safety there was in its smells, its habits, even its mottled stone. She missed Pasqua and her fussing and scolding. She missed seeing the Aldermaston in his gray cassock, looking up from a tome when she arrived with a tray bearing his supper. She missed the laundry nearby and having a spare dress so she could clean a soiled one. Today, she had slowly realized that she lived in the most beautiful and perfect place in all the world. The Bearden Muir was desolate, frightening, and overwhelming in its vastness. As a fugitive, she had to leave the Abbey behind. Memories would be her only comfort, and they were not enough.

Colvin mounted the hillock again, his face pinched with fatigue. He looked grim in the bloodstained tunic, his face a mess of dirt, bruises, and whiskers. The shirt she had cleaned for him days before was fit to be burned, as was the bloodstained tunic from Maderos.

He sat by the saddle, a little away from her, holding the last apple.

"Are you still hungry?"

She shook her head slowly.

"What is the matter?"

Everything since you came into my life, she wanted to say, but remained quiet. She said nothing.

"I have been too harsh," he said with a stern look. "To you. I am...I am sorry."

"It must hurt you to apologize to someone like me, Colvin," she said softly, then added spitefully, "I am glad of it."

Her thrust riled him again. Anger flashed in his eyes. "I am a blunt person," he said. "I speak the truth, no matter how hard it is to hear it. I do not seek to apologize that your questions were bothering me. They were. I spoke what I felt, just as you do. I had no intention of bringing a girl like you with me. I would not consider it now but for Maderos's counsel. Where I go, there will be war. And I did not come all this way for nothing. Those thoughts have...preoccupied my mind today. You are the only one that can take me to my destination, no matter how I wish I could have left you behind in a safer place."

"I have no doubt that you have been distracted today," she said, tearing another bite from the apple. She chewed it viciously.

"What is vexing you?" he asked.

"Can you not imagine?"

"My rudeness? Or what you perceive as rudeness?"

She closed her eyes and shook her head. "From the moment you awoke in my kitchen, I have had little else but rudeness from you. But I still helped you." She did not want to cry in front of him, but the thought of sobbing filled her with fury, and she clung to it desperately, choking the desire.

"Though I am skilled with the Medium," he said, "I am not gifted with reading thoughts. If you would tell me, then tell me! How can I guess what you are thinking?"

She lowered the apple, still savoring its flavor, yet suffering as well. "I left my home today," she whispered. "I will not be welcomed back. Believe me, your rudeness is great indeed, but not great enough to afflict me so much. I suffer because I miss Muirwood. I long to see it again. All my life, I wanted to be away from its walls. Now that I am, I can think of nothing but wanting to go back. Each footstep brings me farther from the place I love the best." Her voice choked up and she could only whisper, "And nearer to the thing I fear the most."

"And what is that?" he said seriously, his eyes finally showing a spark of sympathy.

"That despite anything I may do, you will still die at Winter-rowd, and I will have nothing left in the world. You promised me your man might teach me to read. But you may lose all to the king's fury. Even your steward! Then I have gambled everything to achieve a dream..." She paused, bowing her head. "But in my waking, will have lost everything instead."

His eyes were as dark as shadows. "It is you who do not understand. You are a silly girl. You bound me by the Medium. You will get what I promised you, even if I do not live to fulfill it in person. Did you not feel the Medium when I gave you my oath?

By Idumea, it feels a lifetime ago! What a day. What a haunting day." He closed the saddlebag snugly and then turned back to face her again, leaning forward. "The truth of the matter is that you were and are no longer safe at Muirwood. You were not safe the moment the sheriff came looking for me. It is not a haven for you. Not while the sheriff seeks you. What I do not understand is what he wants from you. There are sordid reasons, for certain, but would he risk the Aldermaston's wrath, or brave a festering marsh like this, without sufficient provocation or motivation? What I cannot understand is why, what reason he could have?"

Her eyes bored into his. "He may think I have his medallion."

Colvin was silent, his eyes widening.

"The night he stole into the kitchen, he was using it against me…making me fear him. I saw a chain around his neck, and when I snapped it off, the fear left me. He chased me out of the kitchen, but then Jon Hunter arrived. When I went back, I hid it."

He rose to his feet instantly. "You did not mention that when you told me. You said you saw the amulet, but you did not…did he…did he hurt you?"

She nodded. "A little. I might have hurt him worse though. I scratched his face."

He stared again. "If he thought you had the medallion, would not he also presume that you gave it to the Aldermaston? Surely he is more powerful in the Medium than the sheriff!"

"That presumes there is trust between the Aldermaston and me. The sheriff could probably see there is little. By hiding you, did I not prove my lack of loyalty? Scarseth stole it when he betrayed me. He has it."

Colvin breathed deeply. "And through the Medium, I just took away his voice. If the sheriff thinks you still have it…of course he will want it back. A thwarted man is dangerous."

Lia closed her eyes again and rested her forehead on her arms. "There is something else," she mumbled.

"What?"

"When the sheriff first came—the morning we snuck into the orchard—I was in the kitchen with the Aldermaston and Pasqua. The sheriff…he said that he knew my father. He told me that night, in the dark, that he was one of the ones who had murdered him."

Colvin looked at her intensely. "Did he say who your father was?"

She shook her head. "But he made me believe that I might be a Demont."

Again, he looked stunned. "Did he say as much?"

"Only that the blood of my Family was still on his sword. That they were cruelly punished after their deaths. My grandfather, my father, and my uncle were all killed. Just like the Demont family at Maseve. I had never even heard of Demont before the sheriff came."

Colvin paced a moment, brooding over what she had said. The sky was nearly black, and the horse was just a shadow at the base of the hill. He walked back and forth near her, struggling with his thoughts. He glanced up, stopped, then stared back the way they had come.

The moonlight gleamed off the river, making it turn silver. But on the far bank, there were torches and lanterns, pinpricks of light against an impenetrable black field. At least a dozen lights were swarming like fireflies.

"Almaguer," he whispered. There was fear in his voice.

CHAPTER
TWENTY-TWO

Fear

Lia had received a new blanket as a nameday present from
Pasqua when she was ten. She had outgrown her childhood
blanket, and she loved that she did not need to curl up her
legs in order to keep them covered. The blanket had its own smell
after so many years in the kitchen. She took care of it, folding it
every morning and storing it in a wicker basket. That was where it
still was—alone in the basket, until another tall, spindly wretched
would claim it.

Those were Lia's thoughts as she fell asleep, shivering, in the
Bearden Muir, wrapped in a wet cloak, dress damp, on hard, poky
ground amidst a thousand brittle oak leaves. The torches and lanterns of Almaguer's men had remained on the far side of the river
and had not moved for several hours. In fact, a bright campfire
shone in the distance, luring her with a false promise of warmth.
Colvin had promised to wake her at midnight so that she might
have a turn watching the sheriff's camp.

Exhausted, she fell asleep, but it was a fitful sleep. She knew she was uncomfortable, her back and legs aching, yet her mind was somewhere else—back at the kitchen with Pasqua, hurrying to prepare the evening meal for the Aldermaston. Memories flitted by, a jumble of past conversations, both spoken and unspoken ones. Then she was back, gazing down at herself on the hillside, her face pale, spattered, and gritty. Colvin was asleep leaning against the tree trunk, hands folded in his lap peacefully. She envied him that. A whisper sounded in the dark, and she heard the crunch of leaves and twigs. Almaguer, robed in black, advanced up the hill, a gleaming sword in his hand. She knew it was him for his eyes glowed silver, illuminating small circles that only just touched his cheeks. Moonlight revealed the medallion around his neck, and blackness emanated from it, stealing through the mistless night and engulfing the hillock like a shroud.

Lia felt like a leaf, hovering on the wind. She screamed, but no sound came out. She had to warn herself, to wake herself. The more she tugged at the immaterial bonds, the more the night breezes puffed her this way and that. She saw Colvin stir, but he slept—he did not waken. In her mind, she screamed out to him as Almaguer advanced up the hill, straight toward them. Colvin slept soundly—peacefully. *Wake up! Wake up!* she screamed in her mind. She pulled at the invisible threads separating her from her shivering body. Still Almaguer approached, the magic from the medallion wreathing in the air like smoke. Only the smoke had shapes—of men, of beasts—like wolves stalking in the dark, each with gleaming eyes of silver.

She was helpless, unable to reach her body again. If the dream ended, it would tug her back inside. She willed herself to awaken. She struggled against the chains of sleep. *Wake up! Wake up!* Almaguer reached the crest, staring down at her body. The smoke shapes circled around them, eyes greedy. Almaguer took his hand off the amulet. Somehow, she could see beneath his shirt—at the black whorl of tattoos that crisscrossed his chest and even now were inching up his throat, across his shoulders, growing with every use of the medallion.

The smoke shapes sniffed at her and Colvin, fingers and muzzles and paws rooting against their clothes, the touch lighter than a gasp of breath. A sick feeling bloomed inside her as she watched them, disgusted, polluted, sniffing at her. She tried to pull herself awake in vain.

Then Almaguer knelt by her. His hand reached out and he touched her hair, running his fingers through its curly tangles. She could almost feel it, those fingers coiling into her hair, and a worm of sickness spread through her whole soul. She shuddered, revolted, and cringed from the tender gesture that was not meant with any degree of tenderness. His fingers stiffened around a thick clump of hair. Moonlight off the edge of his sword blinded her as the tip suddenly plunged into her heart.

"It is your turn."

Her eyes opened to the blackness of night. The moon was pale, only half of its usual brightness. Her arms and legs were sore and cramped with cold.

"It is your turn," Colvin repeated, shaking her shoulder even harder. "Come on. Are you awake?"

"Yes," she whispered, her heart shriveling in her chest with the vividness of the dream.

He crouched next to her and then straightened. "It is past midnight. I let you sleep as long as I could. If I do not rest, I will be useless tomorrow." He groaned. "I have never been this tired in my life. Sit against the tree, but not for long. It helps to stay warm and awake if you keep moving."

Lia raised herself on her elbow. Her heart shivered. The feeling, the blackness, was still there. "Almaguer is coming," she whispered, believing the dream was a warning.

"I think not," he answered. "I have watched their camp all night. The fire has burned low, but you can still see it. They make no effort to hide themselves. They have horses and lanterns. Not even they are fool enough to cross the river in the dark."

He was not listening to her. She stood, grateful to be awake, but fear roiled in her heart. "He is coming tonight. I felt him." She glanced around the hillock, looking for his glowing eyes. Nothing. She was terrified. Her heart beat wildly in her chest.

He snorted with disbelief. "If you see him, let me know. I will keep my sword ready. Now I am going to sleep. Wake me if the lanterns light up again, or you hear something large—I mean larger than a squirrel. There have been deer in the meadow in the night. And I heard a wolf howl once. Have you ever slept out of doors before?"

"No," she said, choking back a sob that he did not hear.

"I used to hunt with my father. The night is full of noises. If a large animal comes up here, wake me. Or the sheriff. Do not wake me otherwise."

Without giving her a second look, Colvin lay down on the earth, his back to her, his head resting on the saddle as a pillow, his hand on the hilt of his maston sword. He had no cloak or blanket.

Around her, in the dark, she felt as if the smoke shapes were still sniffing against her clothes. She did not sleep. She could not sleep. Dread tormented her the rest of the night.

***

Before dawn the lowlands of the Bearden Muir were covered in mist, engulfing even the hillock and its trees. From Lia's earliest days she had seen the mists, and they were comforting to her, but on this morning, they terrified her. Her heart was a throbbing pulp of misery. Her eyes were swollen from all her tears. Colvin awoke with the dawn and set about saddling the horse again, without saying a word of greeting. He chafed his arms constantly, but he did not complain of being cold. His discomfort was plain enough from his expression.

Coming back up the hill, he handed her another apple.

"I am thirsty," she mumbled, taking the fruit from his grimy hand.

"As am I," he replied. "I had a thought while I was saddling the stallion. We are still another two days from Winterrowd, if Maderos was right. I doubt we will die of thirst by then, but if there is a safe spring to drink from, the Cruciger orb would know. If not, we will suffer patiently. But if there is one along our path, or close to it, that would be helpful. You could ask the orb."

Lia had not thought of that herself, and she was annoyed that Colvin had first. After untying the pouch, she emptied the orb into her hand. It was cold and heavy. In her mind, she repeated his request. *If there is safe water along the journey, show us the way.*

Nothing happened.

Colvin looked up at her.

"I do not think there is safe water," she said huskily, her throat raw. "Show us the way to Winterrowd," she then said.

Nothing happened.

Colvin's brow furrowed.

Dread joined the fear in Lia's heart. Then anger. She focused her thoughts—she stared at the intricate spindles and willed them to move. *Show us a safe road!* she screamed at it inside her mind.

Nothing.

"Let me try," Colvin said, holding out his hand. For a moment, she wanted to shove him away, to hunch over and protect it. His hand was extended, his fingernails black with mud and dirt. Reluctantly, she gave it to him.

His brow furrowed even more and he looked sternly at the orb, saying nothing. But it did not obey him either. "Vexing," he muttered, giving it back to her. "Is the orb not working, or is there no longer a safe road? We must determine that. Ask it to show you the direction of Muirwood. Not a safe road there, just the direction."

Lia focused on it, hoping the spindles would whir again. But as she thought about Muirwood, she was met with despair. The orb was silent. "I do not understand," she whispered. "It…it was working yesterday…it…it…"

His face was a struggle to read as he battled to control his feelings. He looked furious, but determined to conquer the emotion. It took several moments for him to master himself enough to speak, and when he did, his voice was more like a bark than a man's voice.

"We do not have time for this!" He turned away, still struggling to contain himself. She was wounded by his reaction, hurt by the anger in his voice. She had no idea why the orb had failed them.

Looking at the beautiful surface, she willed it to heed her. *Show us the road. Show us safety. Show us a way to escape the sheriff. Please!*

"I am sorry," he said over his shoulder. "I am sorry. I am doing the best I can." He turned back to her, his face still twisting with various emotions, none of which she understood. "I am trying to protect you. I am trying to get to Winterrowd. I am trying not to worry about my sister. I am failing at all three. I promise, I never intended to drag you away from your home. Believe me, if I could have done it over again, I would not have let you help me. I should have left on my own as soon as I could stand. I should have gone!" He sighed mournfully.

"Why will it not work?" Lia said, crying openly. "I do not know why it is not. I...I...I do not know what to do. The mist. Winterrowd could be anywhere."

He shook his head violently, his fingers clenching like talons. "No, you are not to blame. I am. Believe me. I am. I know what is wrong. I know why it is not working."

"Why then?" she pleaded, clutching his arm. She needed to touch something to keep the dizziness from making her collapse.

"Because you cannot force the Medium. It knows your thoughts. It knows when you have lost your courage. There is something in your mind that is stopping it from working. It could be your longing for the Abbey. It could be fear. It could be misery." He did not shake off her grip, but she could see him flinch, see his eyes glance at her hand and narrow coldly. "I have seen this before. When I was a learner, it happened now and then among us, especially when something terrible happened. It even happened to me when my father died. I could not use the Medium because I was too angry that he had been taken away, that my sister and I were orphans, and that I had to be both father and mother as well as brother. The Medium knew my feelings and abandoned me to my resentment."

"How long before...how long before you could use it again?" she asked, her hope withering with the look in his eyes.

"Months," he answered bitterly. His jaw clenched. "We cannot dwell here that long. The sheriff's men are hunting us. This is a swamp, not a road. We have no water." He rubbed his mouth on his arm. His look hardened. "Whatever it is, we must discover it. We must not abandon hope. You get what you secretly desire. You claim a right to use the Medium by expecting to receive it. You are strong in the Medium. Very strong. But as strong as you are, you are still bound by its laws and impeded by your own doubts. You must overcome whatever is hindering you."

"How?" Lia asked, confused. "I have never not been able to use it. I have sensed the Medium since…that night of the storm. I know it is real." She let go of his arm and fished the ring out of her dress and pinched it hard between her fingers, letting the edge bite into her skin as she shook it at him. "I know it is real! I do not doubt it!"

"Yes, but you are a wretched. In one way it is a privilege because you have lived inside an Abbey. You have never faced the thousand mutable fears that roam the lands outside those walls. Spirits of aether you cannot see that make you fear and doubt and crave the things that will only do you harm." His eyes burned with passion and he uttered a cough, almost a chuckle. "You are so innocent. I doubt you have ever been fully tempted by the Myriad Ones." He waved his hand around at the trees and the mist. "They live in the world among us, feeding our most selfish selves with their thoughts. This is the world outside the safety of Muirwood. It is a world ripe with things poisonous to the Medium. I know I speak vaguely, for there are things mastons are taught that we cannot share. It is forbidden to speak of certain knowledge outside of an abbey. Trust me, girl. You lived within borders that have protected you from them, where *gargouelles* watch day and night and drive the Myriad Ones away."

He stepped even closer to her. "I studied at Billerbeck Abbey. The Aldermaston there taught every first year learner these words from the tome of Hadrion—'we wrestle not against blood and bone, but against brooding evil in high places and even their puppets called kings.'" His voice changed, softened. "Sevrin Demont fought against the Myriad Ones his whole life and even against his own king when he realized he was but a puppet. Demont failed at Maseve because he gave up hope. The Medium…it abandoned him. Darkness has veiled the land ever since. Mastons are being put to death in secret. I ride to Winterrowd to change that. The orb knows our need. But it also recognizes your fears and doubts. Your feelings are stopping it."

Lia stared at him, wondering what to believe. She knew a great deal about mastons, but she had never heard of Myriad Ones or invisible things that could influence her thoughts. She did know this. She was cold and miserable. She was afraid.

After a period of silence, she said, "I feel what I feel, Colvin. I cannot just change my feelings, like a dirty cloak or a new dress, can I?"

He nodded vigorously. "Yes, you can. It all begins here, with a thought." His finger grazed the center of her forehead. She shivered at his touch.

***

The soul attracts that which it secretly harbors—that which it loves, and also that which it fears. Thus circumstances do not make the maston; they only reveal him to himself. It means that blessedness, and not wealth, is the measure of right thought; misery, not poverty or lack of Family, is the measure of wrong thought. A maston will find that as he alters his thoughts toward things and other people, things and other people will alter toward him. For you will always draw near toward that which you, secretly, most love. Humanity surges with uncontrolled passion, is tumultuous with ungoverned grief, and is blown about by anxiety and doubt. Only the wise maston, only he whose thoughts are controlled and purified, can make the winds and the storms of the soul obey him.

—Cuthbert Renowden of Billerbeck Abbey

CHAPTER
TWENTY-THREE

The Road

They wandered through the Bearden Muir, lost. Even the sun forsook them. Alternately, they walked and rode, giving the stallion as much rest as they could afford. Not that a horse could gallop through a swamp, whether theirs or the sheriff's. Obstacles faced them constantly—wide gullies and ditches choked with foul-smelling waters that were too broad to cross. Often they had to go east to find a way west. Thirst was a constant torment.

All the day long, Colvin spoke to her, instructing her in the ways of the Medium. He did it from memory, quoting from the teachings of the Aldermaston of Billerbeck Abbey and the tomes he had studied there. Lia had many questions, and he answered them—oftentimes impatiently—but he answered.

He explained that learners start out acquiring the skill of reading and engraving so they can translate ancient tomes containing the words of Aldermastons of the past as well as their Family. Only through studying these words, often thick and impenetrable with multiple meanings, can a learner begin to unravel the mysteries of the mastons. The language of the writings is rich with symbols. Reading something again and again, year after year, could bring nuances and understandings that a younger learner could not grasp. She discovered that all the years of learning at an abbey as a youth were merely preparation for a lifelong journey of self-discipline and improvement. It was clear to Lia that Colvin was exceptional. His memory for detail, for example, and the exactness by which he quoted his teacher showed that he had studied hard—the knowledge was written in his heart and not just on his tongue.

"Why is it then," she asked him as they stopped to rest at midday, "that I can use the orb and you cannot? You have studied the tomes all your life. You know the rules of the Medium far better than I. Yet you cannot use it?"

He took a bite from an apple and chewed it slowly. "There are two reasons. Perhaps more."

"And they are?"

He paused and coughed against his arm. "Strength in the Medium is inherited. It does not matter who you are as much as who your parents were. By this principle, I propose that both of your parents, whoever they were, had great strength in the Medium. If their love was illicit…"

"Which means?"

"Unlawful. It was not sanctioned by propriety. They were probably not wedded. Two learners, perhaps, from strong families. If they were ashamed at what they had done, one or both could have decided to give you up as a wretched to hide their shame. It does happen. Every abbey has wretcheds. Bitter shame and the fear of scorn motivate people to commit acts they would not ordinarily do. That is one theory. You are strong in the Medium because of your parents. Stronger than I, even with my legitimate ancestry. If your parents were nothing more than laborers, you would have no skill in the Medium at all. The other reason I can think of is jealousy."

"Jealousy? Whose?"

"Mine, naturally. I have struggled with jealousy since I met you, for I have had to work hard to earn my mastery of the Medium. You can do things that I lack even the imagination to try. Mixing fire with water, for example. It never occurred to me to do that. I have focused so much on learning the prohibitions and to maintain my thoughts perfectly within the proper bounds, that it never occurred to me to explore. Hence, my jealousy. The Medium knows our innermost thoughts. We cannot hide them from it. When I saw you use the Cruciger orb, I wanted to believe that I could as well because my lineage was purer than yours. That belief born of jealousy was not enough to coax the orb to obey."

Sitting on a fallen log, Lia regarded him curiously, then took a bite from her apple. There was so much evidence of the Medium in her life. The ring she wore around her neck. The very apple in her hand—an apple that should not be for it was not even the season. Yet something about the Leering near the tree—something about that Leering kept the fallen apples from decaying. She looked at her torn sleeve. She had never torn a dress before. In her memory, she could not think of a single instance where someone had torn their clothes. New clothes were made for those who grew, their older ones handed down to the younger ones. But repairing garments was foreign to her. She realized, intuitively, that it also had to do with the Medium. There were other Leerings on the Abbey grounds that kept shoes from failing, dresses and shirts from being ripped. They preserved things. Being away from Muirwood, she was no longer under their protection. Perhaps that was what she feared the most, the lack of safety.

"You have an enigmatic look," he said.

Lia eyed him. "My mind is so full, yet I hunger to know more. You have tried to teach me four years of learning and it is barely noonday. I do not know how to think any more. There are so many possibilities."

"Then let me test you," he answered. "How did you and I come to meet?"

"Our first meeting? The night of the storm?"

"The night of the storm. Examine the principles. Let them guide you to the answer." He took another bite from his apple and stared at her while he chewed.

"I will try," she said, wincing. Her mind was jumbled with thoughts. "You are looking for an answer more subtle than Scarseth dragging you there and dumping you at the door. Let me think. You gain what you desire the most. Or should I say, you gain the results of your thoughts. You must desire something, then think on it. Determine to have it. You left your home because you desired to unite with Garen Demont's rebellion. You had to sacrifice something to get it—you sacrificed telling your family. The Medium did the rest. It even intervened when you were betrayed by Scarseth. It led you to Muirwood. It led you to the kitchen because it knew I could help you."

He nodded slowly, a smug smile creasing his mouth. "Go on."

"I desire to read. More than anything else. My desire also brought you to me. Just as I could use the Cruciger orb to help you find Winterrowd, so you could use your wealth and knowledge to help me learn to read. So both of us were harnessing the Medium to achieve our desires. For you, a way to find Demont. For me, the promise to read someday."

He smiled. "Well said."

Lia bit her lip, flushing with pleasure at the compliment, and looked down. "It could have happened a thousand other ways! Why did the Medium not lead you to Maderos? He could have shown you the way or he could have taught me to…"

"No!" Colvin said, his eyes flashing with anger. "Do not tangle it into knots! You had the right answer, but then you doubted. You must never, *never* leave room in your mind for doubt. It chokes the Medium. It starves it. It drowns it. All you must do is believe in those small insights—those little bursts of wisdom that bloom in your mind when your heart is calm, controlled, and peaceful. The Medium brought us together, for those very reasons you mentioned. Years from now, we may look back on this moment and realize there were other reasons still that we have not yet discovered. It is enough though, for now. You wanted to read. And yes, even Maderos could feel that burning in you. The Medium cannot help but respond to your desire."

Lia was not sure, but he seemed convinced. "Should I try the orb again?"

He shook his head. "You are not ready yet."

"Why not?"

His look was intensely serious. "Because each time you fail will make it that much harder to succeed. Do not pull it out of the pouch until you know you will use it and that it will work. Leave it, until then."

The sudden sound of mourning doves flapping their wings and shrieking startled them as the birds took flight somewhere behind them. "We must go," Colvin said, his eyes blazing with worry. "Something startled the birds. Quickly!"

***

Hours later, Lia and Colvin reached a sliver of road. The brush and trees had been cleared, the moors drained sufficiently. It was a narrow neck, wide enough for single wagons or five soldiers to march abreast. By the freshly churned ruts and mashed boot prints, it was clear that soldiers and wagons had passed, and recently too.

Colvin's voice was a dark murmur. "We are behind," he said, sliding off the saddle. Pulling the reins, he tugged the stallion after him.

"Maderos warned us to shun the road," Lia said. The trees were skeletal and sickly. The air was oppressed with the stench of sweat and other vicious odors.

Colvin knelt by the edge of the road, looking at the rut marks. His hand clenched into a fist. "The tracks are fresh. Made earlier today."

"Someone may see us," Lia said worriedly.

"Going back is not a good suggestion either," he said, looking angrier than ever. "We can cover more distance this way, then veer back into the marsh."

"I think we should go back into the marsh now."

"The sheriff's men are behind us, who knows how close. This gives us a chance to outride them a bit." He came back to the stallion and swung up on the saddle. He held out his hand to her to climb up behind him.

She shook her head. "We should not take the road."

His hand hung in the air, fingers hooking. "If the sheriff thinks we took the road, they will ride hard after us. They may not see our tracks shrink back into the Bearden Muir. I know what Maderos said. Trust me."

Part of her was sick inside. Part of her knew he made sense. Maderos's warning haunted her. She did not want to see Almaguer again. The very thought of him made her insides twist and revolt, made her skin tingle with dread. It was as if the smoke shapes were still sniffing at her clothes. Her dream whispered to her and she felt the thrust of steel in her heart.

He leaned closer, his eyes bleary and cragged with veins. "Trust me."

Reaching up with her shaky hand, she took his. The force in his hand, his arm, was powerful as he pulled her up behind him. She clung to him as he kicked the stallion's flanks and started at a full gallop down the road into the twisty maze of trees, reeds, and brush. She saw dirt and sweat on the flesh of his neck. The scenery was a blur of speed. The stallion chuffed and snorted, shaking its wavy mane as it churned the mud and roared ahead. Too far! They were going too far!

Lia wanted to shriek in his ear. Something was wrong. Something was going to happen to them. Get off the road, it warned. Get off the road. In her mind, Maderos's voice was scolding. *The orb tells many things. If you take the road, you will be captured. And so will the girl. The road is not safe.*

Somehow Maderos knew. Somehow he had known. All along, he had known what they would face in the Bearden Muir. They were flouting his advice.

The road is not safe. The road is dangerous.

Each moment made her heart quaver. Each instant was a torment. They had to leave the road. The moors would be safer, even without the orb.

"Colvin," she said in his ear. "Please!"

"Not yet," he shouted.

"Please! Leave the road. Before it is too late."

"A little farther."

"Please! I feel it. Can you? Can you feel the warning?"

"A little farther!"

"We were warned! We do not know how far…"

He looked back, his face a scowl of anger. "Enough! I have heard you. You are nearly blinding me with your thoughts, your fear. Master them! They are not coming from you. These fears come from the sheriff. He is close. He is very close. Somehow he put them inside you. He is plaguing you with them, even now. I will not let him hurt you. Now have faith in me. I know what I am doing. There is a safe path, just ahead. Trust me."

Again the thought of Almaguer struck her mind. His sword plunging into her chest. Glowing silver eyes. Was it just a dream? A dream, not a vision? Or was it? Should she tell him? Would her mock her again? She squeezed her eyes shut, burying her face in the back of his shirt, clutching him so hard she hoped he would scream. If only she were back at Muirwood, safe in Pasqua's kitchen. She needed someone to hold her, to soothe her, to tell her it would be all right. When she had terrible nightmares, she always knew that Pasqua would come in the morning, and that it would be all right again. Even Sowe's presence was a comfort. No matter how a midwinter storm howled, it would be all right.

In her mind, she thought, *Dear Pasqua, I never told you how much I needed you. How safe you made me feel as a child.* There was her scolding, her pinching, her exasperated airs. But more than anyone else, Lia needed her. She needed someone who would comfort her and kiss her forehead and speak in whispers.

Somehow she knew that she could never get that from Colvin.

CHAPTER
TWENTY-FOUR

Hunted

I t was a high-pitched yowling sound, like the rusty hinges of a gate closing. It came from the night, from the unseen expanse of gullies and ravines, and it went right up Lia's spine.

"What was that?" she whispered, clutching her knees.

"I have no idea," Colvin answered, nestling back against the saddle in exhaustion. He hung his head with fatigue, rubbing his eyes on the back of his arm.

"A wolf?" she asked.

He sighed. "If I thought it was a wolf, I would have said that it sounded like a wolf." His voice was straining with impatience.

"What if it comes here? What if it stumbles on us during the night and decides to eat us?" She hated herself for asking the question. It sounded like something Sowe would whimper.

He rubbed his leg. "It may be a bird. A marsh owl of some sort. I am more worried about being devoured by bats."

"Bats?"

"Have you not seen them flitting about at night? There are so many insects here, they must feast like kings." He rose ponderously after a brief rest and then withdrew his sword. After flexing his arms and loosening his neck, he proceeded with drills using the blade, slicing through the air with a whisper of steel and a hiss of breath. She watched him practice, but not secretly as she had when spying him with the broom in the kitchen. The memory alone caused another pang of regret. She watched him, quietly, patiently. She was careful not to disturb him until he was finished.

"You practice for Winterrowd," Lia said, watching the blade slide snugly into the sheath fastened to his belt.

"I must," he answered, mopping sweat from his face on his tunic sleeve.

"Why?"

"Because mastery of any skill comes that way. If I hope to defeat a man who has more training and experience than me, then I best drill and drill and drill harder than that man." He paced restlessly, chafing his hands together. "It also helps me stay awake. I have never felt this tired in my life. My patience is little more than dust when I am tired."

"I will take the first watch," she offered. "I am not that tired."

"Are you cold?" he asked.

"Very. I do not care about being tired. You get used to it. But the kitchen was warm. It was always warm." Again, a stab of pain went through her heart. She leaned forward, hugging her knees.

He snorted. "Given that you summon fire so easily, I would not doubt that you were warm enough. It makes sense that the Aldermaston assigned you to the kitchen. It suits your gifts and passionate disposition. But I would fancy a bread oven right now myself. It is wet and cold in the Bearden Muir." He said it as a truth, not as a complaint.

Lia hugged her knees tighter, grateful she had a cloak, for Colvin lacked one. It was no use asking if he was cold. In the moonlight, she could see his breath.

He turned suddenly and crouched down near her. "I just remembered something my Aldermaston taught. It just came to me. Let me see if I can phrase it properly without my tome." He paused, thinking, then said, "*Inasmuch as you strip yourselves from jealousies and fears, and humble yourselves before the Medium, for you are not sufficiently humble, the veil over your eyes shall be torn and you will see.*"

"A clever verse," Lia said.

"It is a clever verse. It talks about three of the things that keep us from letting the Medium master us. Jealousy, fear, and pride. You do not seem a jealous girl."

"I am," Lia said. "Sometimes."

"No," he said. "I have not seen even a spark of that in you. Trust me—I have seen jealous girls. They speak with venom. They claw each other over trifles. You are ambitious, to be sure, but not proud. As a wretched, how could you be proud? You are in a forced state of humility. But even so, your attitude rises above it. Your demeanor is confident, not sullen. So it is fear. That is what is holding you back from the Medium. It is your fear."

At this moment, she wished she had a sturdy pan she could clench and crack his head with. Rather than screech at him, she kept her voice calm. "Colvin, I am away from my home in the middle of a swamp with the sheriff's men chasing after us. Yes...I am afraid. I am terrified! I am cold. Above even those, I am thirsty. If it rained, at least I could wring water from my dress and drink. We have eaten nothing but apples. This is by far the most miserable moment of my life. I am afraid. But nothing you taught me today helps me to be unafraid."

"It begins with a thought," Colvin said. "As I told you…"

"You do not understand!" she said, cutting him off. "I do not *want* to feel this way. But I do. You taught me that I need to focus my thoughts, that thoughts create feelings. Why can you not understand that all I have are memories of Muirwood? There is nothing else! Being cold reminds me of being warm. Being hungry reminds me of being fed. Being lonely…"

As soon as the words were out of her mouth, she regretted them, for they brought tears gushing. She hated crying, especially in front of him. He crouched near her, helpless as a dolt. He looked poleaxed and impotent, and it made her all the angrier. The tears were hot on her lashes. Why could he never see that she needed someone to comfort her, not gawk at her? Sobs shook her for several minutes, but finally she controlled them again. She would not look at him. Burying a wet cheek against her arm, she looked another way, ashamed and hurting, wishing he would curl up against the saddle and just go to sleep.

His voice was soft, almost a whisper. "When I left Forshee for the first time, I was about your age. I left to be a learner. My pride would never admit it, but I did miss home very much. I missed my sister. I missed my father and his wisdom. I even missed my mother, who I scarcely remember now, since she died when my sister was born. I was five when she died, I think. Billerbeck Hundred is lonely country. I felt it keenly."

Still, she did not look at him or say anything.

"I cannot say the feelings ever left me, but they did diminish over time. That, I can promise you. Muirwood is a beautiful abbey. I went there once with my father when I was very young. I think we went to the Whitsun Fair. I was only a boy, but I remember watching the maypole dance."

The Whitsun Fair—the event every wretched in the Abbey longed for out of the year. The time when the gates were opened and the villagers and Abbey mingled. Visitors from all over the country descended on Muirwood to buy kegs of cider, to trade leather for silk, or to taste the famous dishes that could only be found there. And then when the sun had set, the torches and lanterns would bring a second dawn as the young men and women gathered around the maypole, clasped hands, and danced, weaving colorful sashes down the length of it.

Lia lifted her head, her heart nearly breaking with sorrow. "Colvin, this Whitsunday was to be my first in the dancing circle. My very first. There was a learner...a first-year...I promised..." She blinked away fresh tears. "I promised him I would dance with him. I have broken that promise now, and I will never get that chance again to dance around the maypole."

Colvin said nothing after that, but his eyes were downcast with sympathy. There really was nothing he could say.

***

The crunch of a twig woke her, woke them both. The moon was beyond the horizon. It was dark, and Lia shivered, her body huddled up as tight as a walnut. The horse nickered from the far side of the hill, but the cracking sound had come much closer.

Colvin's voice was a pale whisper. "Did you hear that?"

"Yes," she answered, her heart bulging in her throat.

"Lie still." In the darkness, she heard the faint sound of Colvin's sword dragging clear of its scabbard.

Her heart beat frantically. The sheriff's men had found them. Or was it Almaguer alone, as in her dream? Was the dream a shadow of what would happen? Was it a vision?

She heard the soft hiss of footsteps on the wild grass, of boots coming down delicately on spongy mud, but not quite able to conceal the noise. The sound was close. She trembled, for her back was to it. She could not see. Her ears strained for clues as to how far back. Only one set of boots. Good—that gave Colvin a fighting chance. Suddenly, she was grateful he had practiced earlier, readying his swordsmanship to face this threat.

Part of her back itched, as if its shadow were tickling her. She could hear breathing in the stillness, the huff of breath of someone who climbed a hill. It reminded her of the smoke shapes, and she shivered even more. What was she supposed to do? Lie there? What would Colvin do? Her stomach twisted with fear. What if Colvin were killed?

Somewhere far off, a night owl hooted. That was the moment that Colvin struck. She heard him first, but he charged, his body leaping over hers. She rolled the other way and sat up, watching him attack. The blade whistled down, met steel with a spray of sparks, two blades clashing like lightning strokes. A counterstrike, then another block, followed by several more, each one ringing into the night with jarring sound. The slick, cracking hiss of the blades frightened her. Then the attack stopped, and both were circling each other, swords raised to guarding positions. Their bodies were shadows in the dark.

The pause lasted a moment, then Colvin lunged in, high, low, high—his blade arcing in dizzying circles. The defender parried, high, low, high, stepped in, and grabbed Colvin's arm. Their bodies slammed into each other, wrestling for control, then separated. Colvin hobbled slightly, as if the attacker had stomped on his foot. Again they circled each other in defensive positions, breathing heavily.

Lia was helpless. What could she do to turn the battle in Colvin's favor? Nothing would protect her from the cruel edge of the blade. She had no defense, other than distance.

Colvin lunged the third time—and tripped. It may have been because of a wet stone, the mud and grass, or maybe the injured foot. Lia gasped as she watched him go down, slamming his elbow then fighting to regain his feet. The adversary's short blade pressed up against his exposed neck. It was a short blade, and she recognized it. She recognized the scabbard attached high on his girdle.

"Yield," he said. "I have not come all this way to kill you. Lia—are you near?"

She knew that voice, that gait, and that gladius.

It was Jon Hunter.

***

The greatest achievement was at first and for a time only a dream. Just as the oak sleeps in the acorn, and the bird waits in the egg, so dreams are the seedlings of realities. Beware, therefore, what you dream of. For some dreams are given by the Medium to inspire us by what may yet be. Others are planted within us by others, foul seeds that we harvest to our destruction.

—Cuthbert Renowden of Billerbeck Abbey

CHAPTER
TWENTY-FIVE

Lia's Leering

The drink was from a leather waterskin, and yet it tasted like fresh rainwater from a ladle. Lia swallowed at first, then gulped, and Jon Hunter yanked it away from her.

"Easy, Lia. There is little to share." He handed it to Colvin, who still glowered and massaged his foot, but took it anyway and sipped.

"How did you find us?" Colvin asked, rubbing his hands in the dark and then putting his boot back on.

Jon snorted, breaking a piece of bread in half and handing them each a crust. "I am a hunter, lad." The loaf was slightly stale, but soft enough inside to melt in her mouth, while the outside crunched with little seeds. It tasted like Pasqua's bread. It was delicious beyond words.

"You have no horse?" Colvin asked.

"Easier to follow you on foot. Easier to hide your trail. You took no care to disguise it, so I have followed, concealing it.

Almaguer has a hunter too. He is good, because he keeps finding the trail. They would have caught you by now if I did not meddle."

Lia reached out and grabbed Jon's arm, just to feel that he was real. The leather bracer on his arm was damp, but it was reassuring. His bow was on the ground nearby. "The Aldermaston sent you?" she asked, daring to hope.

He nodded. "I saw you in the village, as you rode away. I called out to you, but you did not see me."

"I remember," Lia said. "That was you?"

Jon rummaged through his pack again. "Oats for the stallion. Not much, but he will not starve. Lia, the Aldermaston wanted me to make sure you were safe. Maderos told us you were taking him to Winterrowd through the Bearden Muir with the orb." He glanced at Colvin. "There was a big argument about that. My duty is to see that you make it safely home when it is finished. If I do not, Pasqua said she would kill me."

Lia's heart spasmed with joy. "I can come back? Even after what I did?"

A half-smile and a nod was his answer. He was never very talkative. Her heart was so full, she nearly started crying again. She clasped her hands in front of her, thinking of it—savoring it. She could return to Muirwood instead of being banished forever.

Colvin's voice was dark. "Why?"

"Hmm?"

"Why does the Aldermaston help me?" He tugged a tuft of grass from the earth. "Why does he forgive her?"

Jon stowed the waterskin and cinched the pack shut again. "I do not begin to understand the Aldermaston's reasons. He is far wiser than I will ever be. He sent me to find you. I found you. Lucky for you both. Your first day in the Bearden Muir went well. You went straight toward Winterrowd as if the Medium were guiding your steps. Then yesterday, your trail wandered to and fro like a pig drunk on spoiled cider until you reached the road. If you had stayed on the road much longer, Almaguer would have caught you. His horses are faster and his men are better riders. They do not spare horseflesh hunting a man. I thought they had you, but you came back into the swamp. I caught your trail before they did. Now they have to double back and see where you came in. I disguised it as best I could. At least I caught you first. What happened? Did you lose the orb?"

"I failed," Lia said, ashamed.

Jon stood to stretch his legs. "It stopped directing you?"

Lia pulled her cloak more tightly around her shoulders. "It is my fault. I have been too fearful."

He was silent for a moment as he considered. "I can tell you this. We will not make it through the Bearden Muir without it. We may not make it through the day. I, for one, do not want to risk being caught by them. Fear stops the Medium from hearkening to you." He looked down at Colvin. "You are a maston though. Why did you not cure her fear?"

Colvin looked up, his jaw set. "Only she can do that. I have been…I have been teaching her about the Medium…"

Jon waved his hand. "She is not a learner! She cannot be a learner. But you are a maston. What about a Gifting?"

Colvin looked shocked. "I have never done one before. I…I… it is not that…"

"You are a maston. You can. You have the right to call on the Medium to lay a Gift on someone."

"But I do not know the words, the right words, they are written in my tome. I do not have it…"

"It is not exactly a riddle, lad. I have heard the Aldermaston do it. He Gifted me before I came to find you. Gift her with courage."

Colvin stood, his face twisting with anxiety.

"How long have you been a maston?" Lia asked him.

"Not very long," he replied, sounding a little ashamed. "I have never done one before. I do not know the right words."

Jon snorted. "It is not about the words. You already know that. It is the Medium. Let it speak through you. She needs courage. Gift her with it."

"Give me a moment!" Colvin said harshly. He turned his back to them, his fists tight, his arms taut.

Jon let him alone for a moment. "Lad, I can help you. I have heard the words. As long as you know the maston sign, you can do it. I cannot help you with that."

Colvin's voice was strained. "I know it."

"Then come on, lad. You have the right, despite your youth. Use it. Or else the sheriff and his men will have us tomorrow. I tell you, they cannot be far behind us."

Colvin turned, his eyes strong like steel.

"What do I do?" Lia asked.

"Just kneel where you are," Jon said. "Put one hand on her head. Make the maston sign with the other. Then you call her by her wretched name. Lia Cook. Pronounce the Gifting through the Medium. The Aldermaston says the Gifts come as thoughts, not words. You have to shape the thoughts into words."

The wind rustled the trees and the marsh grasses hissed. There was a chorus of cicadas somewhere nearby.

Colvin's voice was firm. "Close your eyes. Both of you. You cannot witness the sign." .

Lia straightened her back, though she was still kneeling, and rested her hands in front of her. She closed her eyes, which felt silly. Colvin's boots trampled the grass near her, and she could feel the warmth coming from his body. He knelt down as well, facing her. She could hear the sound of him kneeling, felt the shift of his weight. Her heart started pounding and her mouth went dry. She could feel his hand coming down, but not touching her, as if he dared not touch her. In the dream of Almaguer, he had touched her hair. His fingers had coiled in her hair like serpents. Shivering, she waited, barely able to breathe. The image of the sword plunging through her returned to her mind. She smelled the sweet reek of his skin. She felt smoke shapes sniffing at her, nuzzling against her arms, her back, her legs. She wanted to scream. *Please, do not touch me…do not let him touch me!* Something terrible would happen if he did.

Colvin's hand gently capped the top of her head. It was gentle—yet firm. There was a softness in the way the weight of his hand and fingers pressed down against her hair, bending the kinks, before resting on her scalp. His touch sent new shivers through her.

"Lia Cook…"

It was the first time he had spoken her name. In her ears, there was screaming, raging, cursing, but not from Colvin. It came from inside her. It was as if she opened another set of eyes, eyes that allowed her to look down on herself as a separate person. Colvin was in front of her, but there was a blinding hail of light coming from behind him. Smoke shapes screamed and fled, loping away with a mist that receded from the hillock like water draining from a cracked keg. There was something still in her chest—something that had lodged there since her dream. It slid out and it was like breathing for the first time. Behind her, she could see Almaguer's glowing eyes as he backed away from her, his face twisting with agony.

Then she felt it. Each breath she inhaled brought a sob of recognition. The feeling was back again. Not the terrifying feeling, not the horror and shame and loathing, but the feeling of Muirwood. All her life she had felt it. The subtle feeling of safety, of belonging, of being home—she felt it again, even though the Abbey was leagues away. She understood now. It was the power of the Medium. All her life, she had lived amidst it—breathed it with the very air, yet had never really recognized it before. The same power that defended the Abbey was with her, brought to her through Colvin's warm hand.

She had not heard another word he had said, but it was over and he lifted his hand from her head. Deep inside, she did not want him to snatch it back. She wanted to feel that sense of haven forever. Opening her eyes, she saw him kneel in front of her. His eyes were full of tears.

"They are gone," she whispered. "The fog and the smoke shapes. Almaguer. They are gone. I am not afraid anymore."

"I know," he whispered back, barely able to speak. "The Myriad Ones were all around you. I…I did not know. But they are gone now. They are all gone."

It started to rain.

***

The Cruciger orb led them northwest through the tangled paths of the Bearden Muir. The day was every bit as drab, colorless and uncomfortable as the previous day—but it was no longer soulless. She was still thirsty, but it was no longer a torment. Jon had brought food to share, gathered from the kitchen and assembled in a linen napkin by Pasqua herself. Pasqua, who was worried sick about her. Pasqua, who had insisted on following Jon to the porter gates to hunt for Lia herself, only to be called back by the Aldermaston and threatened with dire consequences if she defied him. Sowe, who Jon said was hidden inside the manor by the Aldermaston while the sheriff's men shouted insults from the gates. He told her how the villagers had finally warned the sheriff's men with the threat of a riot to make them leave.

"Bring Lia back to Muirwood," the Aldermaston had said. "Whatever happens in Winterrowd, she must come back. Bring her home, Jon. Bring her home."

There was no way to describe how that made her feel. That she, a wretched, was worthy of rescue. That the Aldermaston would not only defend her, but continue to defy the sheriff because of her choice to steal the Cruciger orb and her choice to aid Colvin. All her life, she had never felt much in the way of affection for the old man. It was an alien feeling.

The need for fresh water was paramount in the Bearden Muir, so Lia asked the orb for a safe path to Winterrowd that would put them in the course of fresh water. The spindles had pointed the way clearly, and she waited with anticipation for the chance to slake her thirst again.

When it came, before dusk, it startled them all.

The orb led them into a thicket between stark hills. It was thickly wooded with black, mossy oaks, overgrown and filled with stagnant pools with floating clouds of gnats and choruses of frogs. Insects sang and hummed, filling the air with their confusion. Carefully, the orb led them into the midst of the thicket, choked with skeletal trees and brush that clawed at their heads, swatted at their arms, and seemed almost impassable at times, until they reached a boulder in the center. The ground was dry around the stone, and they circled it from both sides. It whispered with power. Sure enough, it was a Leering, with the carved side facing east toward the sun, the western side shaggy with moss and speckled with lichen. There were no other boulders nearby.

It seemed out of place, imposing, permanent—lonely. It was as if the thicket had grown up around it.

Colvin and Jon stared at the carving of its face, their eyes widening in unison. They looked at each other and then at her.

"What is it?" Lia asked, staring at the image carved into the stone. It was a human face—a girl's face fringed with long crinkly hair. She had seen many Leerings before. It did not seem unusual to her, except for the hair which matched her own.

"Idumea's hand," Colvin said breathlessly.

Jon looked equally shocked. "I agree." He looked at it, then at her.

"What?" Lia asked, starting to get angry. The orb pointed to it.

With a grimy finger, Jon reached out and traced the eyes and nose and mouth of the sculpture. "This is the Aldermaston's work. I swear I would recognize his hand. I know his waymarkers. The Aldermaston made this one. But when? How long ago?"

"Look at the moss," Colvin said. "It's been here for years. Here—a single boulder in the midst of a grove."

"The Aldermaston made this?" Lia asked. "Is that what troubles you?"

Colvin shook his head, also reaching out and grazing his fingers across it. "No. It is the face." He looked back at her, his eyes open in wonder. "It is your face."

She looked at Jon.

"It is you, Lia. Even the hair…"

Her world began spinning. Like the games of children when they stand and spin around, arms waving out as they twirl until they are too dizzy to stand. The Aldermaston had carved it. Her face…or her mother's face? Why could she use the Cruciger orb and Colvin could not? Why was she so strong in the Medium?

It was a strange, sickly feeling, but her mind asked it ruthlessly anyway. Was the Aldermaston her father?

CHAPTER TWENTY-SIX

Trapped

T here were no mirrors in Muirwood, they said, except inside a secret chamber in the Abbey. Mirrors encouraged haughtiness, and so they were banned throughout the grounds. Lia did not care much about that. As most girls did, she had a companion like Sowe who could tame her hair or daub dough off her cheek. For the most part, Lia had only seen her reflection in the dirty trough of water at the laundry, or reflected in the duck pond, or off a gleaming spoon.

The Leering bore her face. She ran her finger down its nose, under its chin, then stroked its cheek with the back of her hand. The stone was smooth, cold to the touch, yet power seethed within it. With little more than a thought, water gushed from the eyes of the Leering, bathing her hands. Water—fresh water. After scrubbing her fingers clean, she cupped the water and drank deeply. It was cool, clean, and sent tingles down to her toes. The water puddled at the base of the boulder, then started down a worn track into the bushes, thick with sedge and decaying trees. She drank until her thirst was finally slaked. Colvin rinsed his hands then followed, and then Jon took out the waterskin and filled it to the brim. Then he drank.

"Rest here, but only a little while," Jon said after wiping his mouth. "I will cover our trail. Do not wait for me. I know how to find you."

He started to leave, but Lia caught his arm. "Why did the Aldermaston carve my face, Jon?"

"I do not know, Lia."

She kept her voice pitched low. "Do you think...would he have been my father?"

His eyes were serious. "He is the last man in the world who would father a wretched. No, I do not know how he knew to carve this. But I have seen his carvings before. This one looks like his."

"How did it come to be here, then?"

"Perhaps he knew you would be here someday and would need it. He knows many things before they happen because he is strong with the Medium." He smirked. "Probably why he is an Aldermaston. Let me hide our trail." He tousled her wild hair. "If Pasqua could see you now. Bathe your face ere you leave. You are filthy."

"You are rude to mention it, Jon Hunter. I do not know what Ailsa Cook sees in you."

He suffered her insolence with a grin, shaking his head, then loped back through the twisted oaks the way they came, holding his bow close against his body with an arrow ready.

She turned back and found Colvin kneeling at the Leering, his head under its gushing waters, nearly shivering while scrubbing the back of his neck with his hand. The stallion grazed at the stiff grass. With a thought, she brought a little fire to the water—not too much—not enough to scald him.

"Hot," he said, his fingers scouring through his hair.

"Hot cleans better," she replied with a grin, approaching the other way. Water pattered on the muddy ground, taking his dirt and grime away. She knew him better—knew of his jealousy, his impatience. Something had changed between them. His compassion toward her, the tears in his eyes as he stared at her, something was different. But still she hesitated near him, afraid he might recoil at her again.

"Here, it will go faster if I help you," she said, scrubbing the top of his head as she did for Sowe. He froze for a moment, the water dripping down his face from his nose. It was warm water. What they needed was some soap.

He hiked up his sleeves and scrubbed his arms while she combed his hair with her fingers and tried to chafe away layers of dirt, scaly skin, and chalky crusts from his neck. His shirt and tunic were soon soaked as well, hugging against the chaen beneath.

"Let me see your eyebrow, Colvin."

He looked up at her, swept his dripping hair back, and he looked like someone else. A thin half-formed beard outlined his jaw and mouth. Using the hem of her cloak, she sponged up some hot water and then wiped at the scab along his eyebrow. He winced and clenched his teeth as she cleaned the wound. It did not bleed, but it would scar. The woad had kept it closed.

"There. You smell better too," she said, smiling. "I am pleased it is healing. Your sister will hardly notice the scar when you return."

"She has a gift for astuteness. As do you."

"I like to think I am shrewd. My pride does anyway. I am filthy as well, so help me wash so we can go. We should not tarry long."

"Help you?" he said, swallowing. His eyes looked panicked.

She coiled up her hair. "Hold this up. That is all. Sowe normally helps me, but you will have to do. If you are not too proud to serve a wretched girl."

The water was warm and pleasant, but she liked it hotter still and thought more on the fire. Steam rose from the Leering. Its eyes glowed red. Washing was something she was good at and quick at, and it did not take long to chafe her arms and her neck while Colvin held her hair up. She wiped her face furiously, hoping to get away the smudges and dirt caked in the seams.

"Let my hair fall," she said finally, enjoying the burn of the water as it ran down her scalp. She fussed her hair, smoothing it down with the water until the water dripping from the ends ran clear. Then fishing the ring from her bodice, she washed it until the gold gleamed and sparkled, then stuffed it away again. The metal band was warm against her skin.

"If only Pasqua had packed my other dress," she said, squeezing excess water from her wavy hair. Hers was ripped, tattered at the hem, and filthy. It used to be blue. Now it was a grayish-green color. "You have hardly spoken today," Lia said as they walked around to the stallion. "You have hardly said ten words since we left this morning and it is nearly dusk."

"You were talking to your friend," he replied, gathering the reins and stroking the mane. "I did not want to intrude."

"You can trust Jon," Lia said.

"Trusting anyone does not come easily to me. Even you—it took time before I did trust you, remember?"

"So you admit you trust me now?"

"You have proven your faithfulness, Lia. I require that before I give my trust to anyone. I will requite it in my own way, I promise you."

She reached for the pouch with the Cruciger orb and untied the strings while Colvin fed another apple to the horse. After tugging open the strings, she withdrew the orb and again thought the words—*show us the safe road to Winterrowd.*

Nothing happened.

For a moment, there was panic that she had failed again, but there was no doubt or fear in her heart this time. Nothing that should have barred the Medium from touching her thoughts.

"What is wrong?" he asked.

Words in the same cryptic language appeared in the lower portion of the orb. The spindles did not move; they floated as if a duck on a lake.

Show me the road to Winterrowd, she thought, and the spindles turned and pointed to the northwest.

"What did you do differently?" he asked.

Lia bit her lip. "I asked it to show us the safe road. It did nothing."

The words written on the orb were meaningless, but it was as if she could feel their warning without being told the translation. The orb was warning them. There was no safe road ahead. A thrashing noise in the thicket alerted them both.

Colvin's face turned ashen. "Almaguer's men."

"But if they are behind us, why is it not safe to go ahead?" Lia asked frantically.

Colvin looked the other direction, cocking his head. "Listen. They are coming at us from many sides. Why did the orb lead us down here then?"

"Perhaps this was the safest path—at the time. But we waited too long."

Colvin gripped her shoulders. "The Medium can deliver us still. Believe in that, Lia. Fear will only bring them faster."

She tried to swallow the surge of fear squirming in her stomach like a nest of serpents. Where was Jon? She did not dare call out to him. That would tell the sheriff exactly where they were.

Colvin worked at the saddle straps and freed the second sword and scabbard that Maderos had given them. He thrust it into her hands. "You may need this."

"I do not know how to use a…"

"I know! I will do my best to protect you, but one of them may try to grab you while I am fighting the others. Swing it like a stick if you must."

"It is so heavy," Lia said, feeling its bulk.

"Heavy kills quicker," he snapped. "You do not swing it in the scabbard. If they come, pull it out and swing it. You want to lead with the edge. You…" He stopped, as if hearing something.

"What is it?" Lia asked, turning around the way Jon left. "Should we run?"

"How?" Colvin snorted. "We need the horse. If there was a haven elsewhere, the orb would have told us. Trust the Medium, Lia. Trust the Medium. It will not fail us. It will not. Come on, this way." He tugged at the bridle.

Lia remembered something Maderos had said. *If you take the road, you will be captured.* Her thoughts brought his words perfectly, even the accent. She had assumed that if they had taken the road, they would be captured on the road. Now she understood it differently. Their capture would happen after. Or because of having taken the road.

"Colvin," she said.

A set of riders emerged from the woods ahead of them, toward the direction of Winterrowd. Three of the sheriff's men appeared, their faces haggard with fatigue, their eyes burning with anger. Their horses dripped foam from the bits; their flanks were lathered as well and bloody from the spurs. Lia's heart cringed for the beasts.

Colvin took a deep breath and unsheathed his sword. Three against one.

"Do not do this," Lia warned him.

"I can kill three. If the Medium helps me, I can do it."

"Maderos said it, remember?" He started toward the sheriff's men, but she grabbed his shirt and yanked hard. "Maderos said it! If we took the road, we would be captured."

His face stormed with anger. "Please! Do not infect me with your fear."

Lia wanted to slap him. "I am afraid, but not like before. Listen to me. It brought us here. It knew something would happen here. You are right to trust the Medium. Let us trust it."

"By surrendering? How do you know the orb is not telling us to fight a way clear?"

From the corner of her eye, she saw the sheriff's men approaching languidly. They were in no hurry. The hunt was over—it was time for the kill.

She clutched his arm. "I do not want you to die, Colvin," she whispered. "If your sister were here, she would say it herself. Think of me as your own sister. Please. Do not do this. For her sake."

One of the men spoke, his voice gravelly and rough. "He looks as if he would like to cry. Look at him. All quivery. C'mon lad, do not cry. It has been a hard ride for us."

"A wretched chase," said another, his voice dripping with sarcasm. "You are not going to quit now, surely?"

The third dismounted, sword in hand. "If you will not fight, then shine our boots, squire." The stiff grass hissed as he advanced on them. The other two dismounted. "They are a little mucky.

You can shine them with that stained coat of arms you wear. You sniveling maston! Demont's man!" He hocked and spat.

Colvin looked her in the eye, his jaw clenched with anger. "You are my sister," he whispered.

For an instant, she had hope. It sputtered out.

Turning, he thrust at the sheriff's men, charging into the midst of them, his blade flashing with sunlight from the setting sun. She was surrounded by the rattle of blades and the singing steel, but in her mind, she heard screams. The blood on his tunic was screaming.

It was three against one, and he fell quickly. Maybe his foot was still throbbing from his battle with Jon Hunter. Maybe a loose rock tripped him. She watched him fall and watched the soldiers pounce on him. Lia cringed and buried her face into the stallion's mane, still hearing the screams, knowing what these men had done to other mastons before him. Unable to watch as they started kicking him, she wept.

***

Having conceived of a purpose, a maston should mentally mark out a straight pathway to achievement, looking neither to the right nor left. Doubts and fears should be zealously starved. They are disintegrating elements which break up the straight path, rendering it crooked, ineffectual, and useless. Thoughts of doubt and fear can never accomplish anything. They always lead to failure. Purpose, energy, power to do, and all strong thoughts cease when doubt and fear creep in. The will to do springs from the knowledge that we can do. He who has conquered doubt and fear has conquered failure.

—*Cuthbert Renowden of Billerbeck Abbey*

CHAPTER
TWENTY-SEVEN

Vengeance

Lia heard another kick, then the gasp of pain from Colvin's lips. In her mind, the screams of dead mastons swarmed the grove. Despite the fury of her feelings, she recalled something Colvin had told her—that mastons were being murdered and that Demont was fighting to change that. The decisive moment was nearly there—the slaughter at Winterrowd that Maderos had predicted. If he was going to survive the battlefield slaughter, it would be because of her. She knew it instinctively. Perhaps her knowledge of healing would save his life. Perhaps just being nearby to drag his body from the field would be enough. But if Colvin were to die, it would not be in the Bearden Muir. It would be at Winterrowd.

Unclenching her fingers from the stallion's mane, she turned to the sheriff's men. Every feeling in her heart throbbed with passion and determination. She would see him to Winterrowd. She would fulfill her promise.

"Let him alone!" she screamed at them. With every spark of thought, she willed them to stop hurting him. She did not wait to be obeyed. Rushing forward, she thrust herself on Colvin's crumpled body, shielding it with her own. His face was bloody, his cheeks quivering with pain.

Gazing up defiantly at the soldiers, she saw shock in their eyes. One stepped back.

"Just a wretched," one of them said, his eyes scrunching.

"I said leave him alone!" she screamed again, looking directly at that man, lifting herself higher. "Do not touch him. Do not kick him. Lower your swords, he is not fighting you." The men hesitated, and two of them shook their heads, as if in a fog. "Put them down!" she ordered.

Two of them obeyed, the blades thudding in the mud. The third stepped farther back, holding the sword up as if to protect himself from her.

Branches crackled and more horsemen arrived, Almaguer leading them. His eyes found hers and held them steadfastly. Her courage began to melt. There was something in his eyes—a look—a fearful look. Her teeth began to chatter.

Colvin clutched her hand. "Do not fear him," he whispered hoarsely.

Almaguer dismounted his bloodied stallion. Lia felt as if she were surrounded by things she could not see. Invisible muzzles poking at her back, her arms. Sniffing at Colvin and his wet wounds. Her teeth chattered even more.

One of the three soldiers who had beaten Colvin, the one still holding his sword, waggled it at her. "She...she...Almaguer..."

"Say nothing," Almaguer interrupted. "She is powerful because of who she is. She is Demont's spawn. But still, only a wretched. She does not know what she is doing or how."

Lia looked down at Colvin's face. His eyes fixed into hers. "Do not fear him," he whispered.

"How?" she whispered back, choking down a sob. Every part of her wanted to flee, to hide from this man whose eyes glowed silver in the dark. The feeling of safety was gone. The calm feeling from the night before shredded before the onslaught, leaving only threads.

"Muirwood," he whispered, hunching as another spasm of pain tore through him. He squeezed her hand so hard it hurt. "Think on Muirwood."

"Yes, think on Muirwood," Almaguer said with a bite in his voice, for he was close enough now to have heard. "Think on it, my dear, and imagine every stone broken down. Every window dashed in. The treasures spoiled. The tomes melted for jewelry. Tapestries ripped from the hanging poles and torched. Think on that, child, and know that you caused it. The Aldermaston's head on a spike at the gate. All because of you. Yes, think on that."

His words filled her with visions. She could see his words, could see the Abbey burning.

Colvin's hand clenched again. He tried sitting up, tried to speak, but Almaguer smashed the pommel of his sword against his head and he dropped silently.

"No!" Lia screamed.

Almaguer looked at her coldly, then twisted his head. She could see a scar on his cheek from where she'd scratched him. "Dolbreck, Hutton…Manth and Fraire. Bind him in irons and tie him to his horse. I want him delivered to the king's camp before dawn. I would let you butcher him now, but His Majesty will prefer to do this one himself." His eyes narrowed with hatred. "Colvin Price, cousin to the king, arrested for high treason. Take him."

Lia hugged Colvin's body, shaking her head in disbelief. Almaguer grabbed her arm and yanked, dragging her away from him. Soldiers approached, their expressions grim, and shackled his wrists in iron clamps. One grabbed the stallion, which snorted and resisted, but obeyed when another man seized the reins. Two others hoisted Colvin across the saddle and bound him with strong cords. To her, he looked dead.

Lia tried jerking her arm free, but Almaguer increased his grip with crushing pressure and she nearly shrieked with pain. She tried to speak, but her voice failed. Despair shrouded her, smothering hope.

Jon Hunter!

Almost too late, she remembered him. Where was Jon?

It was as if Almaguer could hear her frantic thoughts. "No one is coming to help you, child. We caught your hunter first and left his body in a ditch. Our hunter is the better shot. He is dead." A smirk twisted on his mouth. "We made sure of it."

A feeling of blackness threatened to swallow her whole. Grief filled her nose and mouth. She drowned in it. Four of the sheriff's men rode away, one holding the stallion's reins to lead Colvin out of the thicket. The sun sank below the nearby hills, filling the Bearden Muir with shadows. As the light failed, so did her courage.

***

After binding Lia's hands with irons, Almaguer thrust her roughly against the boulder while his men settled in for the night. Darkness descended quickly, but soon a pair of fires crackled and snapped. Horses were unsaddled, and they thrashed with weariness and agony. Muddy blankets were spread out, and one of the soldiers set up a makeshift spit. He had a bow and quiver, and Lia knew he was the one who had killed Jon. His expression was remorseless, and she hated him.

Looking down at her mat of swamp grass, she wondered about Colvin. Her efforts had all been pointless. They were all in vain. Everything she had tried to do to help him had failed. In the end, the sheriff had captured her, just as Maderos had warned. Her stomach was sick with worry. She thought about escaping, but Almaguer did not lose sight of her, even for a moment. He studied her with an intensity that made her sicker still. He was looking at her in a foul way. He was leering at her.

Even though she could not see them, she knew the smoke shapes were all around her. The Myriad Ones, Colvin had called them. Something awful was going to happen to her. They knew it and were eager to be part of it.

"It is nearly dusk," one of the soldiers said.

"Past dusk," another growled.

"Almost," Almaguer said. "Feed the fires."

Lia knew somehow that she did not have long. Whatever they were going to do, they were waiting until the sun had set. She leaned her head back against the stone and shut her eyes, not wanting to see anything. Her wrists were heavy, the weight of the irons pressing against her lap.

It begins with a thought.

Those were Colvin's words. The words his Aldermaston had taught him. What then should she think of? As the soldiers bustled about the camp, anxious for the dark of night, Lia drifted inside herself. Muirwood. She focused her mind on the sights and sounds of Muirwood. She pictured the cloisters where the learners studied from golden tomes, the manor where she served the Aldermaston his dinner, a bowl of soup, and a heel of bread. She thought of the fish pond and its oily smell. Then she thought of one of her favorite places—the Cider Orchard. Yes, the Cider

Orchard in bloom in the spring, when a hundred thousand apple blossoms danced in the air like snowflakes.

She felt the corner of her mouth twitch, as if it wanted to smile through her misery. There were the cemetery ruins where she and Sowe ate shrewberries and teased and talked. Another image rose to her mind—a giant mound of ossuaries left to molder in the woods. Laughter filled her ears as she remembered playing there, knowing that she held a secret the other wretcheds did not know. And what of the tunnels beneath the Abbey? She imagined the maze of tunnels that the Aldermaston used to keep his secrets. She could not wait to explore them, to study the mazes until she knew them by heart.

"It is time, child," Almaguer said near her ear.

His words jolted her, turning the skies of her imagination black.

Do not fear him. Lia—do not fear him! The Medium will not abandon you, unless you abandon it.

The thoughts sounded like Colvin's. Was he trying to speak to her?

She focused her thoughts on Muirwood, just as he had told her. She brought the Aldermaston his supper, a crock full of salty soup. He loved Pasqua's soups, especially the warm broth with melted cheese and diced onions and apples.

"You took something from me," Almaguer said. "You have been using it. I sense its power coming from you. Have you noticed the shadows it paints on your flesh? It leaves its mark on your breast. Water will not purge it. The stain spreads with time."

Lia kept her eyes closed, even though his breath gusted on her cheek. The Medium was real. She knew it was. Her memories went farther back—to the night of the storm. There was Jon Hunter, dripping wet, muddy from his fall. There was Pasqua being scolded by the Aldermaston. And there was the Aldermaston, his beard damp from the rain. His will had quenched the storm. How had he done it?

It begins with a thought.

No, it was not the Aldermaston's will that had done it. You cannot force the Medium, Colvin said. If you try and force it, it flees. Instead, you open yourself to the Medium. You seek its will, to understand its purposes.

But why would it have sent her this far to fail? Why would the Cruciger orb lead her to a Leering in the middle of the Bearden Muir and not show a way to escape? Surely there was one path of safety that would have led from the thicket. Surely...

Do not doubt! Do not doubt, Lia!

Almaguer's voice was cold, yet throbbing. "Once you have tasted this power, it grows like a hunger. Do you feel that hunger, child? Whatever you desire, you can achieve. Anything. Anything you desire. I must have it back." She felt his fingers graze her skin, by her throat. But she did not feel afraid. The thoughts of Muirwood lingered. His hands were trembling, his fingers trembling. It was as if some power shook him. He was trying to pull out the ring from her bodice.

"Give it to me!"

Lia kept her eyes shut, thinking of the night the Aldermaston had calmed the storm. She remembered understanding his thoughts, that he dreaded she would learn to use the Medium. He dreaded that she would gain access to its powers.

What would you have me do? Lia whispered in her mind. *I will do it. I will do anything asked of me.*

It was as if a key turned inside her thoughts, and a new door opened to her. That was the only way to describe it. The door revealed possibilities. Connections, thoughts, insights, wisdom— a thousand intersecting strands came together in her mind, like a cobweb. It was a moment of clarity. She understood now. It came as a rush.

The Medium had not abandoned her to the sheriff and his men. It had delivered them into *her* hands.

Suddenly, from the silence of her thoughts, she heard screaming—screaming like a chanting sound, rich with horror and vengeance. The blood of the dead mastons the sheriff's men had slain was screaming to her. Instead of being surrounded by smoke shapes, she felt the blood singing to her. Begging her to act. Pleading with her for justice.

It was time.

Another memory came—of a moment she and Colvin shared in the kitchen. Something in his words had caused a rush and heat through her. *Leering stones help bring the power out of yourself. The stones represent us.* They were exciting words—thrilling words. A great deep thought had brushed against her mind when he said that, so large she could not feel the edges of it. After the last few days, she knew more, and she could feel the edges now. That somehow, the ability to cause fire, or water, or plague, or life slept inside of her, not the stone.

Her back pressed against the Leering boulder with her own face carved into it. The Medium had known this time would come to her. It had inspired the Aldermaston to carve what he did years in advance, not because the Aldermaston had known it would happen. He'd carved it because the Medium had brought all the events together for her to act on it.

Lia opened her eyes as the sheriff fished the ring out.

There it was, a gleaming gold wedding band, dangling on a string that she had worn since she was nine. It was her evidence that the Medium was real.

Almaguer looked at it, confused, his face twisting with shock and surprise. Then he looked at her.

I do not even need a Leering to make fire, she thought.

Flames engulfed her body. The door in her mind was still open. The power of the Medium surged through her, filling the grove with a towering wall of fire. It swept from her like a flood, charring oak, grass, and everything in its path into ash. It burned hotter and hotter—hotter than any fire she had ever summoned in the ovens of the Abbey kitchen.

The iron bands around her wrists melted away, leaving her skin and clothes unharmed. There were no screams as the sheriff and his men died. They were just snuffed out by the Medium's vengeance. It was over in an instant, their intentions spoiled. All along they had believed themselves the masters of the moment. Even at the end, Almaguer had been sure she wore his medallion. Flames raged like a storm, filling the starry night sky. Trees were afire, sending columns of smoke into the air. The ground shook from the intensity. The screams of dead mastons fell silent at her triumph—submitting to the roar of the fire. Behind her, even the boulder cracked from the constant blast of heat.

Lia stood slowly, unharmed by the inferno. Her head was dizzy with the feeling of power. She knew that if the Medium asked her to, she could raise a mountain by lifting her hand. Looking down at her front, she saw the golden ring over her dress and was grateful to the Medium for protecting it. She untied the pouch at her waist and withdrew the Cruciger orb. It shone with radiant light, glowing fiercely with the power of Medium. It was almost too bright to look at.

Bring me to Colvin, she asked it, squinting, and the orb began whirring. It pointed the way.

CHAPTER
TWENTY-EIGHT

Grave

As Lia walked through the blazing hive of fire, she heard her name shouted. The roar was so loud, it took a moment before she realized it was Colvin screaming it. The door in her mind slammed shut, and the power of the Medium rushed back into the void behind her, vanishing into the cracked remains of the hissing boulder. As soon as the power of the Medium fled, all her strength was gone. She stumbled, trying to keep upright. Her hand bit into the charred earth, but it did not burn her.

Colvin was there, catching her. He cradled her and walked away from the crackling flames of still-burning trees. She looked up at him, amazed to see him. She tried to smile, but there was not enough strength in her mouth to twitch.

"I have you," he said, huffing. Sweat dripped down his face, which was pink from the heat. "A little farther."

Her head dipped against his chest and she slept, still clutching the orb in her hand.

When she awoke later, still tired, the pattern of the stars revealed it was past midnight, and the world was still and cold. Mist came from her mouth as she breathed. A calmness settled deep in her bones. Her arms and legs were frigid, but there was no worry at the night noises. All the world seemed contented. Turning her head, she found Colvin asleep near her, his arm pillowing his neck. His mouth was open a little, his face spattered and bruised, lips brittle with scabs. She was still exhausted, but she managed to rise and cover his body with her cloak. He had slept every night without a blanket. Though she had seen him shiver, he never complained of being cold. Nestling closer to him, but not touching him, she shut her eyes again and fell asleep with hardly a thought.

When she awoke again, it was day. Her strength had returned, so she pushed herself up on her elbow. During the night, he had returned her cloak, and it was warm against her body.

Colvin was nearby, eyes open, propping his head up with one arm, studying her. His face was a mess of dried blood and purple bruises.

"Are you well, Lia?"

She nodded, swallowing. The look he gave her was tender.

"I thought the fire was the sheriff's doing. I was so afraid that I had failed you, that you had perished in those flames. But I knew it was the Medium. It felt like the Medium. You have always been strong with fire, I just did not realize you were *that* strong."

Lia smiled. "Neither did I."

"Thank you for sharing your cloak. When I woke this morning, you looked cold. You need it more than I do. I do not mind the cold."

"Well, you shiver too," she said, looking down.

"Strange though," he said, rumpling a bit of her cloak that was near his hand. He took a fistful of it and smelled it. "When you emerged from the fire, there was not even the scent of smoke on you or your clothes. I still cannot smell it."

Lia sat up, feeling awkward. From their vantage, she could see the nearby thicket. Part of it lay smoldering. "It could not harm me," she said, looking at his hand so near that it nearly brushed her arm. She wanted to touch his hand, to squeeze it and thank him, but she dared not. "Thank you for teaching me of the Medium, Colvin. Your words saved my life last night."

"I do not deserve any praise," he replied, fidgeting with tufts of swamp grass. "I arrived too late to save you. You saved yourself."

"How did you escape the sheriff's men?"

"The same way you did, through the Medium. I awoke after they dumped me on the stallion, trussed up. I knew you were alone and afraid. I had to go back for you. The Medium gave me strength to burst my bonds. The strength I felt, Lia. I have never felt that before, like I could crush a stone in my hand. I slew the sheriff's men and rode back until I saw the blaze and nearly lost hope."

She smiled shyly at him. "Not you. You never lose hope."

"Almost," he said.

Lia folded her arms, trying to keep from shivering. "I know why the Medium saved us. I understood it last night. It delivered the sheriff into my hands for all the mastons he and his men have murdered. The Medium demanded vengeance for their blood."

"It does that. I have studied accounts of it before. It was not chance that it delivered them to you. Your family was probably killed by them. Remember what I taught you about the Medium, Lia. Your strength is not about who you are. Whoever your parents were, they were strong. I think they are dead. Have you asked the orb yet, to confirm it?"

"No," she said. "I had not thought of that. Should I?"

"I think you should."

"Where did I put the orb?" she asked, looking around the folds of the cloak.

"I put it back in your pouch while you slept. It still does not work for me." He shrugged and grimaced which made her smile.

She untied the strings and pulled it out. In the daylight, she could look at it without squinting. It rested in her palm, the intricate carvings a little ticklish against her skin.

If my father is living, show me the way to him, she thought. Writing appeared on the lower half of the orb. She knew the answer, even though she could not understand the writing. *My mother?* she thought, wondering if she should even hope. The reply was the same. The spindles did not move.

"I am not surprised," Colvin said, his expression thoughtful.

"Why?" Lia asked, disappointed. She had never known her parents, so she did not know whether to assume they were dead or not. She hugged her knees, staring at the writing that Maderos had said was Pry-rian.

His voice was soft, his expression consoling. "If they were alive, they would never have abandoned you. The night I gave you the Gifting, I felt it very strongly. When I touched your head, I sensed that your parents were nearby. I sensed their feelings for you. Through the Medium, even the dead are near. They loved you fiercely, Lia. You were not abandoned by them."

Tears stung her eyes, and she felt a sudden swell in her throat as she tried to swallow. "That is kind of you to say."

"And I have been unkind to you since I first awoke in the kitchen. It was a struggle learning to trust you. Worse, I have not slept soundly until last night. For the first time in a fortnight, I really slept and rested." He shook his head, chuckling, and stood.

Extending his hand to her, he helped her up as well. His hand was cold from the morning chill.

"Where is your hunter?" he asked, looking around. "I thought he would have found us before now."

Lia's stomach lurched, as if Colvin had kicked her.

***

With the orb's help, they found the body discarded in a gulch. It was in an unburned portion of the thicket, with three arrow shafts protruding from its chest. Lia knelt by it, staring in disbelief. It was too awful to be real. The stiff, pallid body was not Jon Hunter. No, he was full of life, energy, exuberance. Not this thing—this cracked shell. Then she cried, great wracking sobs. Colvin knelt next to her, his bloodied face sharing her grief. He put his arm around her.

She loved Jon Hunter. He was part of her earliest memories, especially those of Pasqua's kitchen. He was one of the Aldermaston's most trusted servants, trusted enough to be sent into the Bearden Muir to save them. It was not fair. It was not right. Her grief had a sharp edge to it, cutting deeply—so deeply.

She looked at Colvin in desperation. "You are a maston. Bring him back to life!"

Colvin was dumbstruck. "Lia, please."

She squeezed her hands together as hard as she could. "I know you can do it. It begins with a thought, just like you said. I know the Medium can bring him back." She frantically pulled the ring out of her dress. "I know it can happen. All those ossuaries were empty. They were empty, Colvin! The Medium can bring him back. He taught you the Gifting. Gift his life back. Please!"

He looked stricken. "Lia, the Medium is strong enough to revive the dead. I do not doubt that. It is written of in the tomes, but there is rarely an Aldermaston once in a century strong enough in the Medium to do it. Do you understand me? It requires an Aldermaston, I tell you. Not a maston. Not me."

"If you believed..."

He shook his head abruptly. "It is not that, Lia. If the Medium willed it, I could turn rivers into sand. I know I could. But right now, it whispers in my heart that I should not even attempt it. You cannot force the Medium."

Lia knew he was right, but that did not make the taste any less bitter. The Medium had its own will. She covered her mouth as another round of sobs forced their way to her lips. Jon Hunter was someone who had mattered in her life. She enjoyed teasing him, matching wits with him, trying to outsmart him. But he was gone. She already missed seeing his beard and hair, always so disheveled, and his clothes that were always mud-spattered and wrinkled. Perhaps it was fitting that he died in the middle of the Bearden Muir.

What would the Aldermaston say? She dreaded having to tell him that because of her, Jon was dead. How would he react? Would his temper burst into flames or would he be all coldness and regret? He had sent Jon to bring her back. Kneeling by the body, she fidgeted with the end of his leather belt. The Aldermaston would be furious, she decided. He might even banish her from the Abbey permanently.

She did not want to leave his body in the Bearden Muir, but they lacked the means to transport it. Instead, she chose to bring something of his back to Muirwood. He was a wretched too, yet she wanted others to remember him as she always would.

Reaching out, she began untying his belt.

"What are you doing?" Colvin asked.

"He died saving us," Lia said, freeing the buckle. "The Abbey needs a new hunter now. I want to bring back with me what I can carry. I want to bring back a part of who he was. We never waste things in the Abbey." Tears trickled down her cheeks. "The new hunter will need these things. I will never forget him. Never." She brushed her eyes.

"Nor will I."

Lia took the parts that made him a hunter in her eyes. She took the leather girdle and belt he always wore, the gladius and ash bow, a homemade leather quiver stuffed with arrows, and even the shooting glove and bracers that protected his arms from the bowstring. She garbed herself in his implements, for there was no other way to carry the items. It was strange, wearing the things that made him who he was. The gladius had a certain feel in her hand. The leather had a smell. On summer days he had let her and Sowe practice archery in the orchard, which resulted in huge purple bruises on their elbows. Tears stung her eyes again. It was too much to bear.

While she dressed, Colvin took his rucksack with the food and then gently removed the arrows sticking into the body and cast them aside. He arranged the body on higher ground and then knelt by it.

"Close your eyes," he told Lia.

"What are you going to do?"

Colvin sighed. "I am going to give him a maston's burial. You should not see the sign."

Lia approached and stood near him and shut her eyes. A part of her heart burned with pain, as if the thicket from the night before was still blazing inside her. There was so much about mastons and their customs she did not know. As a wretched, she never would. It was unfair, but such was the way of the world. She squeezed her eyes tightly shut, because part of her was just rebellious enough to be tempted to peek.

His voice was thick with emotion, but grew stronger. "By Idumea's hand, I do not know all the words. I am a young maston still. But I kneel and through the Medium dedicate this ground in the Bearden Muir as the final resting place of Jon Hunter. By the Medium I invoke this, that when the time of his reviving has come, at some future dawn, he may be restored, every whit. May we always remember this final spot that others may remember what he did for us. May they remember him through our words. Make it thus so."

"Make it so," Lia whispered. She opened her eyes and stared once again at the ashen face. Tenderly, she knelt and kissed his bearded cheek. Then they began fetching stones to cover him up.

***

One of my favorite passages is found in the Tome of Isius. I encourage all my learners to memorize it, for it holds secrets even I struggle to comprehend: "Let a maston be humble before the Medium, without guile, and he will receive of its fullness. He will receive power which shall manifest unto him the truth of all things, and shall give him, in the very hour, what he should say. And these signs shall follow him—he shall heal the sick, banish the Myriad Ones, and be delivered from those who administer deadly poison. He shall be led on paths where serpents cannot sting his heel. And he shall mount up in the imagination of his thoughts as upon eagles' wings. And if the Medium wills that he should raise the dead, let him not withhold his voice. But only if the Medium wills it."

—Cuthbert Renowden of Billerbeck Abbey

CHAPTER
TWENTY-NINE

Eve of Winterrowd

Winterrowd was an ill-looking fishing village surrounded by water on three sides, nestled within the convergence of two strong rivers that emptied into the sea. Lia had never seen the sea before. She had never imagined an expanse of water so vast and blue and never ending. The harbor was thronged with small vessels.

Haze filled the sky above Winterrowd, and Lia realized it was from a hundred cooking fires. Thousands of soldiers swarmed in the town.

"Is it over?" Colvin whispered in shock, turning the horse's head with a subtle jerk to the reins. "Are we too late?"

"No, I do not think so," Lia said, training her eye on the road south. From the vantage of the hilltop, they could see south to the town of Bridgewater. A long, coiled snake—the king's army—still marched on Winterrowd, though much of it was penned up outside. "The town is not burning. It must be Demont's camp in the field there."

Colvin whistled softly. "Yes, and that is the king's army still advancing. They have camped at the outskirts of the village. Look there—you can see the pickets. That is the vanguard of the king's army. Each army will break into thirds. One is the vanguard. They lead the battle. Then comes the main, and it is usually the largest. Then comes the rearguard, the reserve. The vanguard has already arrived. Sweet Idumea, they must have marched faster than the wind! Before midnight, the main and the rear will have arrived. There battle will happen on the morrow."

"So soon?"

"Yes, so soon." His expression twisted into its familiar scowl. "I had hoped to make it here earlier to warn Demont." He shook his head, his face flushed with emotions. "Look at the size of Demont's army. Maderos was right. A tithing…if that. A tenth." He swallowed.

Lia's stomach flittered with worry. "Do you remember what else he said?"

"His words are burned in my memory, Lia. He said I must first survive the slaughter at Winterrowd. He called it a slaughter. How can it be otherwise?"

Lia wanted to touch his arm to comfort him, but could not muster the courage. "He said you may survive, if your sister held a vigil for you. I think…Colvin, I think he was talking about me."

He nodded, his eyes staring blankly ahead. She could feel the fear bubbling inside of him. His face was pale. She could almost see the doubts churning in his mind as he focused on the scene.

"Look at me, Colvin."

He turned his head, his eyes bloodshot and watery. "I am too late," he whispered. "I came too late."

"You are afraid. I can feel it inside of you. Maderos said if I held vigil for you tonight, you may survive. He was right about

Almaguer. He was right about the road. He is right about this as well."

His eyes closed. "May survive. May is not very solid. I thought that we would have a chance. I thought if there was enough time, we could rally others. Or move to better ground. This was to be the starting point. Not the finish." His jaw clenched.

"What must I do?" Lia said, wanting to shake him. "How do I hold a vigil? It is going without sleep, I know that much."

"But what if he was talking about my sister, Marciana? She is finishing her first year at Billerbeck. What if my fate hangs on whether she holds a vigil tonight?"

It was ridiculous. She was having to teach *him* about the Medium. "There is no room for doubt, Colvin. Remember what you told me? Doubt is poison. You must fix your thoughts in your mind. Do not doubt. Believe and then act. Fear stops you from acting. The Medium brought us this far for a reason. You cannot stop here."

He turned away from her. His voice was so soft, she barely heard it. "What if that reason is to die?"

In her mind, she remembered the morning he was to depart from Muirwood. He had just promised her that he would help her learn to read. Even then, he had doubted whether he would survive the battle. Somehow, she had been given a glimpse of his soul and understood his fear. He feared that he would die in battle without anyone to tell his sister what had befallen him. Yet despite his fear, he had driven himself with determination to reach Winterrowd in time. Here they were—not in time to prevent the battle, but to participate in it. His worst fears were about to be realized.

"Colvin," she said.

He looked at her, his expression helpless.

"The Medium brought us together. It brought you to the kitchen because I could heal you. It brought you to the kitchen because it knew I could use the Cruciger orb. And it has brought us both here now, to Winterrowd, for a reason. I still have the orb." She touched his arm, he flinched, and she pulled away. "If you are among the dead tomorrow, I will find you. I will find your sister and tell her how bravely you fought and where you fell. If you are injured, then I will drag you away and tend you and heal you as I did in the kitchen. If you are well, then I will rejoice with you. Whatever happens, Colvin, know that I will watch over you. I know I am only a wretched, but I will not sleep until I see you again on the morrow."

His eyes filled with tears, but he clenched his jaw and held them back. When he had mastered himself, he said, "I do not need to teach you the vigil. You know it already. When you sacrifice for someone else, when you carry another's burden instead of your own, the Medium senses it keenly. It is more apt to help you when you help others. Thank you, Lia. You give me courage to face my fears. I will face them."

She smiled, touched by the depth of his gratitude. "I only remind you of what you already know." She looked down at the valley. "Let us go to Demont."

He shook his head. "It will be safer for you here in the woods. You can hide easily in these hills. How would I explain your presence in Demont's camp? What safety would you have? If our army falls, what would the king's men do to you? No, it is safer here than in the camp. I will rest easier tonight knowing you are sheltered."

She wanted to go with him, but he made sense. She twisted in the saddle to dismount, and he grabbed her hand to help her down.

From the ground, she looked up at him. His face was splotchy with bruises. The corner of his eyebrow was clotted with a scab, his lips cut in several places. The sun sank in the orange sky and only the twinkling winks of campfires prevailed on the fields below. She wanted to kiss him goodbye, but she knew he would flinch away from her again.

"I will find you tomorrow, Colvin."

He smiled at her, hooked one hand around the hilt of his maston sword, then tapped the stallion's flanks and started weaving through the trees and brush down the hill toward Demont's camp.

**

It was almost midnight and the reveling of the king's army continued boisterously. The last of the army arrived to a cheer and hurrah that split the night air and frightened the owls and bats. The laughs and clanking of arms rose in waves from the sea of tents and pavilions in the fields near Winterrowd. Demont's army, on the other hand, was subdued and silent. There were no fires that night, just a piece of earth blacker than the rest.

Lia sat at the base of a thick stunted oak, the ash bow across her lap, waiting and fighting her tiredness. The king's army made a ruckus on purpose, she knew. She recognized it for what it was. They celebrated victory before it happened to fling doubt at their enemies. To show their confidence that winning was foreordained. There were so few in Demont's camp. A thousand perhaps? Maybe less. She imagined that many were like Colvin—not even knights yet, though most would be mastons. A storm had raged around the Abbey the night Scarseth brought Colvin to the kitchen. How long ago it felt. A different world.

Another cheer went up amidst the king's army—another wave of triumph and laughter, and it almost disguised the noise of cracking twigs and branches. Lia sat up straight, her ears seeking the source of the sound. It came from behind her, the crunch and crackle of hooves and men. A sickening fear swept into her heart, like a cloud blotting out the moonlight. She recognized it instantly, the sick fear of the Myriad Ones. Some were snuffling near her, drawn by her thoughts.

For a moment, she nearly panicked. She was a blot in the dark, smothered by the tree's shadow. There was only a sliver of moon in the sky. She focused on memories of Muirwood and drew strength from them. She thought of the sturdy walls with their grim-faced Leerings, the smell of the kitchen before the first day of the Whitsun Fair, sneaking a taste of Gooseberry Fool when Pasqua wasn't looking, and a compliment from the Aldermaston.

With those thoughts and the pleasant feelings they coaxed, it was as if her mind opened and she could see things as they really were. The hillside and valley were choked with Myriad Ones as they skulked with the soldiers, prodding them on with their thoughts. The entire meadow was thick with them as they encircled Demont's camp, grinning, anxious for the smell of blood that would shower the ground at dawn. Her imagination reeled at the enormity of the scene. There were so many! The smoke shapes thronged in waves, thousands upon thousands. Millions. Everywhere she looked, she saw them. They were in every blade of grass, in every fallen acorn. Even worse, she could feel them and their thoughts, drunk with the lust for blood and vengeance. They were ready to gorge themselves on the emotions of the battle slaughter.

Lia turned back and looked up the hill, doing her best to stay hidden. Even though it was dark, she could see black riders. Each wore a cloak to hide the glint of their hauberks and breastplates. Each carried a sword, a knight-maston sword, but she could feel the wrongness of it. These were no mastons. They were imposters. The insight came swiftly, like a gulp of air. The king was sending them around to the rear. They would pretend to join Demont's forces, but turn traitor in the end. The knoll was thick with soldiers and their horses as they lumbered past her solitary hiding place. They moved silently, as silently as they could. Another cheer from the camp rose, and again she realized the purpose. It was to hide the approach of the traitor-knights and to divert Demont's attention to the battle in front of him, not the battle behind.

Lia knew she had to warn them. But how?

Gripping the bow, she started down the hillside, moving as quietly as she could. In the dark, it was difficult to see her footing, and she snapped twigs and brush in her clumsiness.

"Hold. Something is moving down there," came a whisper from behind. "Morris and Severn, see what it is. Might be a scout. Take your crossbows."

Lia's mind blazed with worry. She plunged ahead farther, trying only to touch on the grass, but every other step rang out in her ears. The soldiers dismounted and started down the hillside after her.

"I hear it too. Sounds light—like a doe."

Lia stopped, her heart pounding in her chest. She could not see them in the dark, but she could hear their boots.

"It stopped. Come on then. Go that way, I'll go this way."

Lia started again, glanced backward once, and then nearly walked into a tree. Catching herself, she went around it to hide, but there was no ground on the other side. The hillside gave way to open space and she gasped as she fell into the blackness.

Pain shot up her leg from her ankle as she landed abruptly then fell face first. Fiery darts of agony streaked up her calf, and her whole foot throbbed. She clamped her mouth to keep from screaming. She could hardly breathe through the pain.

"Did you hear that? Over there!"

Part of the hillside had been gouged away. Dirt pattered down like rain. She looked up. The once majestic tree she had nearly stumbled into had been split by lightning and part of it lay shattered around her, exposing some of the roots. The trunk was hollowed out. Rain over the years had washed away part of it, forming a little inlet, a little cave. She had landed in a patch of brush growing at the base, revealing the little opening. There was no way she could crawl to the camp. She needed a place to hide, and there it was. Lia dragged herself and the bow into the inlet, hearing the sounds of the king's men above.

"Which way? Do you hear it?" Their voices were right above her. She hunkered deep into the shell of the tree, shrinking as small as she could.

"I do not. It sounded like it crashed this way. You think it was a deer?"

Another crackle from the woods came farther down the hill. "There it is. Do you see it? A buck, not a doe. Come on."

Lia breathed heavily, feeling the pain in her ankle sharpen as she crouched. She bit her lip, wondering how she was going to get to the camp to warn Colvin.

The Medium.

She remembered something Colvin had taught her. He'd told her that there were people strong enough in the Medium to share thoughts, no matter how distant. Writhing in pain, she tried to focus her thoughts and to push them through to wherever he was. She pictured his face in her mind, remembering the look

257

of tenderness he gave her. A surge of warmth brought a blush to her cheeks.

Colvin?

She could still feel the sensation of his fingers, his strong hand, as he helped her down from the saddle. She remembered how she had wanted to kiss him goodbye.

Lia?

It was less than a whisper. She was not certain she had even heard it, but she went ahead.

Warn Demont. The king sends traitors behind you in the dark.

Lia?

Warn him, Colvin! Beware!

She felt herself tugged away, snatched by a strong, invisible hand as if it grasped the back of her neck. It was not a soldier. It was not physical. But it felt as real as if it were. The jolt came from inside her. A guttural voice whispered in her mind—strong, angry, full of hate.

Who are you?

The thought was loud and crushed against her mind. She was choking. She could not breathe or speak, even if she wanted to. The Myriad Ones swarmed around her in the hidden knoll, with breathless mewling. Who was this creature hiding in the dark, in their dark? The thoughts were bold, hateful. The voice in her mind gripped her like she was an insect—something he could destroy. She realized who it was, recognized the presence without understanding how. It was a memory she did not own, one she only borrowed.

It was the king.

CHAPTER THIRTY

The Battle of Winterrowd

The mind of the king was like a festering sore, a wound that would never heal. It tainted everything brushing near it, and it expanded like darkness and shadows. Though the sky was clear of clouds, it was as if a storm raged in the valley below, harsh with thunder, hail, and wind. Instead of pelting raindrops, the storm was a vision of what would happen the next morning. In her mind, Lia could see the dead littering the fields, each wearing the colors of Demont and the stain of blood. In horror, she watched soldiers hacking those already dead, fixing heads on spears to warn others of the fate of those who defy the king. Lia cowered from the strength of the thoughts.

The battle of Winterrowd would not be a battle—it would be more akin to butchery than any noble contest. The king would not send the soldiers in three battle lines as Colvin said. No, they would attack from all sides at once, engulfing the smaller army like a flood. No matter which way Demont's men faced, they would be exposed. After they were all slain, she watched with despair as the butcher soldiers turned into thieves, stripping the dead of their chaen shirts and tomes and melting them into coins, goblets, or spoons. Colvin would be among the dead. In vain, her eyes searched for him among the indistinguishable corpses. She saw a reaping of corpses.

No!

The violence of her emotions surprised her, especially at how vividly she yearned that Colvin would not die. No, it was stronger than a yearning. She demanded it. She insisted on it. Whatever else would happen on the morrow, no matter how the king's army engulfed them, Colvin would not die. With all the willpower she could summon, she fixed her mind on that thought. Colvin would live. A choking grip strengthened against her. She was going to die. The king's thoughts were going to kill her.

Who are you!

She quailed again, panicking, knowing that she only had moments left to live. Myriad Ones smothered her. She could not speak. She could not breathe. In that moment of nearly pure panic and fear, she clenched her fists, bowed her head, and let loose another thought as if screaming it.

Be gone from me!

The Medium awoke within her, responding to her feelings with a surge of heat. It flooded her heart and flooded her mind, strengthening her. As if the king were a man kept in dark rooms whose eyes could not bear even a candle flame, his will flinched from the fierceness of hers. She could breathe again and gasped for air, more angry than fearful. The thing gripping her mind loosened.

Just as had happened with the Aldermaston and Colvin, she could discern the king's thoughts for what they really were. What she found squirming inside his mind shocked her. He was afraid. He was afraid of Garen Demont, and he feared being weak like his father. In every war he had fought, in every battlefield he had championed, a dark twisted fear had been there, a blight in his soul. He feared anyone who used the Medium for it would not hearken to him. It would not obey him. Only through a chain and a charm around his neck was he able to light the tiniest of candles or summon the gushing waters from a *gargouelle*. But even the chain and medallion frightened him, for he had used them too freely, and now the Myriad Ones controlled him, as they had Almaguer. The medallions had made both men into puppets.

Lia raised her head and looked into the sky, into the milky gauze of stars. She opened herself up to the Medium again. She had sacrificed sleep, but somehow she knew that alone was not enough to save Colvin. To barter for a man's life required more.

I am only a wretched, she thought, speaking softly in her mind to the Medium. *What must I give to achieve what I desire? Colvin is a man of proper Family. He has a sister who loves him and wishes his good health. If justice cannot be satisfied without blood, would my life be enough instead? If one of us must die, can it be me?*

She waited, listening to the stillness, thrusting her petition into the stars. As if to answer her, she felt as if she grew into the size of a giant, and the king shrank to the size of an ant. She saw him clearly in the camp below. He sat in a stuffed chair in his pavilion, staring blankly into a rack of torches, clutching a goblet of cider, his hand trembling so much, the amber pool sloshed.

Who are you? his thoughts pleaded. *I know you. I recognize you. Are you a memory or a shade?*

His thoughts were gibbering with fear. She realized that he did not know whether she was real or a phantom. His thoughts were so consumed with his own jealousies and needs that he could not see beyond himself, let alone see her hiding place. He could sense her thoughts and hear them almost, but not coherently. Her strength with the Medium, how she had used it to pluck his grip away from her mind, terrified him.

Who are you, girl?

Another thought came to her, so small and still that she hardly heard it at all. Yes, a life would be required to spare Colvin's. The weight of the thought and the full rush of the Medium crashed down on her like a mountain. She collapsed.

***

The earth shook. Lia opened her eyes, realizing it was day. She lay against the inner wall of the burned-out tree, her cheek itching with the sooty roughness of the wood. Her ankle throbbed as she moved. A drumming sound filled the air, and she heard the charge of horses and jangle of arms. The hooves caused a murmur like thunder. Lia straightened, her eyes filling with tears. She had fallen asleep! The vigil was not complete!

She stood awkwardly, her legs trembling. Her ankle was sore, but it supported her. How had it happened? How had she fallen asleep? Her mind was scattered with fragments, her memories all tangled and jostled together. Emerging from the shell of the tree, she stared at the fields near Winterrowd and watched as three walls of mounted knights surged across the clods of earth and grass at the tiny army led by Garen Demont. There were at least five rows of black-clad knights in each wall, lances stark against the dawn sun, charging against Demont's men from every corner. Every one of Demont's men were dismounted. She saw their horses tethered beyond their reach.

No! she wanted to scream. The knights charged, closing the gap, as Demont's men waited for them to come. They were arranged in four lines, a square, each man facing outward, shoulder to shoulder with their swords drawn. The gap in the middle showed no reserves. Thunder churned the air, the thunder of war-horses. Lia bit her lip, looking helplessly at the slaughter about to happen. It would be a slaughter just as Maderos had predicted.

Let him live, she thought silently. *Please, let him live! I am not too late!*

Thinking was not enough. She needed to act, to *do* something to aid him. The flutter and color of a dozen battle flags caught her eye, nearer to her than the charging knights. The flags were large and sweeping, fixed on poles and fluttering in the air like huge, forked tongues to rally the king's soldiers. They were held by mounted soldiers on a solitary hill near the wooded glen where she was hidden.

It was near enough that she could see the slope of their helms, the detail on their armor, and hear the nickering of impatient steeds. One battle flag in particular caught her eye. It was red and gold, tattered, and charred black in places. A fleeting memory darted through her thoughts like watery silver, a memory of something she had heard back at Muirwood. She recalled that the king taunted his enemies by flashing the banners of his defeated foes, a deliberate design to crush the will of his enemies, to weaken their resolve to fight, and to seed their minds with doubt.

What was it about the broken red flag that seemed so familiar? Suspended from a long pole mounted on a giant spear, it hung vertically, split into two halves partway across and pointed. A symbol was in the center of the flag—a circle with two slash marks through it. At each point above, below, and to the sides, words had been sewn with gold thread against the red. Not just any words. The script was strange and elliptical and hauntingly familiar.

Reaching into her pouch, Lia withdrew the Cruciger orb and the thought struck her. The text on the flag was Pry-rian. The orb spoke to her in Pry-rian. It was the battle flag of the kingdom of Pry-Ree that caught her eye.

Emotions she did not understand engulfed her. She cried and choked at the same time, not certain which she should be doing but not able to help either. The advancing horses were closing the gap quickly, building speed. Lances glittered in the dawn. There it was, in all its blaze and glory—the battle flag of Pry-Ree. *Her* flag. The flag of her forefathers—her Family. The feelings were so strong, she could hardly breathe.

He is delivered into your hands.

Part of her mind opened again, just as it had in the Bearden Muir. Just as Almaguer and his men had been delivered into her hands, she realized that the king's army was delivered up as well. Their arrival at Winterrowd was neither too soon nor too late. No, the Medium had allowed them to arrive deliberately. From down in the field, she could sense Demont's thoughts, firm and resolute. He did not doubt. He did not fear. He led a small company of raw, young mastons with courage and belief, knowing that the Medium would save them, and he had prepared his lines to defend against the rush of knights on every side. Even as death approached on churning hooves, Demont believed he could win, and he chose action. The Medium had brought her to save them.

He is delivered into your hands.

If the king's thoughts fed his army, if his will was imposed on them, then what would happen should he fall? Lia looked down at the orb in her hand. *Where is the king?*

The orb began to whir until the spindles pointed away from the charging horsemen to the small hill and the tight ring of soldiers holding the battle flags. The one in the center wore a crown over his helmet, but he was not the king. He was a decoy. She knew that in her bones.

He is delivered into your hands.

Then she understood and gasped. The king held aloft the pole with the Pry-rian flag. *Her* flag. He could not have known that the one he had chosen was part of her ancestry. She had barely realized it herself days ago. It amazed her. If the king fell, it would change everything. It would alter the future of the kingdom, perhaps even ending the maston killings. The Medium demanded action from her or Demont's army would fail. She knew what to do.

Reaching down, she grabbed the ash bow that belonged to Jon Hunter. Confidence surged in her veins. She retrieved a single arrow from the quiver. She remembered all the steps that Jon taught her. She remembered how to hold it firmly, how to load it so that the odd-colored feather was on top. Gripping the taut bowstring with the tips of her fingers, she pulled and drew it back to the corner of her mouth. There was no aiming, not at that distance. She had never launched an arrow that far before or hit anything so distant with accuracy. Yet confidence whispered in her mind that the Medium would not let her miss. She never doubted it.

The charging horsemen were almost on Demont's men. A murmuring groan rose up from the field. A collective gasp sounded before the clash.

He is delivered into your hands or Demont's army will fall.

The bowstring twanged and the arrow flew. Suddenly the king jerked straight, the arrow catching him in a chink of armor in his neck, and he toppled off the horse. The battle flag of Pry-Ree dropped from the dead man's fingers, its end stabbing into the hilltop and the wind caught the banner and unfurled it. The power of the Medium surged from Lia into the battle flag, and then spilled throughout the field below, gushing from her like a Leering stone, spreading a web of safety with the breeze.

Spears appeared amidst Demont's soldiers. As the ends were jammed into the ground, the sharp heads lifted, greeting the horsemen with a row of teeth. The stampede of hooves could not stop in time. A razor edge of spear tips awaited them—it was a crush of men and beasts and steel. Had the spears been there all along, hidden in the grass?

She watched the horses crunch against the teeth of steel until she could no longer bear the sight of it, or endure the flood of power that was burning her alive. The weight of the Medium crushed her again and she blacked out.

***

It is the mind that makes the body rich. As the sun breaks through the darkest clouds, so does honor peer in the meanest habit. A maston is as unhappy or as happy as he has convinced himself he is.

—Cuthbert Renowden of Billerbeck Abbey

CHAPTER THIRTY-ONE

The Fallen

Lia awoke to the prodding of a staff into the small of her back. "Wake up. Wake up, sister. It is over, and I am finished scriving. You missed the rest. Can you hear me? Eh? Wake up!"

It was Maderos. Lia sat up slowly, her head a fog of thoughts. Drained—she was completely empty inside. Opening her eyes, she looked over at him, seated on the ground near her on the hillside next to the battlefield. Maderos brushed the crinkled shavings of aurichalcum from the tome on his lap. He looked down at the words again, running his fingers over the etchings, as if savoring some delicious dish. When he saw he had her attention, he spoke softly, clearly.

"The battle of Winterrowd did not last past the morning, and then it was over. The field next to the village was littered with the slaughter. Many from the defeated army of the king escaped into the Bearden Muir, rather than be captured or ransomed, but many were devoured by the moors instead of men. In tales to come, many will ascribe the glory of victory to Garen Demont and to the peculiar arrangement of his soldiers and tactics. How they shied horses and used rings of spears to protect each other. Others will say it was because Demont only allowed mastons to serve him and that they were worthy to call upon the Medium to deliver them from the king's wrath. These are near to the truth. The husk but not the kernel. The battle of Winterrowd was won by a wretched from Muirwood Abbey. None of the witnesses of the battle knew about her or what she did that day, how she used the Medium to defy the army of a king. No one but I alone and those who read this record will know. The world may never know the secret. But I, Maderos, know the secret just as I know the wretched. I will not reveal her name."

Then he closed the tome and set it back in the sheepskin with the scriving tools, folded the sheepskin, and lifted the heavy tome back into his pack. Lia watched, a little jealous still of his ability to read. She wanted to read the other things he had written. She eyed the tome with hunger and then the thought slammed against her like a blacksmith's hammer.

"How many of Demont's men fell in the battle?" she asked him.

"How many *pethets*? Perhaps they all deserved to die. But you will learn soon enough, little sister." He slowly stood, resting his arms on the twisted staff he had poked her with.

"The king's army—it was defeated then?"

Maderos nodded, then waved his staff at the field. "It was a slaughter, just as I told you. Do not suppose that Demont's men did not suffer for their victory. There is not a man among them who is not injured, bleeding, or weary. Each fought bravely. But they do not know why they won." His eyes narrowed pointedly. "They would not believe you, even if you told them."

"You sound like the Aldermaston," Lia said grudgingly.

He smirked. "Perhaps that is so. Perhaps I have lingered near Muirwood too long now. I knew when I saw you, sister. The Medium made it clear to me that you would help overthrow the kingdom. It is in your blood, I think. Go find the *pethet*, child. Go down amidst the corpses."

"Is he dead?" She didn't want Maderos to leave her alone. Her stomach had turned into ice. She wanted him to stay and answer questions, to calm her sudden panic. But she recognized he would never reveal more than he should.

"Use the orb. He is down there. Then you must return to Muirwood. The Aldermaston expects you. There, I have said it. The Aldermaston expects you. That should be enough."

Lia rose, sick with worry, and brushed dirt from her skirt, though it was still filthy. She saw soldiers wandering through the mist and fields below. It was littered with the dead.

***

Find Colvin.

Lia focused on the orb and her thoughts of him and not on the carnage of the battlefield or her throbbing ankle. She tried calming her raging heart and brushed unwilling tears from her eyes. Wagons from the village lumbered amidst the scene, and bodies were stacked and brought to the center of the field. It was strange seeing little children milling about, gazing at the corpses, unafraid. The morning haze burned away slowly, leaving wisps of smoke and fog about the hinterlands.

The smell in the air—there was no way to describe the smell of death. She had been raised in an abbey kitchen and knew her work by the way things smelled. She knew the smell of loaves that had finished baking and the smell of cinders and ash as she swept

270

out the fireplaces. She knew of fragrant spices and pungent aromas mixed, matched, baked, and burned. The stench of the field was overpowering. She gagged, even after she covered her mouth with her hand.

The spindle on the orb led her into the thickest part of the battlefield. New writing appeared on it. Lia stopped and looked ahead, searching the faces of the dead men, and then saw Colvin approaching through the haze. He walked ponderously, as if he dragged a weight of stones behind him. His face was black with smoke and scabs, his tunic a mess of stains, but his smile when he saw her was radiant. It was the sunrise after an endless night. As he drew near, she saw his gleaming collar and a jeweled necklace dangling from his neck and thumping against the mail of his hauberk.

After tugging off his bloodstained gloves, he stuffed them into his belt. His fingers were caked with dirt. But his smile—it was thrilling to see. She wanted to touch him, to know he was real, but shyness forbade her. Relief engulfed her, and she bit her tongue to keep from sobbing.

"Have you heard the news, Lia?" he asked her, his smile beaming.

"What is it?" she said, thrilled to see him alive. Her heart felt like bursting.

He shook his head, as if it were too delicious to speak. "The old king is dead. His son, the heir, was captured on the field. They are already calling him the young king. He is in Demont's tent right now. I just came from there myself. Demont is declared Lord Protector of the realm." One of his hands strayed up, fondling the collar and its jeweled symbol. "Lia, I was just made a knight-maston. Just now, by the young king's hand. I'm now a knight-maston of the order of Winterrowd. The earldom of my

father will be granted in a ceremony soon. Lia, I never believed…
I never hoped…it feels like a dream. That I will awaken and it
will be dawn and the battle will not have happened yet. Is it…is
it real?"

She wanted him to throw his arms around her and hug her,
but he did not. She smiled to hide her pang of disappointment.
"Must I now call you Sir Colvin? And curtsy when I see you?"

His smile did not dim. "No, Lia. Never. The Medium spared
my life because of you. My doubt would have killed me. They
should have killed me. But whenever I feared, I thought on you."
He looked around, as if realizing they were standing in the middle
of death itself. "Come, this is no place for you. Walk with me to
my tent and hide that orb. Come, take my arm. Cover your head
with the cowl and try not to look. It is a grisly scene."

He led her back through the failing mists, talking briskly as
he marched. "I felt your warning last night about the imposters
coming around the rear. I warned Demont that I had a feeling we
would be ambushed from behind. It was a stroke of good favor
at that dark hour. When the riders appeared, there were only a
few and they came claiming to join our force. I think they were
there to stab Demont. One offered to show him his hand, which
is a ritual mastons do to prove one another, but Demont asked to
see his chaen shirt instead. The man balked, for he was wearing a
medallion and his skin was tainted by its brand. When they saw
they could not deceive us, they tried to fight their way clear, but
we easily mastered them and learned of others in the woods and
captured them as well."

Colvin led her through the muddy field and toward the can-
opy of pavilions she had watched the night before. They were the
king's pavilions, with pennants and poles and the battle flags of
fallen foes assembled together.

"Demont knew our trouble, that if we were attacked on all sides while facing the king's army, we would be overrun. In that hour, he remembered a tactic he had learned from his father. A tactic he had discussed at the battle of Maseve, but did not feel confident enough to try. Demont believed that his father had failed that day because he did not trust the inspiration from the Medium. The tactic is called a shiltron square—you use pikes and spears in a tight box. That way, you can repel the attack from any side. It is brilliant but requires great courage. Standing fast when knights are charging you with lances is not easy. It helped us to offset their numbers and withstand their first charge without breaking."

He guided her around the twisted remains of a soldier with a death grimace. "The Medium wanted us to prevail. That became clear during the fight. Lia—none of them could touch me. I felt the Medium coursing through me like fire. It gave me strength to do things I had never dreamed of. It protected me from harm."

It protected all of you, Lia thought. She wanted to tell him what Maderos had told her. But his words of warning kept her silent.

They reached the curtain of pavilions, and Colvin led her to one of the smaller ones, a rich blue color with gray trappings, richly furnished inside with rugs, a table, candles, and a pallet to sleep on, cloaked with fur-lined blankets. The smell of tallow overwhelmed the stench of the field beyond.

"You must be tired, Lia. There, rest on my pallet. There is food on the table and drink. I will send a horseman to Muirwood to tell the Aldermaston you are safe. If he will not take you back, then I will make sure you are cared for, even if I must take you on in my own household." He stood by the opening, staring at her pointedly. "And you will read, Lia, even if I must teach you myself. Get some rest. There is much to be done today."

"Send a horseman to Billerbeck Abbey as well," Lia told him. "Tell your sister you are safe as well. Tell her what you could not tell her before."

His eager smile lost none of its radiance. "I will. And I will tell her about you."

***

When Lia awoke on the warm and comfortable pallet, she found she was being watched by a young man she had never met. His eyes blinked as did hers, and she sat up in alarm.

"Do not be frightened," he said, rising quickly from the chest he sat on. He held up his hands in a placating gesture and backed away. "Your name is Lia. I know of you from Colvin. He asked me to watch over you, to see that none disturbed your rest."

She rubbed her eyes, feeling awkward and embarrassed, for his was a handsome face. Younger than Colvin but older than her. Probably sixteen or seventeen. His hair was long and fair, the color of straw. It was unfashionable, but he was still handsome. His features were slender.

"How long have you been watching me?" she asked, aware of the filthy dress she wore. Part of the sleeve was ripped, and she wore a man's bracers and girdle. "Who are you?"

His eyes widened. "I have embarrassed you. Forgive me. I have had sufficient time to mop the blood from my face while you kept vigil all night. I should have remembered that my sisters are keenly aware of their appearance, yet I thought nothing of it. Again, forgive me. My name is Edmon. My older brother was the Earl of Norris-York."

He stepped closer, looking into her eyes pleadingly while fidgeting with his hands. "I am now to hold that estate, humble as it is." His expression became pained. "Let me explain. My brother was sent to bring Colvin Price to Winterrowd. Our domains border each other. My brother was to find him near Muirwood and bring him here. I have since learned that it was you who led Colvin here because my brother was murdered by the sheriff of Mendenhall. You are the one who found where his body lay in a garden near Muirwood."

He looked down for a moment. "I am indebted to you. Because of you, Colvin brought me our father's sword and chaen shirt. He also brought my brother's bloodstained tunic. I am not yet a maston, but I will be within the year, if the Medium wills it." He stopped, turned red in the face, then bowed his head. "I wanted to thank you in person, Lia of Muirwood. My gratitude may be small compared to Colvin's, but I feel it most keenly. You made it possible for me to fight this day and win my collar. I will always be grateful to you and count you as a friend."

Lia had no idea what to say, she was so dismayed by his gratitude. She had not suspected the maston sent to fetch Colvin would be another earl of the realm. "I am grateful to meet you, Edmon," she said, and it felt hollow. She felt filthy, unworthy of the look of kindness on his face.

He stood quickly then went to the tent flap. "I will tell Colvin you have awoken." He parted the curtain and looked outside. "That is Demont. By Idumea, what is happening?" he said, almost to himself.

Lia pulled away the blankets and joined him at the entryway. She heard the voice before she saw the speaker. The voice was loud and strong and throbbed with emotion. Outside the pavilion, a hundred men clustered around a wagon. The speaker, an aging knight-maston, stood atop. His face was spattered with blood and grime, so much so that she could hardly make out any features except his dark hair, wavy and matted with sweat. A helmet was nestled in the crook of his arm, and his maston sword hung from a scabbard at his side. His voice was hoarse and raspy, and it reminded her of the Aldermaston.

"I am told by the king's herald that many fell on the fields of Winterrowd this day. The numbering is now done. Bodies are being laid to rest in mother earth. In number, over eight thousand were killed from the king's army." A gasp and sigh went through the camp. "All the day long I have been plagued with questions. How many of our brothers have fallen? Do I know what happened to a lad carried away from the field in blood? How many who stood beneath our banner fell this day? I know that Trowbridge and Holland are still with the surgeons. Many of you sustained grave wounds today. But here it is, nearly dusk." He looked up at the red-rimmed sky and swallowed his surging emotions. "By Idumea's grace alone, there are none of ours fallen this day. Not one. I am…I am astonished beyond measure."

Another rush of sentiment began to churn, but Demont held his hand high into the air. Lia saw the gray flecks in his hair above his ears and watched as the crowd fell silent. His lip trembled. "It is through the will of the Medium that we owe our victory. Let no man who was here this day declare otherwise. My brothers…the day is ours."

Lia saw the tears tremble on his lashes, and she knew what he was thinking. His thoughts were choked with visions of Maseve and the battle his own father lost.

CHAPTER THIRTY-TWO

Muirwood Abbey

Before midnight, two days later, they arrived at Muirwood on horseback. Lia had fallen asleep in the saddle again, her face pressed against Colvin's back, while the village around Muirwood showed no signs of life. The gates of the Abbey were closed. A few lamps flickered beyond soot-stained windows in the small huddle of buildings on High Street. The leaves from robust oaks sighed with the breezes.

Colvin approached the gate on horseback, and a porter was waiting there with a lantern. "The gates do not open until morning, my lord," he said blearily.

"Tell the Aldermaston that..."

"He knows you are coming, Lord Price. I was to wait up for you. The Aldermaston left rooms for you at the Pilgrim Inn. Over yonder. Be ready then, in the morning, to present yourselves. You will be summoned when the gates open."

"Thank you," Colvin replied and tugged the reins to turn the stallion around. Edmon and several other horsemen followed him to the inn.

"It did not take long to reach here," Edmon said thoughtfully, then yawned. "Are you still going to hold a vigil for her?"

He stared at the inn, remembering vividly the last time he had come and who had rescued him. For a moment, he was prisoner to those memories. Wordlessly, he nodded.

"I will join you then. For her sake. She deserves the best room." Edmon dismounted and helped steady her as Colvin slid off the stallion and then carried her up the stairs himself.

***

Lia awoke on the softest stuffed mattress, beneath the cleanest sheets, and resting amidst the plumpest pillows in the entire village. Warmth shimmered from the brazier. Lifting her head, she looked around and slowly recognized the room. There was the table where, days before, the sheriff's men had eaten the feast and fallen asleep while she rescued Colvin. The noise that had awakened her was the door as it butted open, and in came a girl she recognized from that adventure, Bryn, carrying a long brown dress and fresh girdle. In the other hand, she carried a tray of bread and some white cheese.

"I am sent to help you," Bryn said cheerily. "The Aldermaston's steward just arrived from the tunnels. He is to take you back now, but we must clean you up first."

Lia swung her legs over the side of the bed, squeezing the sheets and mattress, savoring their softness. "Am I alone? I do not even remember arriving last night."

"Were you expecting mastons to sleep here with you all alone?" She set the tray on the table and crossed to the window, opening the shutters to peek outside. "Most slept in rooms down the hall. Two guard your door even now. The Earl of Forshee, he stayed awake all night in the common room. So did the Earl of Norris-York. We asked them if they were weary, and they said they were not. They are waiting in the kitchen for you now with Prestwich. Do you remember me? Can you not tell me your name still?"

Lia nodded. "Mine is Lia. I have not forgotten you, Bryn. Or what your family did for me."

"Well, neither did the Earl of Forshee," she said smugly. "He rewarded us amply. Come over. I will brush your hair. It is a nest of snags. I can help you wash."

Lia stopped by the window and looked out. Dawn touched the sky with pink, and she could barely see the outline of the Abbey against a sea of purple sky. Her heart was thrilled. Bryn dragged a stool by the brazier, and Lia went to enjoy the warmth.

There was a mirror nearby and what she saw in it revolted her. Turning away, she ate the warm bread while Bryn brushed the many tangles out of her hair, then gathered the mass into a thick bunch and brushed it even more vigorously. Lia's garment was fit to be burned, and she was grateful that Bryn had brought one of her own dresses to wear. It was a little short and snug, but it fit her. She tied the pouch with the Cruciger orb to the girdle. Bryn lifted her hair and scrubbed her neck and ears with a towel and water from the basin near the brazier. Lia washed her face and hands. The water was warm and reminded her of the Leering stone in the Bearden Muir, when Colvin had helped her bathe. She paused at the memory, her heart fluttering. She was anxious to see him. And nervous. He had let her have the soft bed and had forsaken sleep. The thought made her glow inside.

When they were through, Lia returned to the mirror. She looked at herself closely. Her skin was darker than she thought it would be from her days in the sun. There were little cuts and scrapes all over her face and arms, with an especially dark scab on the end of her chin from her fall on the hillside at Winterrowd. In the reflection, she saw the twine string around her neck and delicately withdrew the wedding band she had worn so long. She tucked it back in quickly when Bryn approached.

"What should I do with these?" she asked, carrying over the leather girdle, the gladius, the bracers, and the unstrung bow and quiver. Jon Hunter's face flickered in her eyes at seeing the implements, and it made her heart throb with agony. Yes, she had returned safely to Muirwood, but he was dead in the Bearden Muir. For a moment, she could not speak, her voice too thick with emotion, too fragile to risk with words. She nearly wept, but forced herself not to.

"They must be returned to the Abbey," Lia said softly at last. "I will take them with me. Thank you."

Lia was anxious and wary about seeing the Abbey again in the daylight. There was also sadness in her heart at the thought of leaving Colvin and Edmon, two soon-to-be earls who treated her as an equal. Clutching the implements she had rescued from Jon's grave, she followed Bryn out of the room, glancing back at the bed one last time.

The soldiers guarding her room wore Demont's colors, and they nodded to her respectfully as she passed them. Down the stairs they went, and images of Colvin's fight sent pangs into her heart. She remembered Scarseth quivering on the floor as Colvin took his birthright back, the knight-maston sword that had belonged to his father.

"The Earl of Norris-York is handsome," Bryn said. "He smiled at me when I gave him his breakfast. He is very handsome, is he not?"

"He is," Lia said, but in her mind he was too pretty and too amiable. In her estimation, Colvin was the more striking of the two.

Bryn opened the door into the kitchen, and both Colvin and Edmon stood as she entered. Prestwich the steward was there as well, enjoying a heel of bread dripping with honey. Gingerly, he rose to greet her and finished his bite. He was bald, except for some feathery hair along the crown. He was a short fellow, very deliberate, and used ponderous words.

"Welcome home to Muirwood, Lia," he said warmly. His warmth was genuine. He motioned for Bryn to shut the door, and she did. The family gathered near. She recognized each of them, and her heart bubbled at seeing familiar faces again.

Prestwich gazed down at the floor, clasped his hands behind his back, and then fixed the two knights with a sharp look. "The Aldermaston's instructions are clear in this matter. Lord Colvin and Lord Edmon, he will meet you both this morning after the gates open. You may bring your retinue and enjoy the hospitality of the Abbey. But the hospitality for you and your men will not extend beyond nightfall. This was only a leg of your journey. To dwell longer will raise suspicions as to why you truly came."

He looked at them both pointedly, his jowls stern. "The Aldermaston will give you more instructions later. Again, you are his welcome guests today only. You must make your way to your next destination before sunset. Lia, you will come with me through the tunnel so as not to be seen entering with them."

For a moment, she hesitated. Colvin stared at her, and she could not understand the look in his eyes. His jaw was clenched, but not as if he was mastering his temper. The mud on his face had been wiped clean, his face shaved and smooth, but the scars of the last few days were still evident. He looked as if he wanted to speak with her alone, but dared not demand it in front of everyone, least of all the Aldermaston's steward.

"Come," Prestwich said, waving her to him.

She started after Prestwich, approaching the ladder that led into the cellar with Jon's gear in her arms.

"Lia."

It was Colvin's voice. She turned back and looked at him wonderingly as he drew near. His eyes were deep and penetrating. "I will not forget what you did for me, sister. Nor my promise to you." He leaned closer and kissed her cheek lightly, just a quick brush of his lips, but it sent a tingle down to her toes. But before he withdrew, he whispered in her ear, "Whitsunday."

At the implied request, she smiled at him, a smile that said many words she would not say in front of so many people. The Whitsunday festival was coming, her first year to dance around the maypole. She nodded once, then followed Prestwich down the ladder, her heart afire with emotions. She was filled with the thrill of being back home and the lingering warmth of his kiss on her cheek. What would Reome think—and all the other lavenders for that matter—on the day when a wretched danced with an earl? The thought of it was sweeter than treacle. She smiled at Colvin again before descending the ladder. He smiled back, pleased, and watched her disappear into the tunnels beneath the Abbey grounds.

***

Prestwich ambled in silence during their journey through the secret tunnels. They did not enter through the Abbey itself, but took a separate passageway that led into the manor. A Leering blocked the way, and Prestwich mumbled a word to it, which she could not hear. He turned back and looked at her. His voice was low and serious.

"The Aldermaston will never ask you to lie," he said. "For your own good, however, he desires that others in the Abbey believe that you never went to Winterrowd. Your companion, Sowe, has been in hiding since you left. Neither she nor you have been seen since the day you ran away. Whatever you speak of together, for I know you share certain secrets, we cannot prevent. But you must be guarded in whom you trust with that knowledge. Is that clear, child? The less others know, the better."

"I will obey the Aldermaston's wishes," Lia said.

"I hope so," he answered. "That has not always been easy for you." Prestwich turned to the open Leering. Beyond was another cellar and a circle of light shone, coming from the chamber above. Even from the distance to the ladder, Lia could hear Pasqua muttering under her breath.

"Fits and stones, she should be here by now! Where is that nasty Prestwich? He is taking his own sweet time. By the idle, I ought to…is that you? Prestwich, do you have her?"

"She is with me even now," he replied and motioned for Lia to take the ladder first.

Lia's heart was nearly bursting. She climbed up the ladder, setting down her burdens as she cleared the top, and Pasqua met her with a ferocious hug that crushed her breath away. Sowe was there also, tears gleaming in her eyes.

"Child, child, child, you are home again! Oh Lia—oh my dear Lia!" The hug was strong enough to squeeze tears from her eyes. "Oh Lia—thank Idumea. Thank Idumea you are safe!" She sobbed against Lia's shoulder, squeezing her harder and harder. Lia was surprised by her reaction, at the violence of her feelings. Pasqua hugged her tightly, swaying back and forth. "Never leave us like that again, child. Please…you do not know my poor heart. How I have suffered for you. How I have worried about you." She pressed Lia's cheeks with her hands and kissed her head. "I nearly broke my leg trying to hunt after you!"

"She did," Sowe said, tears spilling down her lashes. "And I had to nurse her."

"Pasqua," Lia said, then stopped, choking on the words. "Sowe."

Pasqua took her hands next and kissed them. "No, child. No, let me speak. You cannot understand my heart. You cannot understand, because you are too young still. But someday, you will be a mother, and you will understand then. So be still. Let me speak. Let me say what I should have said all these years. I have loved you like a daughter, though I never told you." Her hands clenched tightly. "As if you were my own daughter. My own flesh. When you left, and I had not told you, I thought as if the pain would kill me. Dear child, I have loved you since you were a babe. Since the day the Medium left you here. Thank Idumea you have come home. You are home, Lia. This is your home. Sowe, your sister is back!" The other girl was pulled violently into the embrace. "I love you both, do you hear me? You are my daughters. My sweet daughters!"

Lia could not see for the tears blinding her eyes, but she hugged Pasqua and thought her heart would break with so much joy when Sowe joined them.

***

The Aldermaston greeted her with a smile of affection and then turned to shut the door behind her, leaving Pasqua and Sowe in the corridor beyond. "I will only be a moment with her," he told them before sealing it closed.

He walked back to his stuffed chair and eased himself into it. A tome lay open on his desk, a sheepskin covering beneath it. Part of the page was written on. The other part was clean and unblemished by etchings. She recognized it as Maderos's tome.

"Welcome home to Muirwood," he said, his gravely voice so familiar.

"Thank you for allowing me to return, Aldermaston," she whispered, uncertain where she stood in his eyes. The reunion with Pasqua and Sowe had altered her heart in some unimaginable way. Her feelings were like a stew kettle bubbling over. She could not stop fidgeting with her hands.

The Aldermaston leaned back in his chair, wincing with the effort. "I am pleased you made it back safely."

She swallowed, her eyes stinging with tears again. "I did. But I am sorry about Jon Hunter. You do not know how sorry I am…"

He held up his hand and grimaced, as if the pain were still too raw for him as well. "What is done is done. I cannot hold you accountable for his death, Lia. That would be unfair. I sent him, so I alone bear that blame. Now the Abbey has need of a new hunter. I began seeking to rectify that concern when I received the Earl of Forshee's message. Do not burden yourself with it. It was all the Medium's will, surely." He brushed his eyes, whether from tears or dust, but she could see the pain in his expression. "It will be no greater miracle that brings us into another world to live forever with our dearest friends than that which has brought us into this one to live a lifetime with them. Or almost a lifetime. Therefore, we weep when they depart. But we will see them again in another world." A tear ran down his cheek.

She struggled with her feelings for the old man. Never in her life had she seen him weep.

"Lia," he said, then paused, trying to choose the right words. "You may think it was caprice which has prevented me from allowing you to be a learner at Muirwood. I am certain you have assigned any number of motives to my unwillingness. You may even suppose that because of what happened during your adventure to Winterrowd that I will allow you now." He leaned back even farther in his chair and brought his hands together in front of him, his fingertips touching. "I have motives as other men have. But in this thing, I act for your own best good. You must trust me, Lia. You must trust that what I do, I do for *your* own best good. I have felt this premonition since that night of the great storm, the night you stole a ring from my chamber. It was the night that I began to truly realize how strong you were with the Medium already." He bent forward, his voice heavy with meaning. "While I am Aldermaston at Muirwood, you will not be a learner."

A flood of disappointment washed over her.

"Rein in your feelings, child. Until I finish. That may mean many things. It does not mean that you will never learn to read. I cannot foretell how long I will remain as Aldermaston, and you are much younger than I. Those words were spoken to you through the Medium's will at the time. I feel them valid still. You would make an excellent learner, Lia. And that is one of the reasons why I cannot let you."

She subdued her disappointment. "Thank you, Aldermaston. I will trust your judgment in this. I know now that I should have trusted you...earlier."

"Your trust is not easily earned. Thank you."

She turned to leave then stopped. Reaching down to the pouch at her waist, she loosened the strings and withdrew the Cruciger orb. She was loath to give it up. "I am sorry for stealing this from you. I will never steal from you again."

As she was about to set it on his table, he held up his hand. The look on his face—the gesture—confused her.

"I must correct you. You did not steal it, Lia. You, of all people, cannot steal it. For it is already rightfully yours."

She did not realize she had stopped breathing. "What do you mean?"

His eyes penetrated hers. His eyes looked so deep and time-less, like the sea. "We found it with you in the basket. So you see, it did not surprise me that it worked for you or that it led you. Since you have already mastered its powers, I must allow you to keep what is rightfully yours. It is yours, Lia. The Cruciger orb has always been yours."

***

Through the will of the Medium, many devices and implements have been created for the use and benefit of those who believe and are willing to act. There are stones that give off light and shells of glass that fasten into breastplates which allow the wearer to translate languages. Of these implements, the Cruciger orbs are perhaps the most mysterious. No artisan can craft such remarkable and intricate a workmanship. They are ancient devices. All records which speak of them describe that they are gifts found by happenstance by common men and women destined for great deeds and are usually handed down from generation to generation and guarded with the utmost secrecy. The orbs only work for those they were intended to bless. It is my personal belief that they are not of this world at all, but gifts from the world of Idumea.

—Cuthbert Renowden of Billerbeck Abbey

AUTHOR'S NOTE

I am a collector of quotes. Over the years, I have assembled snippets of wisdom from Greek philosophers, advisors of Roman emperors, religious texts of various faiths, and from more modern luminaries like Benjamin Franklin, John Adams, and Andrew Carnegie. Nearly all of the quotes attributed to Cuthbert Renowden of Billerbeck Abbey in fact originate from our world, with some editing for context. There are themes of wisdom from Solomon to Allen that reveal some of the secrets of human nature. I tried to weave these into the Muirwood series as well as I could, bonus point to any reader who figures them all out.

You will find many of the artifacts and traditions within this series to be historical in nature and representative of medieval life. A little delving into Wikipedia on terms like *globus cruciger* and *gargouille* may provide some insights on things very common centuries ago that we do not see much of today. But the story is not set in medieval Europe. Muirwood is set on another world that shares some historical and religious contexts with ours.

Finally, regarding the Medium. Every power demonstrated through the Medium can be found through various religious texts.

Whether it is summoning fire from the sky, water from stones, or preventing death in battle, all have been hand-picked. They show that our own world has a deep tradition of miraculous occurrences. The one exception to this is the use of floating stones, a concept which came from artist Christophe Vacher, someone I admire greatly and whose paintings inspire my writing.

ABOUT THE AUTHOR

Photograph © Kim Bills

Jeff Wheeler is a writer from 7 p.m. to 10 p.m. on Wednesday nights. The rest of the time, he works for Intel Corporation, is a husband and the father of five kids, and a leader in his local church. He lives in Rocklin, California. When he isn't listening to books during his commute, he is dreaming up new stories to write. His website is: www.jeff-wheeler.com